The Twisted Web

Rebecca Bradley

Prologue

The day felt like any other day. Work had given Drew a headache. The kids were unruly. It was the last week of school before the summer holidays and no one wanted to focus on lessons. The heat soaked through the glass windows as though they were sitting in a greenhouse and the smell of overripe hormonal teenagers swelled within the room. He attempted to open some windows but paint had sealed them shut. Only he had never noticed in the past because this was a new room to him and he'd never had the need to open them before because, well, the UK weather, you didn't need to say any more, did you?

He'd been given the room after Mr Forbes had retired the previous year. Five years early. Citing the need to live his life while he was still young enough. The need to see the world. He knew what Forbes really wanted was to get away from these bloody kids. The little fuckers sucked the spirit straight out of you and he was right, he probably did need his life. It was kind of important to you.

So, here he was now, relieved to have made it through another day, with just two more left. Then six blissful weeks away from them. It wasn't that he hated being a teacher. He loved it really. Or he used to love it and he loved the idea of infusing the adults of the future with the knowledge of today. To see where it would take them. Especially in his subject of computers. It was where the world lived and ended. It was where all the huge advances were being made. Though all the kids cared about were the games they could play. There was only the odd child or two who was interested, and this had gradually withered his soul away. Without the symbiotic nature of children needing to be fed, his need to feed them his knowledge dried up.

It was sad really.

Drew was desperate to make his mark and imprint on a child. Have them grow up, make something of themselves and say it was him, he was the teacher who had been the one to spur them on. He was *that* teacher.

As it was, he couldn't even find that pupil. All he could do was turn up every day and do his job. Then wait for the end of day bell so he could release them all back to their homes, their gaming stations, their junk foods, their vacuous lives. And he would go home. To his wife and his children. Who, he adored, he did. He did his best by them. By his wife.

They liked to do things together. Spend time as a family. He nurtured their brains. He loved them.

All this floated through his head as he meandered down the street, sleeves rolled up past his elbows, the summer sun resting on his skin.

In front of him, a street artist was busy at work. One of those who made it appear that the pavement was opening up in front of you, yawning open, the innards of the street below, the wires and the pipes exposed and cracking open. Water bursting forth and upwards. All with a few chalks which she had scattered around her like the hem of a skirt.

He was mesmerised by the image. It looked as though the submerged world was screaming to be allowed out.

People were gathered around the woman and the image. Camera phones wafted in the air. The pavement was choked as everyone stopped to stare.

He looked at the woman surrounded by her chalks, covered in coloured dust. How he would love to have a job so freeing. Or just to feel the love he once had for the career he had chosen. Instead of this heavy weight he carried around with him.

He looked down, marvelled at the detail. At the love that had gone into it. Stepped sideways into the road rather than across her masterpiece. The traffic was steady, aware of the crowd bulging out into their space.

It was difficult to walk and not continue to look down at the cracked-open pavement. The layers of earth, and as he looked closer, the creepy eyes that glowed from within darkened corners.

With each step he could hear a thrum that didn't fit with the rest of the sound around him. It wasn't the mumble of awed voices. It wasn't the regular hum of traffic. This was different. He looked up.

In front of him, also on the road, was a young lad. Tracksuit bottoms, jacket and a woollen hat even though the sun was out. His clothes were dark but they looked dirty, uncared for.

Unclean.

Homeless. About nineteen years of age. His face, like many others, was also turned towards the image on the ground.

The thrum had turned into a roar. Drew looked past the young homeless man and saw a vehicle do a rapid and dangerous overtake. Revving hard. Coming towards them. The driver with a phone in his hand. The car too close to the kerb. He hadn't noticed the bulge of people that distended out from the pavement. Drew stepped back onto the pavement. Gently. Aware still of the cracked-open street below his feet.

He looked at the young man who looked back at Drew confused as to why he'd decided to stand up on the edges of the chalk drawing. Completely oblivious to the vehicle behind him.

The car was racing forward and wasn't going to stop. It was going to plough into the homeless guy. Everyone else had their backs turned.

Drew panicked, grabbed hold of the young man's upper arm, which was slender under the bulk of his clothing, and yanked him sideways up onto the path. The vehicle turned left with a screech of tyres, disappearing out of view.

The homeless lad came flying towards and past Drew, his legs wheeling under him as he attempted to avoid kicking the woman sitting on the ground. He stumbled as he Bambi-hopped over her outstretched leg, arms windmilling before he fell in a heap on the ground, a bundle of bones in a bag of jersey material topped by a woollen hat. The artist's mouth was agape, a sheen of fear glossing her face as the young man's head smashed into the wall with a crunch.

'What the fucking hell!'

To Drew the scream came out of nowhere. He was trying to focus on the boy on the ground. On what had just happened when the high-pitched screech fractured Drew's confused mind.

He ignored it. Presumed the fury was about the vehicle that had driven like it was on a racing track. His thoughts were securely on the boy and if he was okay. With movements that felt sludge like he made a move forward. Panic started to rise and people rushed to the boy. People flapped and fussed. Crouched down beside him. Held his hand, checked his head.

And they pushed Drew out of the way.

He'd saved the boy's life. He needed to make sure he had saved it and not injured him in the process. But he couldn't get to him. The boy was utterly surrounded.

It was almost as though they were keeping him at bay.

As though they didn't want Drew near the boy.

He had saved his life. Drew was confused.

A woman turned from where she was bent over the lad. 'What did you do?' Horror was etched on her face. Disgust. He didn't understand it.

'I saw it. I saw him do it,' another shouted over to her.

And then a young lad behind him piped up, 'I caught it all on my phone. I was taking a video of the chalk drawing. He won't get away with this.'

1.

It was the crack of dawn and we had all been called in as there was an urgent job. The reason I knew it was urgent was because DCI Kevin Baxter was currently pacing about in my office, his face turning more and more red as he spoke.

'You need to get out there now, Hannah.' There was a strong smell of cigarettes oozing from him. He had obviously not long had one.

'Yes, Sir, we're just waiting on Martin, and once we're all in and up to date we're headed out. I believe uniform have the scene?'

I'd said the wrong thing. I knew this the minute the words were out of my mouth. He had already given me a precis over the phone when he called me in and now I'd said the words I could see how annoyed he was over the whole thing.

'You know this is going to be a media nightmare, don't you?' He turned on his heel and faced me.

'We make it clear that we didn't do it and that it was a part of some sick ritual that the killer set up,' I said trying to calm the situation by sitting down in the chair behind my desk.

'I expect you to sort this out, you and your team. You have to clear this up and quickly. From what I've been told it's all over social media.'

I rolled my eyes.

'There's no point in doing that, it's the world in which we live. You have to get used to it.' He spun around again and started to pace once more. I had a strong urge to roll my eyes at him again. Getting this wound up was not going to resolve a single issue. 'Though the way it impacts on us never helps. Everyone has an opinion and they certainly have one this morning.' He rubbed at his face. 'You know the Chief is aware.' It wasn't a question.

'I'm sure he would be. It's the strangest one I've come across.'

'The public actually think we left a dead body out for everyone to see and walked away for our breakfast or something. We need to get on top of this one and quickly.' He looked towards my door. He was losing patience. 'Where the hell is—'

'Morning, Ma'am, Sir.' Martin stuck his head around the door frame. 'We're all here and ready to go when you are. I hear we have a ready-made crime scene waiting for us.' He had a smile across his face, nothing seemed to faze Martin but this wasn't what Baxter needed right now.

'Sort it out, Hannah.' He was about ready to snap. I had to keep my cool. 'They're crucifying us. It's a huge shit show. We need a strong presence out there. We need to show them this isn't us, that we know how to look after a real crime scene. We did not leave a murder victim out on Market Square with crime scene tape around him and walk away.' His voice rose. 'I'm getting pressure on this already, get out there, show them how it's really done and find the bastard who did this.'

2.

'What the hell is this, Boss?' asked Ross as I drove as fast as was possible through the steadily building morning traffic.

'I don't know.' I didn't have an answer, all I had were questions myself.

'Did we do this?'

I let out a deep breath. After the conversation with Baxter I was under no illusion that the body we were travelling to was most definitely not one we had already been out to. And I needed to get there and deal with the shit-show as he'd described it, before more images made it on to Twitter. As far as I was aware with Twitter, if the images were up there, it was already too late. Evie Small, my friend, and our analyst, would be able to give me the definitive.

'No, we didn't do this, Ross. What we need to do now is control it and find out who did.'

A car pulled out in front of me. I pushed my hand down on my horn and cursed. Luckily, uniformed officers had been sent out ahead of us to close down and secure the scene. We would take it from them as soon as we arrived.

Ross whistled at the side of me. I stole a glance at him, his phone was in his hand. He saw me turn.

'The images on Twitter,' he said. 'Unbelievable.' He shook his head to support his disbelief.

'How many?' Traffic was getting thicker and I had no blue light. I slapped the steering wheeling in frustration. We needed to get there. I needed to see this. To figure out what had happened.

'How many?' Ross parroted back at me.

'Yes. Images. How many images are there on Twitter?'

There was a moment of silence. I eased my foot off the gas to look across at him. He was looking puzzled.

'Ross?'

'Are you asking how many different shots there are or how many times each shot has been shared?'

I wasn't on social media. I didn't have the time. Even if I had, I wasn't sure I'd have the inclination. All I had to share was the wine I drank and there were only so many times you could post that. And as for news, isn't that what news websites were for? Or had I been left behind?

'I don't know what I'm asking, Ross.' I turned right onto Friar Lane. 'Give me a general idea of either.'

'As far as I can see the scene has been photographed from different angles by multiple users and each photograph has been shared...' he paused, 'thousands of times.'

I pushed on my horn again and got the two-fingered salute for my trouble.

'You know it's trending don't you, Boss?'

'I had heard. And that means everyone is sharing it, yes?' I wasn't a user but I had a rough idea of how it worked because social media cropped up in so many investigations.

'Pretty much.'

'Great.' This was what Baxter was in such a state about. The public talking and sharing this way, a way he couldn't control.

I turned onto the pedestrianised area, slowed and kept my headlights on so people could see we were here. Though the commotion in front of us gave me no doubt that people were well aware that there would be a high police activity here today.

I slammed on the brakes as close to the scene as I could get. Ross jerked forward and put his arm out. I didn't bother with an apology. It didn't help my mood that we were on the back foot with this. I certainly hadn't needed to be torn apart by Baxter before I'd put my hands on the job, just because someone above him, probably Detective Superintendent Catherine Walker, was on his case.

Martin and Pasha, two other detectives from my team, parked behind me. It was the beginning of December and it was strangely mild still. The sky was overcast but it was dry and pleasant. I saw Pasha shove her phone into her pocket. No doubt she'd been following this trending issue as well. It seemed to have everyone hooked. Even those who were now involved.

'Shall we.' It was more a command than a question. Martin grinned.

'Looking forward to this one.'

I stared at him.

'You know what I mean, Boss. Not the victim. The circumstances are interesting.'

I did know. After the pain and difficulty of informing a family of the brutal loss of a loved one, the investigation itself could stimulate an officer and keep them going no matter how many hours were needed of them.

Martin and I suited up in Tyvek suits, masks and booties and headed to the crime scene.

Ross and Pasha were here to talk to the crowd, to ascertain what time they had arrived, if they had been here earlier, what they had seen or heard. They were here to look for any witnesses.

Even though we now, it appeared, had thousands of witnesses on Twitter.

I provided our details to the officer on the outer cordon and stepped past him. Towards the crime scene.

Not just our crime scene. Whoever had left the victim on the steps of the Nottingham Council Building on The Old Market Square had set him up as a crime scene. They had surrounded him with marked police tape they had bought, as well as yellow number evidence markers and now we, the uniformed officers who had arrived here as the calls had come in complaining that we had left a body out unattended, had set up a taped cordon around that.

This was why there had been a trending hashtag on social media this morning.

Someone had left a body out in the open, right in the centre of Nottingham and set it up as a fake crime scene and then walked away.

3.

At the top of the concrete steps, slumped against the left column on the centre archway, was a white male. His face narrow and pinched. A whisper of five o'clock shadow which looked like intrusive gloom on his bloodless face. His chin rested on his chest and he was wearing jeans, a knitted jumper and a large padded jacket.

The sun was only just starting to rise and there was a grey cast to the day.

'So, were these effects placed here after he died of natural causes or are we dealing with something altogether more sinister?' I asked the team as we moved closer.

Doug Howell, the crime scene manager, approached. 'I've called out the pathologist. This isn't looking like natural causes where he's stopped for a sleep after a couple of beers and not woken up again.'

'What do you have?' I asked as I looked at the gathering held back by the real scene tape.

A CSI was photographing the tape that had been placed around the body before we arrived. As soon as he'd finished it would be collected up, taken to the lab and tested for prints.

'I can't see any obvious injuries but there are blood stains on his clothes. There's no other blood at the site so I'd suggest this is a suspicious death and this is a dump site.'

I couldn't agree with him more. Though Doug was still fairly new in the role as crime scene manager, he'd been a CSI himself until he was promoted. He was good at his job but second guessed his work and worried about the evidence continually until it made it to his lab where it would be secure.

'Do we know which pathologist is on?'

Doug shook his head. 'I'm sure we'll find out soon enough.'

The clock above us chimed seven a.m. More people would be moving about soon. We needed to get move ourselves.

I turned to Pasha and Ross. 'Can you start talking to witnesses, see if we have any?' I indicated to the looky-loos in the square in front of the council house.

Pasha zipped up her coat a little further. 'Absolutely. Let's see if they're ghoulish or helpful.'

Only a month ago I had talked to Pasha about my unease with her having joined the team in a place that was dear to my heart, a place that had been vacated due to the murder of a previous DC on the team, and how I had moved past it. She was a good worker, engaging well with the rest of the unit and more than solid in performance.

'So, this young man,' said Martin as he stepped closer to the male on the steps. 'What is it you have to tell us?'

I looked down at the small piece of card propped against the male with the hashtag in front of it. 'My Kind of Thing? Isn't that also trending?' I asked Martin and Doug.

'Great,' grunted Doug. 'That's all we need. More attention than we already have. It'll be a circus around here.'

I looked across the large flat grey expanse of Market Square. 'I don't understand how he got here without the CCTV operators picking it up. That needs to be one of our first lines of inquiry, Martin.'

He pulled his notebook out his pocket and made a note.

I crouched in front of the male, who, for all intents and purposes looked like, as Doug had said, he had stopped for a nap. 'How did you get here and what happened to you?'

'Let's have a look and see if we can get some answers, shall we?' a voice from behind responded.

Dr Fay Pride smiled when I turned. Her short grey hair was tucked behind her ears and she wore a chequered blue and green scarf wrapped tightly around her neck. 'I know I said I liked working with you, DI Robbins, but that didn't mean dragging me out this early in the morning.'

I returned her smile. The pathologists rotated as we did at EMSOU – Major Crime. EMSOU was the East Midlands Special Operations Unit in which five forces collaborated and covered the area. Depending on which team was free to deal with a job when it came in, determined where they were sent. Our pathologists were now rotating in the same way, and Derbyshire, Leicestershire, Lincolnshire, Northamptonshire and Nottinghamshire pathologists now also covered the same ground. This meant we never knew who would attend a job. Whereas in the past we would always have had Jack Kidner, we now had an array of doctors to help us. We had worked with Fay a couple of times. I found her kind and compassionate. Helpful. Also generous with her time. And in a job like ours, that was a godsend.

'I'm sorry, Fay, you've obviously been pretty wicked recently.'

She laughed, twisting to make sure her back was to the horde of people watching. Laughing at a crime scene would not look good with no context if posted on social media, as it was likely to be. I was glad she was aware.

She rubbed her hands together. 'I've heard all about it already, obviously.'

'You have Twitter?' Martin sounded surprised.

'Something you want to say about my ability to use a social media site, DC Thacker?' She tried to keep a straight face.

This time it was Martin's turn to laugh. He walked towards the body on the steps. 'Doug can't see any visible injuries, but that's not to say there aren't any.'

Fay pushed her spectacles up her nose then flicked her gloves on over the wrists of her Tyvek suit and moved closer.

4

Fay stood from her crouched position over the body. Snapped off her gloves and bagged them. Then closed the medical bag and walked towards me.

'Thanks, can you text me that. I'll see you shortly.' I ended the phone call to the office and turned to Fay.

'What do you have for me?' I asked.

'You have a murder on your hands, I'm afraid.'

'With a sick and twisted after-game, looking at what they've set up here,' I said.

'It's not what I'm used to seeing. Well, it is, but it's usually you guys who set it up.'

I ran my hands through my hair. 'I kind of had it figured for murder with the stains running down his jeans. I imagine it's blood? What has happened?'

'Stab wounds. Three of them in his abdomen. There seems to be an anger to the act. Obviously, this wasn't the murder scene or it would be a lot more bloody. He's been moved. You have a murder scene somewhere else. This is your dump site.'

'So,' I turned back to the male on display. 'He was placed here for dramatic effect?'

Fay tucked a strand of hair behind her ear. 'It would look that way. But those kinds of summations are for you.' She started to walk. 'I'll leave you to find out why someone would do something quite so odd.'

'Do you have a time of death?' I asked as the clang of a tram bell broke through the air and the rails thrummed as it rolled into view. Time of death was the first question we always wanted the answer to. It was a jump off point.

'From body temp and air temp, body weight and clothing, I can provide you with an estimate of five to seven hours ago.'

'What do we know about our scene within a scene victim?' I asked of the incident room once we were back inside.

With a green tea steaming at the side of me, I was ready to work through this. I had DCI Kevin Baxter and Detective Superintendent Catherine Walker standing at the rear of the room, both with a stern look on their faces, Catherine with her arms crossed. Baxter, hands shoved deep into his pockets.

'Who is he for starters?' I clarified, closing the question down a little.

'The ID in his pockets has him as Sebastian Wade, thirty-two years of age.' Pasha read from the notepad on the desk in front of her.

'And what do we know about Sebastian? Do we have his address yet? Occupation? Has he been reported missing?'

'He was reported missing last night by...' She checked for the name. 'Nick Henson. His civil partner.'

I rubbed my hand through my hair. They always had to be someone's son, partner, father, brother. The victim was rarely a lone person who had failed to imprint on the world. The impact of a murder was far more wide-reaching than just the person who would end up on the slab of Fay Pride. There were ripples out from family, friends to colleagues and associates. One death permanently changed the life of many people.

Those affected by a murder often felt as though their life had also been taken once a loved one had been snatched so ruthlessly. But a court, should a murder ever go to trial, only ever counted one life. The media only counted and reported on the one life. Investigating the murder, you soon came to realise it was a hell of a lot more than one life. You don't live in a vacuum. You are more than yourself in the world.

Inside the police, we felt the repercussions of the many lives affected and now we had to go and inform Nick Henson that his life partner would not come home to him again.

I took Pasha with me from the office and drove over to see Nick Henson. Even though we had family liaison officers it was necessary for the SIO to visit the bereaved and touch base with them, assure them that we were doing everything we could. While I was there we could get some answers from him as it was so early in the investigation.

The apartment stood on a beautiful tree-lined street in Mapperley and was set off-road with plenty of room for cars to park on its spacious circular driveway. Pasha and I stood in front of the slightly shabby door and waited. A dog barked from somewhere inside the next-door ground floor apartment. A warning to visitors that his domain was guarded.

Then the door in front of us was yanked open and a man in his thirties, with a dark head of hair that stood up and who had as much hair again on his face, stood in front of us, barefoot, in jeans and a T-shirt. His face was pale, and as rumpled as his hair.

Creased and lined. His eyes dark and hollow. You could sink into them and lose yourself, they were haunted. The missing report had been made late last night and looking at him, this man hadn't slept since.

He spoke before we had time to introduce ourselves. 'You've found him?' His voice was rushed. Pleading. He had made us as police. Last night he had been dealing with uniformed officers and today we turned up on his doorstep. The three words out there in front of us, between us, were loaded with fear, with a barrier, a wall, a demand for us not to tell him anything other than we'd found him safe and well.

'Mr Henson,' I spoke gently, 'I'm Detective Inspector Hannah Robbins and this is Detective Constable Pasha Lal.' She inclined her head in acknowledgement. 'Do you mind if we come in?'

Henson didn't move. Didn't speak. He looked from me to Pasha and back again. The darkness clouding his eyes intensified. Deepened.

The dog continued to bark in muted tones behind its wall.

'Mr Henson?' I took a step closer, to bring this man back to us, to what was happening.

'No.' The sound was brittle. Hard. Suddenly he moved back and the door was closing in our faces.

I pushed my foot forward and blocked the door before it clicked into the frame at the last moment.

'No,' came the shout from behind the half-closed door. 'Go away. I don't want to talk to you. Don't come back until you have Seb with you.'

I looked down the street, caught the confusion on Pasha's face. I gave a brief smile of reassurance. We could do this.

She would have given death messages before, but by the look of her, this was the first time it had been less than straightforward. Where grief was concerned you could never expect a specific reaction. People handled it in diverse and contrasting ways. All we could do was adapt as the situation dictated.

Luckily we didn't have an audience, as my quick glance round confirmed but we were pretty closed off here.

I put my palm up to the door and applied some pressure. 'Mr Henson, Nick, we need to come in and talk to you. You don't need this on your doorstep. Just let us come in, we can make a call and get a friend or family member to come round, but we really need to speak to you.'

He didn't put up a fight. I don't think he had the energy. The door slackened and I stepped forward with the momentum of his move away.

We were in.

And now I had to tell this man the news he so desperately did not want to hear.

He turned his back to me and walked away, bare feet silent on dark stained hardwood flooring. We followed him into a well-lit living room, lined with bookshelves, floor to ceiling. On one wall there were photographs of the couple together and with others, family or friends. Different locations around the world, in restaurants, at home, laughing, enjoying their life together. Their eyes sparkled. Their smiles lit up the images. This was a couple who enjoyed life. The sun that filled the room came from the huge windows at the front of the property. Large bay windows that filled the wall floor to ceiling. They were stunning. The whole set-up was beautiful. It was a space that was loved. A space that was a home.

Nick Henson sunk into the sofa. I took a single chair close to him. Leaned forward. 'I'm sorry we had to come to see you this morning.' I had to get straight to the point. He had made the leap himself. 'You reported your partner, Sebastian, missing last night. I'm sorry to have to tell you this, but it's extremely likely that we have found his body.'

Henson didn't move.

Pasha was still standing, towering over Nick. I indicated she should sit. She moved over to where he was seated and sat at the other end of the sofa. He didn't look as she shifted position.

I inched to the edge of my chair. 'I'm sorry, Nick.'

He shook his head. It was a slow purposeful movement. As though he was feeling his way through each motion. Searching for pain.

It was there. You could see it in the lines within his face. The droop of his body. The way it sagged under the weight of his grief.

'He's only been gone since last night. It can't be him.' Henson's voice was quiet, subdued. Questioning the truth of the information I had given him.

'He had his driver's licence in his pocket.' I pushed the truth towards him. 'We will, of course, need you to identify him...' I tried to get eye contact. Henson refused. 'To confirm it is indeed him. And then–'

'So, there's a chance it's not. It could be someone else. They could have stolen his licence and then got into trouble. It might not be Seb. He could still be alive.' Now he looked at me. Straight on.

Determined.

'I'm sorry. I was...' I couldn't say at the scene, it all sounded so official to relatives, 'there. With Seb. I think he was carrying his own licence.' How to say the person on the ground was the person in the image? 'I am sorry, Nick.'

Death messages broke my heart. They were harder than seeing the actual death and loss of life. The human element of death.

'We need to ask you some questions, if you're up to it?'

Again he was immobile.

Pasha stood. 'Shall I put the kettle on?'

I flicked my head towards the kitchen in acknowledgement.

'Before I do,' I continued, 'is there anyone you want me to call?'

'No.'

At least we seemed to have moved past the denial. I hoped.

'You said you saw him?'

This was also what I hated. This next question. I steeled myself. Took a deep breath.

'I did. Not too long ago.'

'How did he die? Was it an accident? Is that why he didn't make it home last night? Please tell me he hasn't been laid by the side of a road all night, alone and injured, and cold and dying and I could have done something if I'd found him. Please tell me he didn't–' His voice cracked and broke off as the truth hit him. His hand went up to his mouth and he let go of all he had been holding in. He folded in on himself as a deep moan escaped and tears started to fall.

I crossed over to him. Put my hand on his knee. 'Is there anyone I can call for you?'

He shook his head and the tears continued. His body shook with wracking sobs.

'I went out and I looked for him. I did. But I couldn't find him. Please, don't let me have left him alone in the cold.' The words were ragged and torn through his grief.

A fluffy grey cat slinked through the room before it wrapped itself around Henson's legs in a figure of eight. The contact pulled him back to the here and now a little. His tears, still present, subsided somewhat. I grabbed a couple of tissues out my bag and handed them to him.

He took them, scrunched them into a ball and wiped at his face. 'There's no one to call. Well, not family. None that I want here, anyway. And to be honest, I'm not sure I want the company of friends right now.'

I nodded, though I wasn't sure this was the right move I understood where he was coming from. The desire to be alone was high at times like this.

'So, how?'

I hadn't answered his question but I had to. I couldn't leave without doing this. I still needed to ask my own questions.

'We found him on the steps of the council building this morning.'

Puzzlement crossed Nick's face. 'I don't understand. I presumed it was an accident. What was he doing there?'

'I was online this morning, asking for help looking for Seb and the only thing people were talking about at the council building was...'

5.

Pasha handed Nick the mug of tea. She'd put three sugars in it, regardless of whether he took them or not. Nick needed it right now as he struggled to grasp what it was we were telling him. That his partner was not only dead but that he had been murdered and he had been left out in the open for members of the public to come across, and photograph and share on social media like an exhibit in a museum.

Any colour that he may have had in his face was well and truly gone. I wasn't sure I had seen a living person as pale as he was. If sugar was the answer, then I was all for piling his tea up with it.

'What time did you last see him?' I asked after all the questions from Nick had subsided.

'He went out about seven p.m. and was due back about ten – ten-thirty p.m.' He looked into his tea as if it would hold the answers. 'I didn't look at the images properly. That's why I didn't realise. I wasn't there to catch up on the local news I was there to try and raise awareness about Seb. Plus,' he pleaded at me guilty for not recognising Seb in the image, 'there wasn't a real clear shot of his face. His chin was on his chest.'

'It's okay,' I said. I needed for him to focus again. I could only imagine how it must feel to not only lose a loved one but to lose them in such tragic and public circumstances. I tried to manoeuvre him back to the questions. 'And where did he go?'

'To book club. He only went out to book club. But it drags on. They're a bunch of old gossips. Plus, they like a drink afterwards. Seb won't stay too late because he has to get up for work in a morning. So, when he wasn't home for eleven-thirty p.m. I started to worry and phoned a couple of people. Then obviously called you at half past midnight.' He pulled at his eyelid which was looking sore at the corner.

'I'll need details on the book club, obviously.' I looked at my notes. 'Did he walk or take a car?'

'He walked. It's only a ten-minute walk, it's held at the Copper Café bar, on Woodborough Road. They just grab a couple of tables and have a chinwag about whatever book they've read that month. Have a drink, maybe order a bit of food. Generally have a good evening between them. It's their thing. They focus on non-fiction with a leaning to true-crime, which is why Seb went,' Nick continued.

I turned to the bookshelves on the wall and for the first time noticed the titles. They were mostly true-crime reads. I realised this fascinated a lot of people. Seb was amongst those intrigued by it.

'Anyone he has any problems with? Or have you noticed anything of concern recently? Have you had any problems?'

Nick shook his head. 'No one would want to hurt Seb. I know everyone says this.' He turned to Pasha. 'Please, you have to believe me, no one has a bad word to say about him. He's loved.'

Pasha nodded.

He turned back to me. 'I just can't believe they would do that to him. The crime scene. It's so sick.'

'I know, I'm sorry.' I had no words to comfort him other than to tell him we would work hard on this and bring him justice.

'But they did it to Seb.'

'I know, it's difficult to take in. We'll provide you with a family liaison officer who will be here to support you and to guide you through the whole investigation and hopefully prosecution process.'

He rounded on me. 'It's not that. I'm not talking about that. Don't you realise who Seb is?' He shook his head, wiped at his face with the tissues that were now dissolving in his hands. 'What he did?'

I glanced at Pasha who lifted her eyebrows in response. What were we about to find out? What had we missed?

'Seb was a true-crime blogger. His blog had a massive following. That they killed him and turned his death into a crime scene, well... what does that say to you, DI Robbins?'

6.

Drew watched the Twitter feed and the hashtag feed and greedily soaked it in. The shock, the horror and outrage that the police had left a crime scene, a body, out in public this way, for anyone to come across. Old people, sick people and children, anyone could have come across it. The police were taking a real slating.

They were being shamed.

People had strong opinions and he felt a flutter in his stomach as he read the comments. His body tingled at the mounting drama on the screen. His face was lit by the light of the monitor, heavy curtains drawn closed and the rest of the room in an eerie toast coloured glow with a cream edge of light around him.

The level of affront and offence grew by the minute as person by person the information filtered through and the images permeated the new day.

He heard movement downstairs. A tap being run, water flowing, a flick of a switch as the kettle was turned on, a mug dragged from between the many in the cupboard – how many mugs did two people need? – before it was slammed with too much force onto the worktop. He peered behind him. Would this be the day he would be interrupted?

What would he see? It was Twitter. The world lived on and lived by Twitter.

The flutter in his stomach turned heavy and he swallowed.

Viewed the screen again.

What turned his stomach was how the shock, the disgust, the so-called distress they talked about, didn't stop them talking about it. Didn't stop them sharing it. Didn't stop them adding a fancy goddam hashtag to it. Because it was social media and a hashtag had to be added. This wasn't real life, after all, they were behind their keyboards safe and sound, being violated by what had happened out there. They could say what they wanted, spread the image of a dead man on the street and then they could go about their day without having to deal with the repercussions.

They could vent their disgust in their nice warm homes. Regardless of the facts of the event. Who needed facts when you could share an image? Slate a person? It was much more fun to attack a large organisation, especially when you were doing it with the herd, than it was to wait for any facts to emerge.

If the herd said this was Nottinghamshire police's fault then so be it. Nottinghamshire police were going down. How dare they leave a crime scene this way?

Shame on them.

7

The bank of screens in front of us was huge. There were three walls filled with monitors.

This was the nerve centre of Nottingham's CCTV. People and vehicles were moving about the monitors, going about their business like a small insect colony.

The room was near dark other than the glow coming from the moving images. The quantity of monitors provided a decent amount of light for anyone working in here. But still, it was a grim environment for a workplace. There was not a single window. It wasn't possible due to the data protection issue surrounding the monitoring of people and vehicles. The smell of leftover food hung in the air of the confined and closed in space. Like microwaved meals just left out in the open to congeal. I wouldn't fancy being locked up in a room like this day in and day out.

'How do you focus on all this?' Pasha asked Scott, the wiry male who was responsible for keeping an eye on it all. His colleague was currently biting what was left of his nails in the corner, a worried expression on his face.

'You get used to it,' Scott answered. 'If something's happening, we need to call you guys out for, it kind of leaps out at us. We're tuned in to it. Like a sixth sense.'

Pasha was listening while she watched the screens.

'CCTV Jedis, I suppose,' he continued, practically salivating over Pasha.

I looked at him. 'And last night?'

His face paled. 'Ah, ah, I wasn't on. It wasn't me. I'd have called it in. Of course.'

I turned to the guy eating his way through his fingers, who pulled them away from his mouth long enough to hold them up in a submissive gesture and deny he was at work either.

'So, who do we need to speak with?' I was losing patience with these Jedi operators.

Scott moved to a desk and flicked through a folder, peeling over pages until he came to the one he wanted. 'It was Smithy. Smithy was on last night. With Louise.'

I raised an eyebrow.

He flipped the cover of the folder closed. 'David Smithson and Louise Burton.'

'I'll need their details. Addresses. Contact phone numbers,' I said.

'Okay, but I have to check with head office first though.' His eyes never left Pasha as he spoke to me.

'Check now please. This is a murder inquiry and we don't have time to mess about.'

His head snapped round. 'Murder?'

Jesus.

'And I'll need a copy of last night's recording for Market Square as well as recordings of the surrounding areas, so we can attempt to ascertain where they came from.'

The finger chewer finally spoke up. 'I can't believe someone wheeled a dead body straight onto Market Square and dumped it and those two idiots didn't notice.'

'How does something like that happen?' asked Pasha.

'Beats me.' He shrugged. Then returned to his silent act.

We thanked them for their time, took copies of the night's recordings and seized the originals for evidence then made our way back to the car.

'How can that happen, Boss?' Pasha was driving as I needed to make some calls to the incident room.

'What's that?' I was distracted. I had two missed calls from Baxter and a follow up email telling me to contact him and update him on where we were. It hadn't been that long since we briefed. What did he expect to have happened in this period of time?

'That the killer got Seb into Market Square without anyone, the CCTV crew, calling it in while it was happening? It doesn't feel right.' She turned to look at me. 'We could have caught him as he was leaving the scene.'

She was right. I didn't understand this either. I put a call in to the incident room and spoke to Martin. Gave him the details for Smithson and Burton and asked that he contact them and get them into the station. I wanted them to feel a little pressure. They had let a murderer dump a body right under their noses and I wanted to know not only the how, but the why. Why had this happened? Was it negligence on their part, were they screwing around, figuratively or literally, or was it more sinister than that?

We needed to find out. And a witness interview room would apply more pressure than if we spoke to them at their homes where they would be comfortable and confident.

'The DCI has been in looking for you,' Martin said before he rang off.

'Yeah, I have a couple of messages from him. I'll get to him. Thanks, Martin.'

I'd return his calls at some point. I couldn't focus on the investigation if I had to chase up Baxter at every turn, if I had him chasing me for updates every hour. I understood how difficult this one was. I could imagine the pressure he was getting, especially with the social media aspect.

'Straight back to the station?' Pasha asked.

'Yes, hopefully Martin will get those two in, even if he has to get a uniform car to drag them in.'

My phone rang in my hand. It was Baxter again. I let out a sigh and pressed the green answer button.

'DI Robbins?'

'Yes, Sir.' I looked at Pasha. Her eyes were firmly on the road.

'Why haven't you been answering your phone?'

'I've been busy. Working this case.'

There was a silence as he caught the unsaid annoyance in my words.

'We have a problem.' He had let it slide.

'What is it?'

'Obviously the local media are interested in this morning. It was going to happen because of the hash things, what are they called? It doesn't matter,' he snapped. 'They were always going to be interested. We've had a call from one of the Nationals. They've been paying attention to that Twitter and want to know if we did leave a body unattended. They want our response before they go to print.'

8.

I wanted to get the team together for another briefing, based on the information Nick Henson had given us. It was a disturbing slant on the murder.

'It looks as though we need to up our game and learn a lot more about the online world than many of us may be comfortable with.' I looked at the team, Pasha was smiling. 'Though, I acknowledge some of you will be fine with this aspect and will therefore be our guiding light.' She nodded enthusiastically.

'So, he talks about crime online and is murdered and left to be found in what is made to look like a crime scene?' Ross asked, clarifying the situation in his own mind. A situation we all needed to get our heads around.

'That appears to be the gist of it, Ross. I'm going to bring Evie in on this and ask her to do some research on his blog for us.'

'But, what the hell?' Ross again.

'It is pretty sick,' Pasha confirmed.

'And that's the precise reason we need to get on top of this one as quickly as possible.'

The door to the incident room opened and DCI Kevin Baxter strode in. All heads turned to look at him, then back to me.

'Don't let me stop you, DI Robbins.'

I knew I was in trouble when he used my official title. I had decided working the case was more important and had started the briefing before seeing him to discuss the press issue.

'I'm informing the team of our victim's active interest in true-crime, Sir. According to his partner, his blog was extremely active and had several thousand hits every month.'

Baxter raised his eyebrows. 'Seriously?'

'Yes, Sir. His main focus was Nottinghamshire, but when he couldn't find anything to blog about locally he would look further afield. He was very good at what he did apparently and was talking about setting up a podcast in addition to the blog.'

I knew about podcasts; I subscribed and listened to a few of these. A couple of travel ones and a couple of science ones. They were great because you could listen while you were doing something else.

'Podcast?' Baxter looked blank.

Ross smirked.

'It doesn't matter,' I clarified, 'because he hadn't got that far. His blog was popular and the manner in which he was found has to be considered in terms of his interests.'

'Jesus, Hannah. This is all we need. What mind fuck is going on?' His face hardened.

The team looked down at their desks.

'We're working on it now, Sir.'

'I'll speak to you when you've finished the briefing.' He stalked over to an empty chair, sat and crossed his arms. He had no intention of moving. He wanted to know what was happening. If he was stressed about this case then I was obviously going to be stressed; that was the way it worked.

I grabbed the remote control from the desk at the side of me and turned on the screen that I'd positioned at the front of the incident room. 'Pasha and I went to the CCTV hub earlier and we've seized the footage of Sebastian being dumped on the council building steps. They're already logged into evidence. We also had a couple of copies made, which is what we're going to look at now.'

Pasha had set the disc up so it was already in place. The screen was a murky blur. CCTV at night was notoriously difficult. Luckily Market Square was well lit but in essence a fuzz of dots made up each image and we knew if anyone was visible, it would be an incredibly difficult to identify them.

I pressed play. Everyone in the room leaned forward. Even Baxter had his eyes glued to the screen. Silence lay heavy as we waited for what we knew was about to happen.

The camera faced the council building, but had a view of the whole square. A bird swooped into view, landed near an empty packet that was floating about, investigated the contents then flew off.

'Here he comes.' Pasha was nearly falling out of her chair.

And she was right, we had already viewed this at the CCTV hub.

It definitely looked like a male. Dressed pretty much as the victim had been, in jeans, but with a large hoody pulled over his head, his face obscured. Gloves on his hands. They didn't look like medical gloves. Normal gloves that wouldn't draw attention to a person walking through the streets at night.

'Wow, he's brazen.' Ross was incredulous.

The reason: the male was pushing a wheelbarrow and in that wheelbarrow was our victim, but the way he was hanging out of it, from the dark fuzzy image, he looked like a Guy Fawkes, especially bearing in mind the time of year. Yes it was late, but you could still be forgiven for believing this was what was in the wheelbarrow.

There were also two small cones, narrow nozzle end pushed into the barrow, one either side of Sebastian.

We watched to see what would happen next. Though Pasha and I were the only ones who knew exactly in what order our killer did what, we all knew the end result. Sebastian Wade left out in the open to be found and be turned into a public topic of discussion and outrage.

The man on the screen made his way, without hurry, over to the council building. The camera followed him, one or both operators obviously interested, to some extent, in the lone male with the wheelbarrow crossing the square. He stopped halfway, rubbed at his back as though the load in his barrow was too much for him and he was struggling. He stretched out. Pulled at his muscles.

'Camera!' Baxter barked as the killer lifted himself to full height in his stretch. 'Where's the other camera? We need his face.'

I shook my head. 'The one that would have been useful was on automatic rotation and was pointing the wrong way. As you can see, the operators are following him, but only using one camera.'

'Damn those incompetent idiots. What have they said for themselves?' He was pacing about now.

'They're on their way in. We'll be speaking to them after this briefing.' I needed for him to calm down so we could get on with this and I could then speak to Smithy and Louise.

I un-paused the image and we continued our vigil of Sebastian, who was already dead, and now a prop in his killer's sideshow.

When he had finished easing out his aching muscles he picked up the barrow again and started to move. No change in his direction. A perfect straight line towards the council building. Not a falter or sense of apprehension came from him.

At the council building the killer put the barrow down and stretched out his back again, then pulled down the peak of a baseball cap he was wearing underneath the hoody. Being extra cautious.

I looked to Baxter and before he had chance to ask the question I said, 'There's a partial view of him, but it doesn't cover his face.'

He swore under his breath.

The male pulled out the two cones and popped them on the ground a short distance from the steps. The camera continually trained on him. It definitely was not on automatic rotate. He dug into the side of Sebastian, down into the barrow and brought out what we knew to be the crime scene tape and we watched as he tied it around the decorative lion at one end of the steps and then wrapped it around one of the cones, moved along and wrapped it around the other before dropping the reel on the ground.

There was a gentle murmur around the room as the team voiced their disgust at how organised this guy was. I didn't silence them. They were still paying attention and I felt pretty horrified myself by what I was watching, what I had seen.

It was when he lifted Sebastian out of the barrow and dragged him over to the steps that the wave of revulsion grew louder. He did it in such a way that Sebastian looked just like a ragdoll that no one should pay any attention to. He hurled him out of the barrow, half tipping him out, half lifting him, with an appearance of weightlessness, then dragged him with one arm up the steps to the top. It was maybe because they were only five shallow steps that he was able to do this with such ease, because I doubted he would have been able to make this look so effortless if the steps had been deeper or higher.

With a little flourish, he had Sebastian in the position we found him in and with his head dipped he strolled back down towards Market Square and the camera. The peak of his cap pulled low, and the baggy sweater hood over the top of it casting shadow around the sides of his face. In the pixelated grey of CCTV darkness, his face was completely hidden from view.

'Dammit,' Baxter cursed from the back of the room.

'He's very aware,' said Martin. His voice quiet and respectful of what we were viewing.

'He's not made it easy for us,' I admitted.

The killer moved to the cones, bent to pick up the crime scene tape, walked to the lion at the other end of the steps and tied it off, completing the closed off appearance of a crime scene.

Then he stepped over the tape and dropped the cardboard notice down that had the hashtag written on it. In this lighting, it wasn't possible to see the words.

With another adjustment to his cap, the killer picked up the handles of the wheelbarrow and moved off, head down, away from the camera that had been following him. As though he was aware.

Then he was gone.

And Sebastian Wade was propped on the council building steps awaiting the dawn and judgements of others.

9.

Awed silence filled the room as everyone took in what we had viewed. How calm and collected the killer had been.

Unruffled.

'And what time is this?' asked Baxter.

I looked at my notes. 'Two-o-nine a.m., Sir.'

'And what time is the post-mortem?'

'Fay said she can fit him in at the end of the day.'

He nodded.

I returned my focus to the team who waited patiently for our exchange to end. I'd noticed a couple of them had made notes on the time the victim had been dumped.

'We need to check out Nick Henson. He said he was at home but that he went out to look for Sebastian. We need clarify his whereabouts; his being out could have given him opportunity to commit the murder. Get the recording from when he phoned Sebastian in missing. What time it was, bearing in mind this footage at two-o-nine a.m. And I want the report from the officers who attended his home address, their pocket notebooks, plus I want to speak to them in person. To see what his demeanour was when he reported his husband gone. Was he upset he wasn't home or distressed because he'd just publicly dumped his body? Though this guy on the CCTV looks far from distressed.' I looked at the screen again, at the still image of the killer walking away, calm and slow. As though he'd just dumped a bag of rubbish on the side of the road. Not a human being who had a life, a husband. Loved ones.

I hated to do this when a loved one was grieving so obviously, but very often a murder was committed by someone close. We had to at least rule Nick out. This image on the screen. It didn't correspond with the man we had seen. The coldness on the screen. I couldn't feel it in their home.

'Martin...'

He lifted his head at me.

'Can you check the Family Liaison list and see who's available to put in the home with him, please?'

He made a quick scribble in his incident book.

I turned my back on the room. Other than Nick Henson, we had the book club, who will have been the last people to see Sebastian alive. Plus we had the whole blog issue. I scrubbed at my face and turned back to the room.

'I want every last person identifying from that book club, and I want them speaking with, and statements from them all. I want to know where they went after book club finished. Check their statements, CCTV, ANPR, witnesses, anything we have at our disposal.'

Baxter nodded at the back of the room.

'It's held in a pub. Speak to the staff, I want to know who else was there that night, if they have CCTV inside or outside in the car park. I want statements from each and every one of them. This has got off to a sticky start. We're on the back foot. Let's catch up and catch up properly.'

I looked to Aaron's desk. He would usually run point on the actions that needed to be dished out but he wasn't here. I missed him. I missed his calm. How he never became flustered. I missed my friend.

Christ, I was tired. My bones felt heavy as though I was dragging them around in this soft frame of mine, like it was hard work. There seemed to be a permanent headache threatening to burst out from behind my eyes and the point at which I had been knifed in my upper arm dragged at me, reminding me how fragile I was, how fragile the human body was.

I turned to Theresa and Diane, our two civilian staff who were responsible for the majority of the HOLMES work. Theresa was the inputter: it was her job to make sure everything made it onto the system. Diane indexed, processed, researched and analysed all the information on there.

Theresa was already nodding before I even spoke, a gentle smile on her face.

'You don't mind?' I asked.

'Of course I don't mind. It's no bother to me. I'm sitting here on my computer anyway. What difference will it make?'

Both these women made our lives so much easier with their professionalism with HOLMES. Though I still liked to go with my gut. It was great to have a system in place that tied all the information together and found the links, but you couldn't take people out of the equation.

'You all have something to do. Let's get on with this.' I looked to Baxter. His face was tight and closed. He wasn't happy. I had to get this over with.

Baxter's office was sparse. Impersonal. He waved at the chair in front of his desk and sat down. Behind him the grey day slipped quietly into the room through the large window behind him.

'Have you seen what's happening online?'

I understood why public perception was always so important to the bosses, but it was a problem I didn't worry about myself and it was the reason I didn't want to go any further in the promotion ladder. There was too much paperwork, not enough policing. Too many meetings and not enough interviews. Too much bullshit, not enough humanity.

'I can't say spending time online has been a priority of mine today,' I said.

His face soured, his chin crinkling below his lip.

I corrected myself. 'I'm sorry. I mean, I've been too tied up to have looked. Is there more I need to be aware of?'

'It hasn't stopped. In fact it's growing. Because it wasn't us, they're even more interested in what happened.'

I looked at him. The man who had made comments earlier today and called it That Twitter. How did he know what was happening online? 'Sir?'

He waved a hand outwards. 'Kirsty.' He indicated towards his PA who was sitting at her desk outside his office. Her head was down, fingers tapping away at her keyboard. 'She showed me how to follow the hashtag and check for any new or trending hashtags.' He paled. 'It's like the Wild West on there, you know.' He didn't wait for a response. 'The press want a statement.'

I nodded. Of course they did. Even if it hadn't have been online they would have been interested in a body in the middle of our city this morning.

'What the hell am I going to tell them?'

I hadn't seen him this stressed before. Baxter was still relatively new to the department. Only having been here a few months. He liked to give the impression of control. Wanted to know what we were doing at all times and was more hands on than the previous DCI, my friend, Anthony Grey. And I was aware that this was a stop-gap; Baxter wanted to further his career. He wanted to climb that ladder. A shitstorm was not what he needed on his watch.

'We give them the bare facts as we would any murder investigation,' I replied. 'We treat it as any other murder investigation. Just because people have an opinion doesn't mean we investigate differently, or behave differently.' Even as I spoke I knew it wasn't quite true. For him and for Catherine, our Detective Superintendent, it was all about perception, answering to supervisors higher up. Christ, even the Chief Constable had to answer to someone, and that was the Police and Crime Commissioner, the civilian role responsible for providing efficient policing in their areas. They were elected positions, so yes, they, at the top of the chain, were most definitely concerned about what the public thought about the police and what the police were doing and very slowly that concern trickled down. With a high profile case like this, our PCC's eyes would be all over it. No wonder Baxter was tense. He could see his promotion prospects slipping out his grasp. Not that the PCC could influence them, but if a job this big went wrong, it wouldn't look good on his CV. He wouldn't be classed as up to the task.

'Shall I get Claire to draft a media release for you?' I asked. I didn't want to be dragged into this. I had enough to do. I wasn't sure why he had dragged me in here when he could have contacted Claire Betts, our media liaison officer, himself.

'I can phone her.'

I clenched my teeth together. Kept my mouth shut.

'The reason I asked you in here...'

Ah, I knew there was something, other than him feeling the pressure.

'I've had a message from HR.'

I lifted myself taller in my chair. I was interested now.

Baxter leaned forward and placed his arms on the desk. 'Aaron has been in touch with Occ Health and wants to come back to work.'

Yes! This was the best news I'd had in months. 'This is great news.' I looked at Baxter. 'And great timing, we could do with all hands on deck. I presume he has to have his assessment at Occ Health first?'

Baxter's mouth twisted and he leaned back in his chair. His face wasn't matching my emotions. 'Yes, he needs to be assessed as fit to be operational, but...'

But? What the hell did he mean, but? My stomach sank. Aaron had been away from work for the past six weeks after suffering a minor heart attack at the office following a pretty tough case. I had since learned the proper name was a myocardial infarction. I had been speaking with him during his enforced absence from work and I knew he was hating it and was desperate to return, though I hadn't known he was about to contact HR to make the request. I was desperate to have him back. What was wrong with Baxter? Why so reticent?

'What?' I asked him.

'After a heart attack, do you really think a high stress team like Major Crime is the right place for him?' He gave me a look. I wasn't sure what he thought he was conveying but he looked to be in pain. 'Honestly?' he pleaded.

'I do think we're the best team for him,' I replied. So that's what this was about. Just prior to the heart attack Baxter had threatened Aaron's position on the team. He had clashed with him. Disliked Aaron's manner, not realising Aaron had Asperger's. And Aaron had refused to allow me to inform him. I had been stuck between wanting to support Aaron's decision and helping him. 'I think if we move him now we would add more stress to him that he could most certainly do without.'

Would he really do that to him? Could I still keep Aaron's confidence? Or was protecting him more important? This ball was now in Baxter's court.

'Let's see how his assessment with Occ Health goes first, shall we?' he conceded.

I stood to leave.

'I'm of a mind to get a replacement DS in here, Hannah. I think it's for the best, for the team and for Aaron.'

10.

David Smithson, or Smithy as he'd introduced himself when he held out his hand in the witness interview room on the ground floor of St Anne's police station, was petite for a male, standing at only about five foot five. Louise Burton towered over him. Her frame tall and willowy. A good meal wouldn't have gone amiss though.

I didn't know if they worked the night shifts in the CCTV unit on a permanent basis and therefore never saw daylight, but the pair had a sallow look about them. Their pale skin had a slight rubbery sheen to it.

They were witnesses so I needed to separate them, to speak to each of them alone. I explained this and Martin indicated to Louise that they would leave and use another interview room. Her already pallid face turned grey and her eyes widened as she looked to Smithy.

'It's normal in these circumstances,' I reassured her. 'If we catch whoever did this, we may need your help at a later date and we can't have the prosecution saying you conferred during this interview.'

She gave a slight nod and Smithy bared his teeth at her in an approximation of a smile.

I suggested we sit and Martin ushered Louise out the door before she could protest.

Smithy dropped into the plastic seat and let out a breath. 'She's scared, you know.'

'Why's that?' I asked, curious why she would be afraid of talking to us about what occurred during the night.

'She's got a couple of kiddies.'

I frowned, confused.

Smithy pulled on his bottom lip with his teeth.

I leaned back in my chair opposite him. Gave him time to think about his next statement.

'She doesn't want to lose her job.'

I looked at him.

'You found a dead body and we followed the guy with the camera and did nothing!' he exploded, spittle flying from his mouth. I tried not to wince as it hit my face. It wasn't as though he had spit at me as an assault, this was emotion.

I rubbed my nose and tried to discreetly wipe the damp patch from my cheek with the side of my palm. Smithy watched me. His eyes hard. Waiting.

'Tell me what happened,' I said eventually, after I had managed to clean my face.

'You saw the video?' Funny how we still referred to anything that wasn't a still image as a video, even though video recorders were long gone and everything was now digital. It was simply a digital recording on a disc.

I acknowledged that I had.

'We thought he had a Guy Fawkes.' His voice was plaintive now. He ran his hands through his hair. 'He was so goddamn relaxed we seriously thought the guy was a prop. That it was staged. Especially when he put the crime scene tape up first.'

He pulled his hands down from his face. 'It's not like you expect someone to walk a dead guy out into the middle of Market Square right under your CCTV nose, is it?'

11.

We'd been in the morgue for over an hour now and my back was starting to ache as well as my upper arm. I rubbed at my arm as I listened to Fay talk into the microphone hanging from the ceiling over Sebastian Wade. A strong scent of disinfectant lay heavy over us in the clinical setting, the strangest of medical rooms. The floor sloped towards drains for easy cleaning and every surface was wash and wipe clean, tile and metal. It was a large well-lit space with multiple tables in the centre.

Today we were the only people in here and all that had been done so far was the outer examination. Fay was thorough. Not only was she thorough, but she wasn't in any hurry.

I kneaded my arm.

Fay cut off Sebastian's clothes, and Martin had bagged them individually in brown paper evidence bags, sealing each one and signing the exhibit label. The bloody items would be placed in the forensic dryer back at the station once we returned before being sent to the forensics lab for analysis. Sending damp items through to them was a big no.

Sebastian was laid before us in the very condition he entered the world, other than the extra stab wounds he possessed.

I hadn't asked Nick if he had any parents still surviving. No one wanted to survive their child. It was always the most difficult task I had, informing a parent about the loss of a child. No matter how old that child.

Here, in the mortuary, the dead were quiet. Peaceful. The pain they suffered was finished. They were here to give us their answers. To talk to us about their last moments. I could cope with that. With their help, we could stop another family going through what their loved ones were going through.

And it was with this reasoning that I was able to stand here as Fay took her scalpel, leaned over and made the first incision into Sebastian Wade.

Fay looked at me. 'He didn't stand a chance.'

I nodded. I'd watched and listened to the examination of the three knife wounds in his abdomen.

'He was never going to survive unless he got to a hospital in pretty quick time,' said Fay. 'His liver was pretty badly damaged and I would say he died within minutes.'

'He would have known what was happening?' I asked.

Fay walked to the side of the room, bent down and retrieved a clean sheet from one of the shelves under the work-counter. 'Oh yes. Death wasn't instantaneous. He would have been able to look his killer in the eye. Ask him the obvious question: why?' She placed the folded sheet on Sebastian's feet and ankles ready for when he had been stitched back up. 'He wouldn't have said much more. Blood loss would have been rapid.'

'And the type of weapon we're looking for?'

Martin was placing all the evidence bags we were going to take away with us into a larger bag for carrying.

'I'd say it was a kitchen knife. An average kitchen knife. One you can find in any knife block. The slim filleting one.' Fay snapped off her gloves and bagged them, then handed the bag to Martin. 'I don't believe it was found at the scene so we can't do a comparison.'

I shook my head.

'Well, if you find it,' she continued, 'we can match it up with the wound and tell you if it's the right one.' She looked at Sebastian laid on the slab.

I followed her gaze. Sebastian, now pale and waxy-white as his blood had pooled as his heart was no longer pumping it around his body. A man who had been filled with life and had interests and love, but had it torn away from him.

He'd tried to talk to us today, but he hadn't been able to say much.

Fingernail clippings had been taken, but there were no visible signs that he had scratched at anyone. There were no defensive marks on him. All we had found were the three knife wounds in his abdomen.

Whoever had killed Sebastian Wade had managed to do so without him putting up a fight.

This either meant it was someone he knew, or someone had got the jump on him.

He'd gone out last night not realising it was his last night. His last book club. His last goodbye with Nick.

Sebastian Wade had not said goodbye to anyone. And he hadn't said much to us either.

12.

Drew couldn't concentrate on work today.

All he could do was watch the online explosion about the body found on Market Square that morning. The speculation and finger-pointing was incredible to witness. It was mesmerising. Every person had an opinion on what had happened. They knew whose fault it was. Who should be castigated for such a heinous act, leaving that poor man out there on the steps that way. The poor people who'd seen him would be traumatised.

Though it didn't stop them sharing the images.

Twitter was doing its best to take them down. It had put a formal request out for them not to be shared but then there had been further uproar about citizen journalism, and how images of warzones and riots where people were hurt and beaten were shared with no consideration for the effects on the viewer of the image.

The police had denied they had created the crime scene and said they were now dealing with it and advised people to stay away and requested that any images not be shared on social media but be forwarded to a Nottinghamshire police email address they had set up for this incident.

It was a complete mess.

And he could not drag his eyes away.

How could these people not see the horror of what they were doing? How could they not see that they were turning this death into something even more ugly?

His phone rang.

He ignored it.

There was a particularly angry outburst happening right now that he didn't want to miss.

It rang again, the back of the phone rattling against the kitchen counter as it vibrated. He checked the caller ID.

His ex-wife.

Damn.

'Yeah?' He didn't have the time for her now.

'Do you have to answer like that?' She was pissed off already.

'What do you want?'

'It's Libbie's birthday at the weekend.'

He ran a hand through his hair. 'You think I don't know that?'

There was a long sigh down the phone. 'I'm trying here. You could at least meet me halfway.'

He barked out a laugh. 'You left me, remember? This is what you wanted.'

'Don't.'

'I'm sorry, was that not halfway?'

There was silence.

He watched the screen as it scrolled. Life and death brought alive in two hundred and eighty characters of pure anger and hatred and it fizzed through his veins in a rageful hot ball.

She finally spoke. 'Are you coming over at the weekend?'

He rolled his eyes up to the ceiling. He knew what she was saying but he couldn't help but go there. 'I thought I'd take them for lunch.'

The silence was loaded.

Why did he do it?

'It might be better if you came here,' she suggested. Her voice softer now.

'I'd really like to take them out.' His hand tightened around the phone. Knuckles turning white.

'You know...' she paused.

'Just say it.' He could feel a dull ache starting behind his eyes.

'You know that they won't.' Another pause. 'I'm sorry. But after all the press. It's been hard on them.'

He wanted to throw the phone against the wall but he held on even tighter. The ache pushed into his eyes. 'Hard on them?'

'I'm not doing this with you again.' He heard her shift position. 'I can't. Drop by if you can.' And with that, she ended the call. There was nothing but silence.

And the scrolling anger on the monitor in front of him.

With a rigid hand he placed the phone back down and returned his attention to the screen.

It was this very screen that had changed his life, that had destroyed his life. They were the reason Melissa said his children didn't know if they wanted to see him. Someone that day, well over a year ago now, nearly eighteen months in fact, someone had taken a short movie clip of him pulling the young lad to safety. Because they had originally been taking movie footage of the chalk woman and her drawing the whole picture hadn't been captured. What was out of shot was the car behind them and what was in shot was him pulling and pushing the lad and him landing in a heap with his head in a wall.

It had gone viral in hours. People were calling him all the names. Someone had identified him and then they'd called for his dismissal from his job. It had been endless. His family couldn't take it, especially the kids. The school had taken a lot of grief and not knowing how to move forward with it they had suspended him pending a thorough investigation. Meanwhile his life had spiralled ever downwards and eventually the school had asked him to resign before they had to take any further action. They said he was a valued member of the teaching team but the furore was having a negative effect on both the school and the children. They didn't want to fire him and it go against him in the future and they were unsure of their footing, but if he quietly resigned it would be better for all of them.

So he had and his fall was complete. All at the hands of an internet mob.

So now he would show them how ugly they looked when something happened that went online. They had brought the events of today on themselves. They had gradually broken him and it had taken some time to find a way to show them how ugly their world was. Now he finally had.

13.

The two cops who had attended Nick and Sebastian's house weren't on duty until ten p.m. Now this had now turned into a murder inquiry so they came as soon as they woke up and were informed that they were needed. Sharon Bell and Lynette Gregory looked tired as most uniformed cops did when they were working nights. I used to hate that shift. The four a.m. wall did it for me. Yes, we could be on late, or called out in the middle of the night, but we didn't actually work night shifts as such.

'Thanks for coming in.' I handed both women a mug of coffee and they looked at my desk, I knew, wondering where they could place them.

'I'm sorry, let me shift something for you.' My work space wasn't popular with Baxter. He gave me a look any time he had cause to come in to my office. I moved a pile of folders and dumped them on top of another stack that was already teetering. I held my hands around it for a moment while we gauged whether it would fall or hold and when it stayed upright I sat and thanked them again.

'I'm not sure what we can do to help,' said Lynette, the older of the two women. 'We only took the misper report. We weren't at the house very long. It was late, there were no other jobs at that moment in time so we took the call and paid him a visit.' I nodded. There was a public misconception that you had to be missing twenty-four hours before you could be reported missing, but it just wasn't the case and police assess and grade missing calls and deal with them appropriately. 'Mr Henson had already been out looking for his husband,' she continued. 'We took details and told him the morning shift would pick it up after us and someone would be in touch with him again.'

I smiled, reassured them. 'It's not the practical events themselves I'm interested in,' I said. 'It's his demeanour. How was he? In himself?'

Sharon looked to Lynette then back to me. 'He was distraught. Well...' she rubbed a hand through her cropped bleach blonde hair, leaving it looking as good as before she touched it. 'He was a contained distraught if you get what I mean?'

I did, but I needed her to explain. I needed it out in the open so there could be no mistakes. 'Tell me.'

Lynette jumped in. 'He was pacing about. Talking quickly. Trying to give us lots of information. Information we didn't need.'

'Which indicated his level of stress. He wasn't visibly upset, if that's what you're asking,' finished Sharon. She was the most nervous of the pair. Lynette had experience on her side. She knew jobs could go in any direction. Sharon, by the look of her, was still learning the ropes. She may even still be in her probationary two years. She was only young. Just thinking this made me feel old.

'What time did you get to his house?'

Sharon pulled her bag from the floor at the side of her and rummaged inside. Eventually she pulled out her pocket notebook. Lynette let her. Though I had a feeling she knew the time, but was allowing her young colleague to finish what she was doing now she had started, to prevent her feeling uncomfortable.

Sharon flicked through the pages. Came to the one she needed. 'We were State 6...' at the scene 'at zero one twenty-six hours.' She kept her book open and looked at me.

I nodded. The call had come in from Henson at a little before twelve-thirty. The killer was roaming the streets with Sebastian's body at two-o-nine a.m.

'How long were you with him?'

Sharon checked her pocket book again. 'We left Mr Henson at zero-two-fourteen, Ma'am.'

It wasn't Henson. He was in the clear. I was glad about that. Though we now had a sadistic killer on our hands who we had to find and quickly before they decided to play any more games.

14.

As the car headlights swept across the front of my apartment I saw someone crouched on the step. It was dark and they had a hood pulled up over their head obscuring their face. Body curled in on itself. I had no idea of size or gender. My skin prickled. I checked around. There was a group of young men walking on the other side of the road. They were oblivious to what was happening here. Though I wasn't sure what that was. Other than them I saw no one else. It was me and this person.

I decided not to park in the gated secure car park as I might need to make a swift exit. I pulled my phone from my bag. Brought up the control room ready to press dial should I need to.

The figure didn't move. They must have known I was here.

When I opened the car door they stood. With the darkness and the hood I still couldn't make out who it was, but they were too short to be the male on the video I had watched earlier in the day.

They moved a few steps towards me. 'Hannah.'

Shit, I recognised that voice. Why had I come home now? If I'd have left it another ten, maybe fifteen minutes, my front doorstep might have been empty.

'I've been waiting ages for you. I thought you were never coming home.'

I didn't want to talk to her. I looked back to the group of men who were now nearly out of view. I would rather have a conversation with them.

'If I'd known you were here waiting I might not have come back yet,' I replied.

She was closer now and she pulled her hood down. I could see her face under the street light. I couldn't get used to the fuller cheeks, the roundness of her face. But she looked pale. I had no sympathy.

'Won't you just talk to me?' she asked. 'Can't we talk?'

A stony look was my response.

'I've said I'm sorry,' she continued, 'and I mean it. Dad has forgiven me.' There was a whine in her tone. This irritated me more and the headache that had been threatening started to deepen.

I rounded on her. 'Dad didn't nearly lose his job because of you did he? His career. In fact, Dad doesn't even know what you did to me. How you nearly screwed my career over for your own selfish needs.' I ran a hand through my hair.

He would forgive her even if he was aware. Following Mum's death Dad had latched on to me and Zoe for his emotional support. We were the people filling that huge void that had been left in his life. He couldn't cope if he lost one of us and not through a family fall-out. It broke his heart when Zoe was sent to prison for dealing drugs and he'd lost her temporarily. He had visited as much as he could.

Zoe stuffed her hands into the pockets of her hoody, bunched up her shoulders. 'I was a different person, Hannah.' Her voice was quiet. I had to strain to listen to her. 'Can we go inside to talk about it?'

I walked past her towards the door. It was cold out here now.

'Thank you.' It was barely a whisper.

I turned and looked her in the face. Tears had welled up in her eyes. I closed my own eyes for a brief moment. Tried to clear my head.

'I'm not letting you in, Zoe.' I could feel my chest constrict as she dropped her head to hide her face.

'I'm clean, Hannah. It's all the past. I want to make it up to you. I was a different person. It was the drugs. I never wanted to hurt you. Please.' This last word was dragged out. Painful. Caught in her throat and in her eyes as she faced me again.

'I can't. Do you have any idea what you did?' I turned my back to her and pushed the key in the lock.

'I never thought...'

'Exactly. You only thought about yourself. And here you are again, thinking about yourself and your own feelings. This little display here, it's not about me. It's about you and how you feel and about what you want. You aren't considering me in this scenario. How I might feel or what I might want. If you did you might have gone about it a little differently than accosting me on my doorstep after a long day at work. For Christ's sake, do you not listen to or read the news?' My voice was raised now.

'You won't speak to me when you come to Dad's!' She was shouting herself now. And we were still outside, for my neighbours to catch every word. This was so damn typical of her. To have this conversation this way. Rather than in a private place away from prying eyes and ears.

'In fact, you've started to avoid Dad. He's noticed, you know. That you only come when you know I'm not there. It's upsetting him. I had no choice but to come to see you at your home because you won't give me the time of day at mine.'

'It's not yours.' Why couldn't I control myself around her? 'It's Dad's home. He's letting you stay there while you get back on your feet.' I barked out a laugh. 'Which you won't, will you? This is you. You'll suck the life out of him.' I was getting warm now. My whole body reacting to the stress she was creating.

She took a deep breath, 'You're so self-involved you can't see anyone else's point of view. How the hell do you help people, Hannah? You help so many people but when it comes to one of your own, your family, you close off.' Tears spilled down her cheeks. 'I was a mess when I stayed with you that time. I didn't know what I was doing. I was out of my mind. The drugs controlled me. I would never hurt you that way. Not on purpose. You must know that.'

I turned my back on her. I was tired. Worn out. 'I have to go, Zoe. I've got another long day ahead of me tomorrow.' I stepped into the hallway.

'I was worried sick when you were stabbed. I thought I was going to lose you without being able to make it right again. Don't let that be the way this plays out.'

I closed the door. Leaned my forehead against it and let the tears flow.

15.

I'd decided to start my day by checking the online news pages. I wish I hadn't bothered. All the mainstream news websites were leading with the murder of Sebastian Wade and the public response to the mimic crime scene that had been set up around his body. They had done their homework, though it wasn't difficult in the world of the internet, I was finding out, as they linked him up as a true-crime blogger. And how it was strange his own murder had been staged the way it had. They had obviously picked up this information from the stream of noise the public made. Though much of what had been online the previous day had been rubbish and emotional hysteria, some of it, like the fact that Sebastian was a true-crime blogger, was factual, and the press had selected this information out of the pandemonium, researched for truth, and run with it.

The blog, Sebastian's blog, was an area we still needed to get to grips with, to see how it impacted on the investigation. What he may have said on there or who he may have upset.

Yesterday had been a long and busy day. There were many lines of inquiry on this case and it wasn't one that would be resolved in a matter of hours. Now that Nick had been ruled out, there was no clear suspect for us to home in on. We had to trace Sebastian's steps. It had also been made complicated by the very clear message that whatever was behind his murder, his blog was involved and we needed to dig deeper.

I pushed the door open to Evie Small's office. Our station analyst and my best friend was already in, as I knew she would be. Her trademark curls were piled up on the top of her head today, tendrils falling down randomly where she hadn't managed to tuck them in. She did organised messy brilliantly.

Me, I just did messy.

She turned from what she was working on. 'Hey, lovely. How's things with you this morning?' She pulled open her drawer and pulled out a third of a packet of chocolate biscuits, pointed them at me like a weapon.

I shook my head. She frowned.

'I didn't bring a drink with me,' I said in response.

'Biscuits don't need tea. It's the other way around. Tea needs biscuits. It's too wet otherwise. Didn't you know that? Why do you think I always have a pack?'

I grunted at her in response and wondered how she managed to stay so slim.

'Please yourself.' She fished one out the pack and shoved half into her mouth. 'What can I do for you?' she mumbled through the crumbs.

I adored this woman.

I pulled a chair over from the corner of the room and sat beside her. 'What do you know about blogs?' I asked.

'The same as you, I imagine.' She swallowed the biscuit. 'The ones I read have their own niche and are updated on a regular basis. What is it you need to know?'

She followed blogs?

'You use Twitter?' I asked instead.

'Don't you?' She gave me a look. 'Of course you don't.' She shoved the other half of the biscuit into her mouth.

'What do you talk about?' I was digressing. But, Twitter, I was too busy to living my life, to stop what I was doing and put the details online for people to ignore. I didn't understand it.

Evie chewed, her eyes twinkling as she regarded me then she fished out her phone from the drawer at the side of her. Unlocked it, tapped the screen then handed it to me.

I took the phone. 'What am I looking at?'

She raised her eyebrows.

'I can see it's Twitter.' I grabbed for the pack of biscuits on her desk.

She smiled as I picked a biscuit out and started to eat while still staring at her phone. 'It's my feed. It's what I tweet out. If you look at that, I can then show you the feed I look at when I'm on. It's what other people I am following are saying.'

The last thing she had tweeted was a brief review of a movie she had been to see the previous evening.

I looked at her. 'Date?'

She took the phone out my hand. 'Might have been.' And tapped the screen a couple of times before handing it back to me. 'That's the feed I follow of other people.'

'Tell me more about this date.' I pushed.

'What was it you came in here for?'

'Information on your date, obviously.' I laughed at her. We were both hopeless when it came to our love lives. In different ways. Evie was afraid to get close and always backed away after she had been with a man for a while.

'If you don't need to see that, I'll have it back.' She made a move for her phone.

I tightened my grip on it. 'Let me just have a look.'
I started to read through her feed.

'I thought you came in here about blogs?' she asked.

There was still a lot of chatter about Sebastian and the crime scene from yesterday. Today the focus was on the connection to him being a true-crime blogger.

'I did, but it's kind of connected,' I answered as I read outlandish theories about why he might have been killed the way he had been.

'You're investigating that blogger?'

I handed her the phone. 'Yeah and I want you on the team for this.'

'Okay. I'll make sure I'm at the briefing. What do you need from me?'

I nodded towards the phone. 'People talk about real stuff like this murder in such ridiculous ways just because they can and because they have the space?' I asked instead.

'What do you think he did?'

'Who?'

'Your dead guy.'

'Sebastian Wade?'

'Yeah. He had a true-crime blog right. That's what you wanted to know about. He will have blogged about crimes and he will have also given his opinions on them. Whether they were factually correct opinions or not.'

This was fucked up.

I nodded.

'You want me to look at his blog and analyse his traffic?'

'Yes. I want to know who didn't like Sebastian Wade's online opinions.'

16

Drew didn't usually have anything to get up for. Not since he'd lost his job and had to take on the role he was in now. It was demeaning.

Tutor at an online university.

Yes, he was still teaching. But he could do the hours he pleased. He could work in the nude if he wanted. Though only in his room because he wasn't sure his housemate would appreciate it if he wandered around the house naked.

He wasn't teaching children. He wasn't moulding the minds of the young and impressionable. He'd been cast aside, like yesterday's news.

He had been yesterday's news, hadn't he, and it had lasted a hell of a lot longer than yesterday. With the rise of the internet and citizen journalism, he blew out a breath in frustration at the phrase, stories that caught the public's imagination could and would run and run. And those pushing to keep them alive had no regard for the person behind the story.

He licked his lips. His mouth was dry and tasted like week old coffee and a cat's litter tray.

They didn't have a cat and he didn't drink coffee.

Walking into the kitchen he saw through the window that his housemate's car had gone from the drive. He'd left for work. To a day job with walls made of brick and mortar and real human people to interact with. Drew pulled a bottle of orange out the fridge, unscrewed the lid and gave it a sniff. Deciding it was still within consumable parameters he took a glass down from the cupboard and poured himself a drink.

His day would consist of being alone, sitting at his computer, checking the forum where the students talked and asked questions and marking the last few assignments he had to do. There was also a webinar he was booked in for later in the evening. He'd actually have to get dressed for that. It was the closest he got to talking to people.

And it was all because people decided they were the ones to select the facts and then be judge, jury and executioner.

It was brutal.

Now it was his turn.

With his juice in hand he turned to the dining room where he'd set up the laptop. No need to close himself off in his room. There was no one here to disturb him, to see what he was doing.

Bringing the computer to life he opened three windows. First Twitter, then his news site of preference, and then the Nottinghamshire police website.

Time to see what had progressed overnight.

He was thrilled to see the murder was still high in the listing for the news website. They were leading with the unusual fact that the victim had been a true-crime blogger and the crime scene had been set up like, well, like a crime scene.

He had to laugh. It had been ingenious really.

The reason he liked this news site was because they tended to report the news quite impassively, leading with the information they knew rather than opining on it.

There were plenty of other news outlets he could obtain a warped version of world events, depending on the political leanings of said outlet. Opinions were ten a penny.

Reading the news with an opinion attached wasn't news in his eyes. News was information. People were easily swayed and if you were told how to feel about the latest NHS crisis over your cornflakes then it wasn't news it was an op-ed. And once you spoon fed the public with what they should be thinking they ran with it. In full technicolour. Berating anyone who held a differing point of view.

Watching these flare-ups used to amuse him. Not since he had been the target of a social media pack mentality attack. Not since that day on the street with the chalk artist.

The day that had changed his life.

He switched to Twitter.

This was the place that would decide if his actions had accomplished what he had set out to do.

To hold a mirror up to their ugly hate-filled face.

To show them the grotesqueness of their mutual actions.

He clicked onto the trending icon.

Amongst the trending topics was *True-crime blogger* and *Nottingham*.

He smiled.

They were still talking about what he'd done. This was a good start. Maybe he had shown them.

Maybe they were horrified and were considering what social media was.

Maybe this was a tipping point for them.

Clicking on *True-crime blogger* the screen filled with all tweets that contained those words. Tweets discussing the man the police had found the previous day. The man Drew had left for them. The trending topics started initially with the top tweets. The ones that were most popular, that had been shared or liked the most.

True-crime blogger found in his own crime scene.
True-crime for true-crime blogger, maybe we need a true detective?

The glass of orange juice whipped off the table with a sudden ferocity as Drew's arm sliced across the table and knocked it flying. The amber liquid splashed down onto the wooden floor before the glass hit it and splintered with a loud smash. His anger flaring at the comments he was reading, Drew barely noticed the damage on the floor.

Where was the introspection? How could they not see this was aimed at them? That their online life had turned into a nasty reality and one that they controlled and it would only stop if they stopped. If they reflected on their own behaviour instead of the behaviour of others. They had caused this and they were the masters of what was about to happen next.

The fury raged inside of him like a white hot ball in the pit of his stomach that wanted to consume him and the only way to stop it was to find peace. But this wasn't peaceful. Here they were basking, in how sick they thought it that the man had been left in such a way. No matter how sick, it didn't stop them soaking in it. Covering themselves in it. Making sure they were a part of what was happening. Even if they were in no way involved and never would be.

But, he was.

He controlled this.

He controlled this narrative.

This time.

A quick stop at the Nottinghamshire police website revealed little. A brief statement that they were investigating the death of a male found on Market Square and anyone with information needed to come forward.

He would come forward all right.

Just not in the way they wanted him to.

17

Aaron poured the boiling water into a mug and squeezed half a lemon in. Fresh droplets hung in the air as he squeezed, light and clean and tangy. Lisa had decided it was what he needed to drink first thing in a morning; she said it was good for his health. He had done the research but couldn't find anything to back it up, but he went along with her anyway because he actually liked the flavour. She had been obsessive since his heart attack and ruled the kitchen but had worked with him to figure out what he was willing to eat and drink. Knowing that he liked a menu routine she read all the literature and talked with him, then meticulously listed his meals for the days of the week. Meals he could eat if he was in the house or, when he returned to work, easily pack into a plastic tub and take it with him. She wasn't going to let him slide just because his return was on the horizon.

She had also changed her own diet and those of the children, in an effort not to isolate him.

Not that he would care. He was more than happy to do what he needed to do, regardless of what others needed.

Lisa loved him and his heart attack had scared her. That had been one of the things that had amazed him out of all this. The utter love that had shone out of her. Not that it hadn't before. She had always been good to him. This, it had been on another level. Like she had genuinely thought he was going to die.

But he hadn't. He was here, wasn't he?

Lisa came up behind him. Told him she was there and leaned into his shoulder and whispered into his ear, 'Do you have one of those for me?'

He could smell her familiar perfume. The one she had been wearing when they met and he had liked and bought her every Christmas since.

He pulled another mug down from the cupboard and filled it with water. Squeezed the other half of lemon into the water, turned and looked into the eyes of his wife.

She gave a slow smile. Took the mug out of his hands. 'How are you feeling?'

'I feel okay. I tell you that every day.'

'You have an appointment with occupational health this afternoon.'

He did.

Lisa sipped at her drink.

Aaron turned his back to his wife and picked up his mug.

'Are you confident about the appointment today?' she asked.

He could hear two sets of music coming from two different bedrooms as both kids got themselves organised to leave for school. It was always the same, every morning. He hadn't usually been here to see it – having already left for work, but since his enforced leave he had found out what his family's routine was. And noise, it appeared, was a part of the morning as much as it was in the evening and he hated it. It would be bad enough if there was one noise heard coming from upstairs, but two competing against each other made his skin crawl. He'd had to use his own earphones as he adjusted to morning life in his own house.

Lisa pulled on his arm and turned him back to face her. 'Well?'

'The doctor said I'm fit to return to work, so yes, I'm confident in the appointment. There's no reason for me not to be,' he replied.

She reached behind him and placed her mug on the counter-top. Let her hand linger behind him, dropping to his hip. 'How do you feel about returning to work, honey? It's been a difficult few weeks.'

He closed his eyes. It had been difficult for her. He knew that. She had told him that much. She had been scared. Scared of losing him.

He opened his eyes. Looked at her.

He hadn't been afraid. He had listened to the doctors. Understood what they told him. Believed what they said. That the heart attack was caused by a blockage and not stress and that so long as he continued to take his medications and follow a balanced diet and kept physically active he should be okay.

'I'm fine. I'm ready to go back,' he told her. And he was. He loved his family and having a routine set up from the hospital had helped him adapt. He needed the familiarity of work. Of the office. Of getting up in a morning, getting showered and leaving for work.

Lisa put a palm on his cheek. 'I love you.'

'Muuuum.' The screech came from the kitchen door as Beth stood there in most of her uniform. 'Kyle won't tell me what he's done with my tie.' The whine in her voice was nothing new to the family home. It had appeared the moment she had turned thirteen and hadn't left for the following fourteen months.

Lisa let out a sigh. Mouthed 'I love you' again at Aaron and walked towards their daughter. Beth smiled at her dad, happy to get help coming her way. Aaron shook his head. It was easier dealing with the offenders at work than it was parenting two teenage children. He was going to be damn glad to get back to work. It wouldn't be too soon for him.

18

I brought the room to silence and made sure I had everyone's attention before I started the morning briefing. As well as the investigating team we had the presence of Detective Superintendent Catherine Walker and Detective Chief Inspector Kevin Baxter, Evie and Claire, the media liaison officer, who had the sunniest disposition I had come across in this line of work, though she used it to keep people off guard. She always managed to get her message across and brooked no messing.

Everyone had their notepads out, pens poised.

I updated them on the post-mortem from the previous day. Quickly ran through what we had from our lines of inquiry, which as it turned out, wasn't a lot.

A male had managed to walk into the middle of Market Square with a dead body and dump him there, setting him up in his own private crime scene for members of the public to come across on their walks into work that morning.

The huge furore online was why Claire was here. There had to be a determined effort to deal with what we had, to make sure the public felt safe, were assured they were safe.

'We really have no idea who this male is?' asked Catherine, incredulous.

'He knew the cameras would be on him and he made allowances for it. He dressed for the event. We don't have a shot of his face so we don't even know his ethnicity,' I responded. There was no point in being coy about our lack of forward movement.

'And what are you plans for today?'

Well, if she let me finish the briefing she might just find out. I ran my hand through my hair. 'Today we have multiple witnesses to identify and locate. We're going to speak to everyone who saw Sebastian at the book club before he died. We're going to speak to the members.'

Catherine nodded.

'We're going to find out what kind of mood he was in. If he arrived anxious. If he raised concerns about anything during the meeting. If they noticed anything when they left. If anyone was waiting for him. If he met with anyone. Someone has to know something.' I looked at the room. 'I'm not buying that it was a completely random attack. Not with the crime scene set up around him.'

I paired the team up so that we could work through the interviews at speed. Nick Henson hadn't known much about the people at the book club. It wasn't his thing and though he had hated to admit it, he had only half listened when Sebastian told him about the people he had spent time with.

'He's given us the location where they met and the website, because whoever ran the meeting had set up a professional looking website in order to attract more members. Nick said it was with a lot of help from Sebastian,' I relayed.

Catherine looked concerned. Baxter leaned in to her and whispered in her ear. I hated when they overshadowed my investigations like this and it only tended to happen if there was the possibility of a negative outcome on the department.

Catherine nodded, lifted her chin and spoke up. 'And the blog, Hannah?'

I tried to let out the sigh as silently and unobtrusively as I could. 'Evie is looking in to that for us. As soon as we know more then we can action it.'

With a curt nod my update was dismissed and she and Baxter turned on their heels and left us to it.

I looked to Aaron's empty desk. What the hell was I going to do about this? I desperately needed Aaron back and it was great news he was healthy enough to come back, but I was concerned about the ability of Baxter to block him returning.

There was movement in the office now as staff started to collect their coats and slip them on. Pool car keys were collected from the key-rack. It was time to find out what happened to Sebastian Wade the night before last.

The Copper Café was a lovely pub to hold a book club in. It was on the busy Woodborough Road in Mapperley and was located within a row of shops, but inside, you felt away from the hustle and bustle of the high street outside. I had taken Pasha with me and paired Martin up with Ross. They were still at the office until I contacted them with the details of other book club members.

We were met by the manager, a young man who looked as though he could barely be out of school. It didn't help that he wore a pair of Harry Potter spectacles perched on his face. He was energetic and effusive. Eager to help. Offering us a warm drink, which we gladly accepted after walking in from the light drizzle of the day.

Once we were seated I asked him about the meeting, about what he had seen that night, anything out of place, and if they held any CCTV.

Unfortunately the only CCTV was directed in the grounds, to protect the customers' vehicles.

'But I was here. I served the group all evening. I can help in any way possible,' he gushed.

I asked him if the group felt different in any way. If there appeared to be any friction. What their usual demeanour was when they attended meetings here.

'They're a great bunch of people,' he said, leaning forward. Pleased to be involved in the investigation. You often found this in people on the periphery of cases. If they weren't directly involved and hurt by events, it was quite exciting for them to feel they were in the know a little. Especially, if, like this case, it was garnering some press interest. Worldwide internet interest. He could tell his friends he was involved.

'They're never any trouble. In fact, I keep meaning to join in myself.' He lowered his voice a fraction, though the bar was closed as it was still too early to open and there was no one to overhear him. 'I have quite an interest in true-crime, you know.' He lowered his voice even more, into a stage whisper. 'I have quite a keen eye.' He winked.

Pasha shifted in her seat beside me and I knew she would be hiding a smirk.

'Okay,' I acknowledged. 'So, nothing of note Wednesday night?'

'Oh no, absolutely not. They really are the perfect group to have around. They come in, grab a table or two, order drinks, maybe some food and chat about their stuff.' His fingers spread out in a fan against his breastbone, the tips of his fingers just tickling his throat. He seemed shocked that I should suggest there would be a problem.

'What about other people in the bar?' I asked.

'In what way?' His face creased in confusion. Small lines furrowing down between his eyebrows, crinkling his otherwise youthful face.

Pasha picked up her mug from the table in front of us.

'Did you see anyone in the bar that night that looked to be paying the book group, or Sebastian, particular attention? Negative attention,' I clarified.

The eagerness of a minute ago slipped off him like a silken coat as he remembered Sebastian Wade had been brutally murdered and left out in such a public way. His eyes darkened.

'No.' His voice was quiet now, but not the same hushed excited quiet. Now it was a somber, apologetic tone. 'I didn't see anything that could help you, I'm afraid.' His final admission, that he had nothing to offer the investigation. That this was real life and people were hurting. He couldn't help.

Often, people didn't know when they saw something that was helpful. Because, at the time, it didn't seep into their consciousness.

I leaned into the conversation. 'Look, Joel, you might know more than you realise. Let's just run through the evening. What you saw and what you heard and let us decide if you know anything of substance or not, shall we?'

He scrubbed at his face. Nodded.

I pulled out my notepad and we walked through the events of the evening.

19.

The person who ran the book group was Andy Denning. A slim, quiet forty something.

We were in his living room, a tidy place, which if I was honest, didn't have the feel of a home. It was sparse, functional. There were no photographs or books, no newspapers or magazines, no cushions, nothing of comfort. The room held no emotion, no feeling. It was cold.

Andy, though, was upset when he realised it was Sebastian who had been found in Market Square and dabbed tissues at his eyes. 'He was a good guy,' he said. 'Popular. Why would someone do this to him?'

I couldn't tell him as we had no idea. That was why we were here. Andy looked genuinely shaken and I wondered if this, even at his age, was the first death he had encountered. It was unusual to get to your forties and not to know someone who had passed away. He wasn't particularly helpful, he couldn't think of a reason anyone would want to hurt Sebastian. He repeated that as the founder of the book club Sebastian was one of the most treasured people there and knew so much more about true-crime than the rest of them. And how awful it was that he was found the way he was. Did we really not leave him that way?

I told him that we hadn't. How anyone could believe police would walk away and leave a crime scene with a murder victim in it, open like that, and alone for anyone to walk into, was beyond me.

'I thought the book club was yours?' I queried him. 'Joel at the bar said you were the one to speak with.'

Andy nodded. 'He would do. I took over the administration of the group as Sebastian got so frustrated with it all. He enjoyed the group and the books, but he wasn't one for the background stuff, so when I joined I offered to take it on for him. He was more than happy to offload it. I keep track of all the members and send out the emails reminding everyone of what book we're reading and what date we're meeting each month.'

'On that point then we need a list of the book club members,' I said.

Andy nodded, swiped at his face with the tissue again and stuffed it in his pocket. 'Let me get a pen and paper,' he said. He walked towards the television, stopped in front of it, paused, seemed to consider what he was doing then turned and rapidly left the room.

Pasha looked at me and raised her eyebrows. I smiled in response. The poor man was a gibbering wreck. He didn't know what to do with himself. Murder wasn't a crime that many people experienced. If you were going to be close to a crime it was likely to be anything other than murder, depending of course, on your gender and age. Teenagers and young adults are more likely to have mobile phones stolen. Young men to be the victims of violence and so on and so on. Murder is something you think you'll never encounter. You read about it and watch television dramas about it, but you never expect a real life experience. We scare people. It's part of the job. We recognise that and allow for all the reactions that will come our way.

Andy walked back into the room, a small notebook and pen in his hand. He gave us a weak smile that did not travel to his eyes. He sat down and started scribbling into the pad. We silently let him work. When he'd finished he tore out a sheet and handed it to me.

'This is a list of all the members of the group.'

'Is this all of them?' I asked, with emphasis on *all*.

'Of course. I keep meticulous records,' he said.

'Including past members?' I clarified.

'Oh.' He looked perplexed. 'No. I'll need to download those for you. I can't remember them all. I'll send them to you, shall I? I'll need to find them out first. My computer isn't the most organised of places.'

I agreed that we would indeed need the list as soon as he was able to send it to us and gave him my card with my contact details including my email address.

Andy told us again that Sebastian was the vital beating heart of the club, with a very real passion for true-crime, what with him having that website and all that, he said.

There were no bitter rivalries within the group. No romances. It was a book group, he repeated again.

'We read a book in a month, then meet up and talk about it for an hour,' he said.

What on earth did we think was going to happen in a book group, he asked. He looked confused by the questions we were asking.

I couldn't answer him having never been to a book club meeting, simply because I never had the time, not because I didn't read. I loved to read. Science fiction was my thing, escapism from my day to day. Obviously someone had something against

Sebastian and it did have something to do with his interest in true-crime.

Pasha asked him for his movements after the session ended. He said the group stayed at the bar for a few drinks and then everyone broke up and wandered away home. Some of the group stayed to be sociable but he left when the meeting finished because he had a headache that evening. He usually stayed but not that particular night.

'So, Sebastian stayed behind?' Pasha asked.

'He did. He liked the company of those who enjoyed crime as he did.'

'Do you know who saw him last?'

Andy looked to the ceiling for the answer. 'I don't know, you'd have to speak to everyone who was there. I don't know if they staggered their leaving or if they all left at once.' He looked at us. 'It had been a good meeting, everyone was in good spirits.'

Pasha wrote down the details of everyone who stayed after the meeting for a drink.

I turned the heating up in the car. The light drizzle outside made it feel cooler than it probably was. Pasha was on the phone to Martin, passing him half the list of members we needed to visit.

Pasha hung up her call. 'All done.' She looked out the window at the house we had just left. 'What did you think?'

'Of him?' I asked.

'Yeah. He seemed...' She trailed off.

'He was a little odd. Then again, doing this every day, I tend to think those who have an interest in true-crime are a little odd. Real crime isn't fun or interesting. It hurts. It's painful and it's devastating, as I think he just found out.'

I rubbed at my arm. I was still having physiotherapy but it didn't help the pain that lingered. That throbbed deep inside whenever I was cold, I was tired, if I had done too much, if I'd been too busy or if I'd put too much strain on it. It didn't help with the way it needled at me when I wanted to forget it was there. How it reminded me of past events. A permanent reminder of that evening when I had got everything so wrong and discovered I was fallible. Real crime left its mark. Outside and in. It was easy for those who decided to take their magnifying glass to a case and examine it, but they would never know or never understand the pain and hurt caused by the crime.

I dug my fingers into my arm. I needed my painkillers but I hated to take them in front of staff so it would have to wait until I was back in the office.

'Boss?' Pasha jolted me from my thoughts.

'Sorry, I got lost there a minute. I just don't understand the fascination with crime.'

I looked at her. 'Why did you join the police, Pasha?'

She fiddled with her phone. Stared out of the window. Then back at her phone. It wasn't usually a question that was difficult to answer.

'I'm sorry,' I said. 'Shall we make a move, to our next group member.'

'It's okay,' she rushed in. 'It's just it's more personal than the usual, *I want to help people*, story.'

'No.' I was firm. 'I don't need to know, Pasha.'

I didn't want to make her uncomfortable by forcing her to disclose personal details to me because she felt the need to bond more with the team, to get closer to the boss when we had not quite got off on the right footing in the first place.

Her face dropped as though I had admonished her.

I looked her in the eyes. 'It's not that I don't want to know, I don't need to know right now. Tell me when it's a good time for you.' I held her gaze. Her eyes were slightly glassy with a sheen of unshed tears. 'Okay?'

She nodded.

'Okay, then let's go and talk to these book fans and see what they know.'

20

This girl was only just old enough to be interviewed on her own without an appropriate adult, at seventeen years of age. Her dad had told us she was at work and we had tracked her down, her boss giving us space in the back room of the coffee shop to talk. His ruddy face was practically bursting with the need to know what Verity Shaw was involved with the police for.

For her part, she looked slightly terrified.

Pasha attempted to put her at her ease. Difficult in the tiny space we found ourselves in. The two of us were crowding her as the table and chairs for staff lunch breaks took up most of the space, the coats on the coat hooks extending out into the room. A damp smell invaded the room from the heavy material.

'It's okay, you're not in trouble,' Pasha calmly explained. 'We just want to know about your book club and particularly about last night's meeting.'

Verity looked surprised. 'The book club?'

I gave her a look, raised my eyebrows at her.

'Oh shit.' She pushed herself backwards at the chairs. Her hands floundered behind her until she found one and pulled in under her, dropping onto the seat. 'Oh no. It's not one of us?'

We didn't speak. Gave her a moment.

'No.' It was little more than a whisper in the air. 'I tweeted about it yesterday.' She looked at us, horrified. 'I didn't recognise the photo. I joined in. I shared. I talked about them as though they weren't real.' A tear slid down her cheek. And yet she didn't even know who it was.

Pasha pulled out one of the other chairs, forcing me sideways. I sidestepped so she could sit beside Verity. She leaned towards her. 'You weren't to know,' she soothed. 'How could you?'

A genuine question. Now we had to see if she would answer it.

Instead she scrubbed at her face with the ball of her hand. Scrubbing away the tear tracks.

We waited in silence to see if she would offer anything up. Silence was a tool you could use. People hated it. Tended to fill it. It made them uncomfortable and they would use their words to stuff the empty space rather than suffocate in the void.

The sound of porcelain clattering came from behind the door. The gush of the coffee machine and the low hum of conversations seeped through under the gap below the door and through the thin cheap wood. But in here, the vacuum ballooned and was about to smother us.

Instead of filling the empty space with answers Verity Shaw started to cry even more. She looked like a child. She was little more than a child.

'What is it, Verity?' I asked.

'I'm sorry,' she mumbled through the tears. Hands up in front of her face suffocating the words. 'I just can't believe the man in the Market Square was someone I know.' She cried even harder.

I crouched down in front of her. 'I'm sorry, Verity. We really need your help right now. You were one of the last people to see him alive. We need to know about the meeting. We need to know everything you can tell us about Sebastian Wade and who exactly was the last person to see him alive.' And with that she cried even harder, all sounds of the coffee shop beyond forgotten.

21

We visited a couple of other book club members and obtained basic details from them. It was the same story from everyone. They didn't see anyone of concern before or after the meeting. Sebastian hadn't mentioned any worries. That night or in the run up, in the weeks preceding.

I gathered the team together again once we had visited everyone that had been in attendance at the meeting. We had arranged for them all to attend the station at one point or another to obtain official witness statements.

'They can't believe he's dead. "He's the nicest person" and "who would want to kill him" was all they offered up,' said Pasha. A sad smile. For all it was trotted out, it appeared to be a true sentiment.

We still needed to talk to members of the book club who hadn't been there that night but who still might know something of relevance. They were names now listed on HOLMES waiting to be actioned, but we had talked to those who had seen Sebastian last.

'We haven't come away with anything useful.' I wrapped my hands around the mug of green tea I had made, grateful for the warmth. I was feeling the chill of the day. The constant drizzle outside made me feel cold. The heat from the mug seeped into the bones of my hand. 'Everyone we spoke to said that Sebastian seemed to be his usual self. He didn't mention he was concerned about anyone or that he'd had a run in with someone on the way in to the meeting or anything at all. No one mentioned problems on leaving the meeting. Just that Sebastian had a couple of drinks with them, then left to walk home to Nick.'

I turned to Martin and Ross.

'Same here, Boss,' said Martin. 'There were some shocked faces. Some upset and no real understanding of how or why this happened.'

I nodded. 'There are still a lot of people to talk to but it looks like we're not going to get a solid lead from the book club.'

Evie had her laptop open. She was poking about at her keyboard. 'Evie?' I asked.

She looked up. 'Sorry. Me?'

I nodded again. Took a gulp of the tea. It tasted good. I needed it. 'What do you have on his website? Anything yet?'

'I've applied for access to his provider to get details of who visited his site and to be able to see his messages. See if anyone messaged him and threatened him. As soon as that authority comes through then we'll know more.' She looked down at her laptop screen. 'I've been trawling through what's visible to the public, his blog posts and comments left on those posts, and I don't see anything of concern. He had a specific interest in crimes linked to Nottinghamshire, but would talk and look at any true-crimes anywhere, countrywide, then worldwide if something caught his interest. He also reviewed the true-crime podcasts that have become popular over recent years. He was a big fan and wanted to set up a podcast of his own. He'd started to discuss with his followers what case he should or could investigate or follow for a potential podcast.'

'And what were the possible cases he was looking at? Do we think this might be what got him killed?' I asked.

Evie rubbed the tip of her nose, bent over her laptop again and started scrolling down the page. 'Let me find the couple of posts where he talks about it and I'll tell you in a minute.'

I let Evie work and focused back on the team. 'We obviously have to wait for forensics to come back, but as you're aware, it takes time. I looked to Aaron's empty chair again. Prioritising the forensics submissions was usually his job. As well as missing my friend, I was missing a hard-working valuable member of my team and I desperately needed him back. I had to stop Baxter preventing his return.

'Uniform have collected all the CCTV from the surrounding areas between the Copper Café and where Sebastian was dumped. It involves a drive and coverage is patchy, but we need to see if our offender or Sebastian pops up on it.' I put my mug back down on the table.

The list of actions at the start of an investigation was never-ending. It was good job we had the HOLMES and Theresa and Diane who kept it in order, because keeping track of it all would be difficult without it. Without them. Though I didn't like to rely on it solely. I did believe in people and intuition.

'There are a lot of witnesses still need statements taking. We have a lot to be doing. I hope you've all warned your loved ones that they won't be seeing much of you over the next few days or weeks?'

There were nods around the room. Ross had a wide grin on his face. He loved to get stuck into an investigation. No matter how many hours it took out of his life.

'Boss?' Evie piped up, respectful in front of the team.

'You've found the cases he was talking about looking at?' I asked.

'Yep. I don't know if they'll be of interest, but, I imagine you'll want to consider them anyway.'

'Let me have them.' I opened my major incident notebook, scribbled today's date on top of the page and the time and waited for Evie to speak.

'He was considering a woman who had two husbands and one died in mysterious circumstances. Not Nottinghamshire based. Then there was a farmer whose crop was poisoned, he was losing his livelihood and after he accused his neighbour the neighbour ended up dead. That one was Notts based. And finally he was interested in a gun that has been involved in four crimes, all crimes of passion but the weapon mysteriously disappears before it can be destroyed. That's not even in the UK so I presume he was planning on travelling to research that one.'

'Great, thank you,' I said. 'Another line of inquiry then. Each of these cases has to be looked at.'

The whole office seemed to quiver as everyone sighed. Another three investigations had just opened up to join the one we were running and that was a whole lot of work on top of the live case we had.

22

Drew decided that a walk and some fresh air would do him good. He was too often cooped up in the house by himself. Yes, he had his housemate for company in the evenings, but he had his own life. He didn't stay in every night like Drew did. He had a social life. He had friends and a girlfriend, or a couple of girls on the go. Drew wasn't quite sure as he never saw them. He just heard them through the night and then in the morning as they washed and had breakfast or sneaked off in the early hours.

His own life was quiet. His friends had fallen by the wayside since the incident. The majority of them had made the right noises and said they believed his version of events but, with time, and not even with a respectable amount of that, they slipped away. They stopped texting, stopped calling. Didn't check he was okay. Yes, the polite messages asking after him came in when he lost his job and then when he and Melissa split up, but that was it. It was an obligatory move to ease their own consciences. So they could soothe themselves later when they realised they had eventually abandoned him. They could tell themselves that they had done everything they could. Or at least, everything they could possibly do in the circumstances.

He drove down to the city, parking at a park and ride, and jumped on the tram to get into the city centre. The tram was half empty. An old man in a flat cap was sitting alone opposite him, his shoulders hunched up, rounded forward. The toes of his feet dipped downwards as he attempted to ground himself on the floor of the tram. He was a small man. Shrunken with age.

Was this what Drew had to look forward to?

A ding in the carriage alerted him to the next tram stop. The doors opened and the cold air whipped in. The old man shrugged into himself. Tried to make himself even smaller. A woman with three children under five climbed aboard and bundled them where there was room for all of them. Right behind Drew.

He clamped his jaw down.

He loved kids. If he didn't he wouldn't have done the job he had done, but today wasn't the day for screaming kids. Little kids like these. Especially not after the morning he had had.

The tram arrived at the next stop with another electronic beep and he rose from his seat, happy to leave behind the rabble of children. The overwhelmed mother. The sad sunken little old man and the many other people going about their business.

He exited the tram on Market Square and took in a deep lungful of the cold November air.

This was where he was taking his walk.

Market Square.

A smile tugged at the sides of his lips. He looked around. If only they knew. Those people who were only here because of what had happened. The crowds that were here today, not all of them were the natural ebb and flow of people that would normally be on the square. There were people here who had been drawn just for the spectacle. For the murder scene. The closest they had ever got to the scene of a death.

How they decided in a morning that they would get up, get dressed and come and look at where a man was found stabbed in the side, was beyond him.

On the other hand, he had every right to be here.

This was his domain.

He had created this.

This was his image.

What they were here to look at, to stare at – it was all his creation. They wouldn't be filled with this...

what? Morbid fascination was one way of phrasing it. Looking at the knot of people over by the council building on his right, he would say there was a thrum of excitement. A grisly joy at getting this close. Because it was so public. It wasn't inside a building the police could close off and stop them getting near. This was in the open. In a public place. Free for all to huddle around. To push and shove for the best vantage point for the instacrime photograph.

Arms were lifted in the air as fingers tapped at phone screens to capture the steps of the building where Sebastian Wade had been found.

There was nothing there now.

No dead body.

Drew moved towards the tangle of people that screened his view of the stage of his nocturnal activities.

What was it that remained?

What was it they were so fascinated by?

What had he left for them?

His chest swelled with pride. Then heat rose through him as anger grew. This what he wanted to stop. To prevent.

Now he was getting caught up in his own story. He had to get it under control.

This wasn't about him.

It was about them.

He pushed his hands into his pockets as the cold air pinched at his fingers. The trundle of the tram as it moved away behind him was a constant soundtrack to this area of the city. Climbing the few steps to the higher level of the square he continued forward, frustration gnawing at him as people pushed and shoved around him. Moving around. Some were doing their daily business and some were headed in the same direction as he was.

'It's just over here.'

'Left on the steps.'

'Do you think he's still there?' one girl whispered to a huddle of friends as they moved towards the building.

His clenched teeth ground together.

What was it with people?

Finally he was in front of the building.

It felt as though all the air had been let out of him, like a balloon shrivelling up in the air when it had been let go. His heart shrunk in his chest. His breath hitched in his throat.

He clawed at his top buttons, pulled down on them. Tried to get some air.

For all the people taking photographs, there was nothing here.

Drew had expected something. Some remnant of the scene. Some reminder that he had been here. That he had made a statement.

There was nothing.

People were crowding, were photographing, nothing.

It was the council building steps as they always were.

It was as though Drew had never been here. The large and extravagant display was no more.

Wiped away.

And yet... He blinked in the cold dry air, and yet, the people, they continued to crave what he had delivered.

Instead of shrinking away in horror, they were here, trying to get as close as they could. To be a part of the story.

If that was what they wanted, then he would give them it.

He would make them part of the story.

He would make them the picture.

23

The Occupational Health department was a small one-level building, in fact it was a temporary building that had gained permanent status over the years. Tucked away at the back of headquarters. Tucked into a shaded area, down a dirt track, down the steps, hidden away.

It was almost as if they were ashamed of themselves, thought Aaron. Being Occupational Health. Ashamed of the issues that were brought here. The stress and depression that officers very often brought through the doors. Though he knew probationers also came through these doors for their initial health checks. It held an air of secrecy, of hiding away.

Some may say, it was peaceful.

Aaron thought it was secreted. Hidden. And everything that came with those two words.

This made him uncomfortable.

It wasn't a good start to his appointment, that he already had these two words inside his head.

Secreted.

Hidden.

They clicked into place and spun around on repeat as he walked down the long ramp towards the glass door. Damp soiled leaves underfoot from the tree canopy.

Secreted.

Hidden.

He couldn't remember the last time he had had to attend occupational health. If he was to hazard a guess he would probably say it was when he was a probationer. And that was way back in his history. At forty-one the days of learning to police seemed so far off. There had been so many experiences between then and now.

Secreted.

Hidden.

Aaron pushed on the glass door and entered the small waiting area. Pressed the buzzer at the tiny rectangular reception window for attention. He just wanted to get back to work.

A young woman, slim in a red jumper and black trousers came to the opening, a smile on her face. She opened it. Smiled again. Aaron waited.

'Oh, who is it you're here to see?' she asked.

'Aaron Stone to see Doctor Willis.'

The young woman smiled again. 'He's expecting you, take a seat, he won't be long.'

Secreted.

Hidden.

24

I managed to shove a couple of painkillers down my throat before there was a brief knock on my office door and then it was pushed open. I looked up. Aaron was standing in front of me. I couldn't get out of my seat fast enough. I was about to rush around the desk and hug him but stopped myself in time as I cleared my chair. Realised my contact wouldn't be welcome.

'Aaron!' I practically screeched, instead. 'It's great to see you.' It was. So good. 'How are you?' Instead of reversing back into my seat I continued forward, slower though and grabbed one of the two chairs that were in front of my desk. I pulled it away slightly, so as not to crowd him.

Aaron smiled. 'It's good to see you.' He took the empty chair and sat. 'I'm good. Ready to come back to work.'

I took my cue and sat myself. 'I'm so glad. We could really do with you around here.' I couldn't tell him about what Baxter had said. Could I? Would it help to tell him? Would we be able to do something about it together, if he knew? Keeping him in the dark, well, what good was that doing?

'I went to Occ Health this afternoon.' There was a smile creeping across his face as he spoke.

'And?' I prompted.

'I have a clean bill of health.' There was a fleeting frown. 'Which I had anyway from the hospital.' And then the smile returned. 'Which means I can come back to work.'

'That has to be the best news I've heard all day.' And it really was.

'They've signed me off immediately.'

'Can I get you a drink?' I stood, my stomach churning.

'I don't want a drink.' There was a puzzled look. He knew me. The years we had worked together, he had learned to read me. Even if he didn't always understand the emotions behind how I behaved, he had learned to read the signals and know if there was something amiss.

'Is there a problem?'

What should I tell him? I so very desperately wanted him back and I wanted to fight Baxter with this. Just not at the expense of Aaron's health. He was going to find out in some way. Which would be the better way? Through Baxter being a twat, or me trying to resolve it with him?

'Baxter is being Baxter,' I said.

137

'In what way?'

I sat back down in the chair. 'Remember what he was like before you had your heart attack?'

Aaron was silent a moment. I gave him the time to think back and to process. Fiddled with a strand of hair that was falling in front of my face. Then pushed it out of the way. Looked Aaron in the face.

'I need you back on the team though. We picked up the Market Square job.' I scratched at my head. 'I'm presuming you heard about it on the news.'

He nodded.

'And there's so much work involved. I need you by my side to help me run this. It's huge, Aaron. I can't do it without you. No matter what Baxter thinks or wants.'

'What did he say?'

I flicked some lint off my trouser leg. Then scratched at the invisible mark it had left behind. 'He thinks the position might be too stressful for you with your heart.' I paused. 'Oh, Aaron, he's not right, is he? You said Occ Health said you could come back to work, but is it restricted?'

One of the traits I liked about Aaron was how calm he was, even when I was getting myself worked up.

'No. It's not restricted duties. I can come back to my usual role. And because Occ Health have said that, then Baxter doesn't have a leg to stand on.'

I let out a breath. 'Why the hell didn't I realise that?' A big grin spread across my face.

It was mirrored by Aaron. 'Because you get too emotional about the subject first without thinking it through.'

'And this is why I need you by my side.'

'So, tomorrow then.'

'What about Lisa and the kids?'

'I think she'll be glad to get me out of her hair. I may have been a little bit much for them in the house this past few weeks. Don't tell her I noticed.'

'She was worried sick about you, you know.' I looked at him and waited for him to return my gaze. 'We all were.' A small, barely perceptible nod. 'The team will be thrilled to see you.' I smiled. 'Tomorrow.'

25

It was Saturday, but we were at work and it was early.

I used the stairs instead of the lift to get to our floor, fully expecting to be the first one in, as I usually was, but as I strolled down the corridor I saw a light on in the incident room. Not that the whole room was lit up, but a small light was glowing from one corner. I moved towards the room, wondering who had made it in before me, and on a Saturday of all days. It wasn't as though we had something major planned today. It was an investigative day ahead of us, but one we couldn't afford to take off at this early stage in the case.

Pushing the door open my heart lifted as I saw Aaron hunched over his desk. From here I could see the narrow wires sneaking over his shoulders and into his ears. He was wearing his earphones. I smiled.

It was great to see him back and in such a familiar position. Even if it was this very item, his earphones, that had rubbed Baxter up the wrong way in the first place.

Aaron needed his earphones to keep him calm when the noise levels got too much for him in the office, when he wanted to focus on his work and drown out the sound of his colleagues. He was diagnosed with Asperger's and this simple act of listening to music, or audiobooks, or podcasts – I hadn't actually asked him what he listened to – helped him immensely and it wasn't detrimental to anyone else.

I approached him now and leaned into his view slightly. He turned, pulled out his buds.

'Morning.' I smiled. I really was happy to see him.

'Morning,' he replied.

'You beat me in this morning.' I nodded to his desk.

'I thought I'd check, to see if I needed to catch up with anything. See how bad my email inbox was, but I see you had it switched off in my absence.'

'Yes, I contacted IT. I didn't want your return to be bogged down with emails.'

'Thank you.'

'It's so good to see you.'

'You only saw me yesterday.'

'I mean at work. This is where you belong.'

'It's good to be here. I think Lisa breathed a sigh of relief, though she really did fuss this morning.'

I laughed. 'She was up in time to see you off this early?'

'Oh yes. There was no way she was going to allow me to walk out that door to work without checking I was okay and handing me the lunch she had packed me.' He grimaced.

'She packed you a lunch?'

'For my heart.'

'Ah.'

'Enough about that. Are you going to get me up to speed with this job we have in?'

'Shall we go and put the kettle on while we talk it through then?' I started to move away from his desk, not waiting for a response. He knew I needed a drink of green tea to get me going in a morning. As I walked into the kitchen Aaron followed me in and then, as I flicked the kettle on, gently dropped his mug on the worktop at the side of mine.

I filled his mug with a splash of milk. 'Did you contact Baxter?' I asked.

He stayed quiet.

I turned and looked at him, sitting at the small circular table pushed up against the wall. 'You didn't?'

'This is my job. This is where I work. No one has told me otherwise and Occ Health has passed me fit to be back at work. As far as I'm concerned, there are no issues with me being here.'

He had a point. If it wasn't for the conversation I'd had with Baxter neither one of us would have known that Baxter wanted Aaron out of the department.

My phone vibrated in my pocket. I frowned. It was still early. I pulled it out and looked at the screen. Six forty-five a.m. Message sender was Zoe.

I pushed the phone back into my pocket without checking the message.

'Not reading it?' asked Aaron.

'It's Zoe.'

'Same question.'

The kettle started a slow hum as the element heated up.

'She paid me a visit a couple of days ago.'

'How did that go?'

'I'm not interested, Aaron.'

'She's your sister.'

I was well aware of that fact and had often wished that she wasn't. 'Is that supposed to mean something?' I asked. 'You know what she did. I nearly lost my job because she stayed with me and left her bloody drugs at my place.'

'Does she know what she did?'

Why was everyone so damn keen on resolving this issue? Why couldn't they leave well enough alone?

'She says she's sorry,' I told him.

Aaron opened his mouth to speak but I cut him off. 'It's easy enough to say that. Sorry is just a word. A five letter word. Look, sorry. See? Easy.'

'Hannah.' He looked at me like you would a child.

The kettle clicked off and I poured the drinks.

'You're doing a very good job of detracting attention from the Baxter situation,' I said as I handed him his coffee.

'You're doing a good job of detracting attention from the Zoe situation,' he replied. 'And I don't know what you want me to say. What am I supposed to do? I've gone through the official channels and had my return rubber-stamped.'

He was right. 'He wants you out, Aaron. That is a problem. And one I want to support you with.'

He nodded and walked out of the kitchen.

It was two days since Sebastian Wade had been found on the steps of the council building on Market Square and we were no further forward in finding out who had killed him.

Going through the CCTV footage was a long and arduous job, as was getting all the statements from people who may or may not have seen or known something.

What we were really waiting for was results from the forensics tests. Maybe the killer had left a stray fibre on Sebastian or at the scene, or we would find DNA in the nail clippings that had been taken from him. A fingerprint left carelessly on the length of crime scene tape he had put up around the body.

Or he could simply have looked up at a camera on another street after dumping or while carrying Sebastian.

Our job was about waiting.

And it frustrated me.

People often thought a murder investigation was all excitement. But, for every ten minutes excitement, there were days and weeks, and even months of tedium as the case crawled by.

I held the briefing. Martin had called in at a local greasy spoon on his way in and grabbed a box of sausage and bacon sandwiches. Grease filled the air as we discussed what we had and what we needed to progress. No doubt there would be grease marks inside incident books as well.

Pasha was eating a bowl of muesli and laughing at Ross, who was managing to make a mess of himself as he ate. If anyone was going to dump his food inside his major incident book then it was going to be Ross.

'So, today,' I caught their attention again. 'You all know what you're doing?'

Ross nodded vigorously, his fringe flopping over his eyes. With the back of his hand he pushed it back. He'd probably find some fried egg in there later.

'What's the social media side of it like?' I asked Evie.

She wiped her hands with a square of paper that had arrived with the sandwich. 'It looks to have died down considerably,' she said. 'Yes, there's still a few stragglers talking about it. But Twitter is a fickle beast. They're talking about today's subject and won't talk about this again until, or unless there's something new that catches their attention.'

That was good at least. Baxter was not happy with the pressure of having the most chatty social media site focused on our investigation. And if he was unhappy, it rolled down to me.

'Let's keep it that way then shall we?'

Evie rolled up the paper bag that had contained her breakfast, aimed her arm and with one shot, threw it in the bin.

Ross whistled.

'What? You think because I'm a woman I can't do that?' said Evie in mock outrage.

146

'No, I er, no, it–'

She laughed. 'Calm down, kiddo. I'd hate for you to hurt yourself.'

Ross, never sure how to take Evie, partly because of her good looks, quickly shut up.

The door to the Major Incident Room opened and Baxter walked in. Looking relaxed in a jeans and a shirt, obviously not here for a full day's work, but coming in to check up on us. He smiled as he moved into the room, catching the eye of different staff members. He knew how to keep people onside when he wanted to.

Then his gaze fell on Aaron. The chair which had been vacant for the past six weeks was now occupied. The smile slipped from Baxter's face and his eyes drifted to mine. They turned to cold granite and they begged the question, what the hell?

26

Drew stood in front of the door. The cold air was no longer clean and crisp. It was damp and seeped into his lungs as though they were a sponge, soaking up any available moisture. It made his chest feel tight.

At least, he thought it was the damp air.

This door, he used to be able to turn the handle and walk straight into the house. Feel the warmth of the central heating, click the kettle on, kick off his shoes and get a hug from one of his children, depending on what mood they were in, depending on what else had snagged their attention.

Yet, here he was, standing in front of the moss green door, staring at it as though it held the answers. Or as though it was the one in the wrong.

Because this front door used to be his front door.

With sluggish movements he lifted his arm, his frozen hand clenched tight, rigid with built-up anger, and rapped on the glass pane.

Waited.

Waited to be allowed into his home.

Waited to be allowed in to see his children.

Waited. To be allowed.

The anger was a red hot spot in his core. Buried deep. So deep, he could feel the acid burn in his stomach.

He stayed there, waiting. Listening to the sounds of home beyond the door. The muted sounds of the television. The sound of his daughter upstairs in her bedroom, singing along tunelessly to some current pop song. And the spot inside him burned and his lungs choked him.

'Drew.' There was a hint of surprise in her voice as she opened the door. As though she hadn't expected him. And yet she had been the one to tell him about today. Who had said to come round.

Who had invited him into his own home.

'You said to come.' He was sullen.

'Yes. Yes, of course.' She stepped back a little, pulled the door with her. 'Come on in.'

An invite. He'd been invited into his own house.

The spot deep inside him swelled. He rubbed at where his diaphragm sat. Then he stepped over the threshold, into the house that used to be his home, and he smiled.

'Is she about then?' He grasped the bag in his other hand. The handle was all knotted and twisted round his fingers, turning them white where they were cutting off the blood flow. A small token held within.

Mel pushed the door closed behind him. He felt her energy as she stepped closer to him. The electricity that used to flow between them. The gentle layer of her scent floated into his nose. A memory of evenings on the sofa when the children had gone to bed. Of better times.

Of good times.

'Drew?'

He shook himself. 'Sorry.'

Mel walked down the hall, turned right into the living room. He followed.

Like a puppy.

Bag still clenched in his hand.

'Libbie upstairs?' he asked.

'Shall we sit down?' She waved at the seats. As though they were in some strange room, not a place they had made their own. The cornflower blue sofas had seen many an evening in front of a flickering television playing to itself.

'I thought I'd give Libbie her present before seeing if she wanted to go out for something to eat.'

Mel didn't answer.

'And, of course, I can see if Dylan wants to come along as well. Just because it's Libbie's birthday, doesn't mean I'll leave him out. He'll probably want to spend the day with his sister.' He paused. Realised what he had said.

Mel gave a gentle incline of her head.

'He's fifteen. He's not going to want to spend time with his sister. What was I thinking? Libbie's only just turning thirteen. She won't mind spending an hour with her dad. Not yet anyway. I have a year or two in me yet, I'm sure.'

Mel sank down into one of the single armchairs. 'Drew, why are you doing this?'

'It's her birthday.'

She put her head in her hands.

Drew felt the heat spread. The day wasn't going the way he planned. There was an underlying current here he didn't want to acknowledge. He pushed it away and tried again.

'Shall I shout her down?' He moved back towards the hall, to the stairs.

'Drew, no.' Mel was up and out of her seat, but Drew was gone, already out of the room.

'Libbie,' he shouted up the stairs. The music hummed through her door. 'Libbie,' he raised his voice.

'Drew. No. Please. Stop.' Mel was close to him now, her hand resting on his arm.

'Libbie!' A roar.

The music stopped.

Drew turned to Mel and smiled. The colour drained out of her face. Resignation flitted into place as her shoulders slumped.

Footsteps stomped across the floor and then Libbie was standing at the top of the stairs. She looked to have grown a foot overnight. Her legs were clad in black skinny jeans that were more holes than jeans. A tight fitting T-shirt topped off the look. Her usually straight hair had been curled as he'd never seen it before. And was that lipstick?

'Happy birthday, Libbie.' He ignored the lipstick and pasted a smile to his face. He was the absent father. If her mother had had the make-up discussion, he couldn't come in and go against her. He respected her far too much for that.

'What are you doing here?' She leaned against the wall.

He turned to Mel, not sure if he had heard her properly. Mel shrugged.

'It's your birthday, and on a Saturday. How good is that?' Drew forced cheerfulness into his voice. He could feel the joy sliding away from him, an ugly darkness seeping in. This wasn't going the way he had imagined, or at least hoped for.

'You want to go out for dinner with your dad, don't you?' Should he have asked the question? The silence enveloped the small hallway. Smothered them all.

'Libbie?' he prompted.

'Mum?' Libbie whined towards Melissa.

Drew looked at her. 'What's with Mum? Of course it's okay with your mum for you to come out with me. You know that.' His voice was getting more and more high-pitched.

Libbie's eyes pleaded with Melissa. Just catching her eyes over the bannister rail. Please Mum, they said. Please Mum, help me.

Mel stepped towards him, arm outstretched. 'Shall we go back into the living room a minute, Drew?'

He jerked away from her. To accept her comfort would be to accept this, whatever this was. And he wasn't going to accept this. He looked at his daughter. Her face was now downturned to her feet. Shoulders heavy. Hands tied up in front of her.

Melissa's hand caught his elbow. 'Drew?' Her voice was gentle, low. 'Let's talk about this in the living room. You can say...' She stopped mid-sentence. 'You can speak to Libbie again in a little while.'

Her fingers wrapped around his arm and she tugged at him as he continued to look at his daughter and she continued to refuse to face him. Eventually he allowed himself to be steered back into the living room where he sagged into the cushions of the sofa.

'She doesn't want to come out to eat with me, does she?' he asked when he could bear the silence no longer.

'You need to give her time. Give them both time, Drew.' He stared at his ex-wife. 'They're teenagers,' she said. As though this explained it for him.

'What does that mean? That they don't eat any more? I presumed it meant they ate a hell of a lot more,' he snapped. He couldn't help it.

Mel held her tongue, let the silence play out again.

'It's me?' He was incredulous.

'Not so much you...' She hesitated. 'It's to do with the incident.'

'You know I didn't do what they said I did.' His anger fired up like a match. Fast and bright.

'Drew, it was brutal.'

'I did not attack that homeless boy. I did not just randomly see a homeless boy in the street and decide to push him over. There was a car coming, behind him. I had to get him out of the way. I was trying to save his life.' His voice filled the room, his anger a living breathing entity that he struggled to control. It happened whenever he thought of what he had lost due to the stupidity of how everything was recorded nowadays and how this incident had been recorded from only one angle. 'Why does no one believe me.' He stood now.

Melissa followed suit. 'Drew. Lower your voice,' she hissed.

He clenched his jaw, fury vibrating through his body.

'You said all this when it happened. But still–'

He interrupted her. 'But still, you left. But still, the children were ashamed of me, believing I had hurt a homeless boy and for all to see. For all their friends to see.'

'It wasn't that, Drew. It was the furore that we couldn't cope with.' She softened. 'And then what it did to you. We, me and you,' she moved to stand in front of him, her face just a whisper away from his. Her breath silky on his face. 'We couldn't cope with what it did to us.' Her eyes were dark pools now with a sheen covering them. 'It wasn't about the video, it was about the social media campaign and how they managed to get you fired from the school and how the press targeted our lives. It blew out of all proportion. We were in no position to withstand that. We didn't have the tools to start with. We're average people, Drew. That kind of scrutiny...' Her hand rested on his arm. 'Your anger.' A tear slid down her cheek. 'We couldn't survive it.'

Drew looked away from her. He had heard all this before. She had abandoned him when he needed her the most. When it seemed as though the entire world had turned on him baying for his blood. For not only had they castigated him, they had been made demands for him to lose his job. They had rejoiced when the papers had reported the separation. They had wanted his life destroyed. And they had succeeded. And Mel and the kids had done nothing to stop it.

'The kids?' he asked. Surely they had moved on by now. It was he who had borne the ridicule, the torment, the derision.

'They had a lot of problems at school, you know that.'

'After I left though...'

'Even then. They're only just starting to settle back in. Dylan was suspended for punching a lad who called Libbie the spawn of the devil.' A hand brushed away the tears that were flowing freely now. 'I'm sorry, Drew. Give it time. They're kids. These things, especially online problems, they affect children. You're their dad, they love you. They just don't know how to deal with it all. So, they're burying their heads in the sand. It's the only way they know.'

Drew moved towards the door.

'I'm sorry, Drew.'

He turned. Threw the carrier bag he was still clutching onto the sofa. The box inside rolled around in the bag then settled. 'One of the latest wireless speakers. I thought she'd like it for her room.'

Mel gave a weak smile.

Drew stalked out of the house without a backward glance.

His day had just been freed up.

27.

Drew had watched the ghouls gathering at the steps where he had left the true-crime blogger. Not only were they using their phones to photograph the steps – even though there was nothing to see – but they were turning around, their backs to the building, their arms outstretched, taking selfies of the place the blogger had been found.

His stomach curled in on itself at such crass and disturbing behaviour.

As much as Libbie and Dylan were distant from him now, they were good kids and would never put themselves in such a position. Though, Libbie looked up to some girls in the media he thought questionable. Girls that were famous for being famous.

He hoped that Libbie would grow out of it. See the girls for what they were. Leeches, absorbing anything and everything that was online and thrown their way.

He had his next plan. It was vague. He had to work on it. He was good at making a decision, researching it and then putting a plan together. Teaching had honed that skill.

He had a photograph of the four of them; him, Melissa, Dylan and Libbie, on the beach in Corfu, smiling. Fresh-faced, no make-up, not posed. Natural and happy. They thought they had all the time in the world in front of them. Life was good. They had jobs and security, each other, and that was all they needed. The Ionian Sea sparkled behind them. The sun glinted on the waves, creating a beautiful crystal blue backdrop.

Libbie had only been ten. She had been carefree. Not worried what she looked like or what boys may or may not think of her. Still a child. Mel had mused about having another baby after they'd had a few drinks and the warmth of the evening kissed their skin on the walk back to their apartment, kids strolling away in front of them. They'd reluctantly agreed that they were probably getting a little too old, though Mel had said with a wistful tone that she was only thirty-five. Three years younger than he was. They could if they really wanted to.

And he'd been tempted. That night. As a gentle breeze lifted their hair from the sticky napes of their necks and the dark velvet night enveloped them with a scent of shellfish, garlic and wine, he'd been tempted. He'd never felt so calm, contented, settled and happy.

Little did he know then how his life would change and would be torn apart by someone with a camera phone. How three years ago a camera phone would snap a beautiful image on a beach, capture a moment of love, and two years later it would distort and lie and destroy everything he held dear and he would lose it all.

He placed the photograph back on the top of his drawers. Remembered the final decision that they wouldn't bring another child into the world. They had all they needed, they decided. Why rock the boat? Start again when their children were so old? It would mean going back to the start, when now they could travel and enjoy each other's company. They had a future in front of them that was filled with so much potential.

He nearly laughed.

If their decision had been different, he would have a two-year-old child now. A child who would not judge him. Who would be happy to see him. And who would be a link to the rest of his family.

Turning back to his laptop he cleared the search bar. He had research to do. He needed to find someone local, that he could reach.

It didn't take long. They made it so that they were easily found. It was what they wanted.

Well, you got what you wanted this time.

I found you.

And, I'm coming to get you.

I'll show them.

In fact, you'll show them, pretty much as you've been showing them all this time.

This time is yours. I'm just going to give you a helping hand.

28

After the briefing had finished Baxter threw me a look, twitched his head sideways in a way that said he wanted me to follow him to his office. I thanked everyone again for coming in on a Saturday and left them to get on with their tasks. We had plenty to be getting on with.

I followed Baxter out of the incident room and we walked to the stairs. His office was on the floor above.

We walked in silence. Usually he was quite chatty. He liked to come across as the friendly, even if quite meddlesome, boss. His shoulders were tight as I took the stairs behind him. His steps determined and his strides long.

He was a man on a mission.

He hadn't been happy when he had seen Aaron back at work, but it had been expected. He had been the one to tell me about the possibility himself, so if this was what it was all about, I wasn't sure why he was this tense.

He closed the door behind me as we entered his office, made his way around his desk and took a seat, indicating I should do the same.

'DS Stone is back, I see,' he said with no preamble.

'Yes, Sir. It's great to have him back. He's an integral part of the team.'

Baxter didn't flinch. 'He's been passed fit to work by Occupational Health then I take it?'

I wasn't sure what the point of this conversation was, but as Aaron had pointed out, Occ Health had given him the all clear so Baxter had little say. 'Yes, he came in to see me yesterday evening and let me know how it had gone. He's pretty eager to get back and to get stuck in.'

Baxter leaned forward and steepled his fingers under his chin. He was obviously not a happy man and was assessing the information. 'Here's what you're going to do, DI Robbins.'

This didn't sound good.

He leaned back again, happy with his decision. 'Starting today you are to keep a detailed log of every action DS Stone takes, every decision he makes and every mistake and error of judgement he makes. He's going to find it hard to come back to work, I am sure he will slip up and we will be there to record those errors. The job—' he made steady eye contact. 'This job, demands officers of the highest calibre and if he is not up to the task then we need evidence of that.'

I was shocked. Nearly at a loss for words. 'I can't vouch for DS Stone enough,' I said. 'In all his time on the unit he has never let us down.'

Baxter rolled his eyes. 'DI Robbins, this current case necessitates everyone is on the ball, we can't have a weak link right now. Everyone is watching, in case you were not aware.' His tone hardened.

'I'm well aware of the case, Sir, and I'm well aware of Aaron's capabilities–'

'You will keep that log,' he said, not allowing me to finish my sentence.

I was incensed. He was asking me to look for evidence he could use to kick Aaron off the unit in an official capacity.

29

Even though the night was cold, the streets were filled with revellers. Men wore jeans and shirts, some even with jumpers and jackets. The women though, they had insisted on coming out in the skimpiest clothes. Skirts just below their bottoms, and tops so low it was as though they wore strips of material. Drew could never understand this disconnect. He supposed it came from being a father of a teenage girl now. More aware of young women and, not only what they looked like when they were out, but how they handled themselves. And he wasn't happy.

He needed to remind himself he wasn't here to get all judgey. There was a task to be completed.

Castle Marina looked particularly beautiful at night, when the darkness enveloped it and the Magistrates' Court across the river was all lit up. The court was a huge dome of glass. Not an upright dome. But sideways, coming out from one side wall across the front of the building like a bow and onto the other side wall. The front was a tower of lit-up glass with circular steel girders holding a semicircle of roof over the top. It was stunning in the night.

The river, on the other hand, was dark and ominous. Or it would have been had it not been for the noise of the marina, the people in the bars, spilling out and feeding in.

Plus, Lacey Lane was going to do a brief photo shoot on a canal boat this evening. She had announced it on her Instagram page and there was a crowd filling the area, waiting for her. Drew's research had told him that she liked to take photographs in unusual places. It was one of the reasons her account had gone viral the way it had. The canal boat was one of the more ordinary settings she chose. Disused railways, empty parking lots... she'd even risked standing on train tracks – which was utterly beyond him and from what he had read after seeing the images, there had been a huge furore in the press because young and impressionable teenagers followed her account.

She could have lost money, the sponsorships she had, but it was her risk-taking and unusual scenes that made her so popular. In the end the fuss had died down and she had continued to do what she did.

It was this devil-may-care attitude that also made her perfect for this evening.

He had to make it different to the last one. There could be no blood. He had to consider how he would get in and out. There were cameras all over this city, so he wore his woollen hat and baggiest hoody with the hood pulled up and over. The plainest jeans and trainers. And gloves. It was cold, of course he needed gloves.

In his backpack he had a baseball cap because there was going to be a changeover. He was taking a big risk. If you wanted to make a big statement, you needed to take a big risk.

Life couldn't get much worse than it had since that day with the homeless lad. So, here he was, standing on the side of the river. Mingling with the inebriated crowds waiting for Lacey Lane to make her arrival.

He took a slurp from the bottle of beer he was clutching. It was prudent to look like one of the crowd. Like one of the regulars. He would be taking the bottle with him though. Everyone knew how the police worked nowadays thanks to all the cop shows on the television.

After twenty minutes in the cold, Lacey Lane made an appearance. She was unusually wrapped up in a large parka with a bright purple woollen hat on her head, pom-poms bouncing around on top of it, and a massive scarf wrapped several times around her neck in a multi-chequered pattern. She was a tiny thing. So much smaller than she appeared in her photographs. She can't have been any taller than five three. Her frame disappeared beneath the layers she wore.

Sensible girl.

Lacey greeted the crowd with a megawatt smile. Signed some bits of paper that were shoved at her then climbed aboard the boat, and he was surprised about this, he had expected a lush clean boat, but she climbed onto a beat-up old thing. He thought back to the images he had seen online and yes, though the photos appeared glossy, they were set in glum and rustic-looking settings. She didn't have a bag with her. Drew presumed she had everything she needed in her pocket. A phone for the photographs.

A friend clambered aboard with her. She was taller, a flash of blonde hair. And less clothing. More like the girls that were swarming the banks around them with their drinks.

The deep water of the Trent looked inky blank as he peered down. A screen hiding a hurtling rush of freezing water below the surface.

The blonde friend started to take photographs of Lacey, who posed and laughed on the deck of the canal boat. She was uninhibited. Unafraid to do as she wished in front of the waiting and watching throng who were here braving the cold night air. Drew stamped his feet in an effort to keep warm. From his distance it was fascinating to watch. Both Lacey, and the gathered crowd. How they lapped it up. As though a movie star had come to town. And how Lacey lapped up their adoration. She had been born for it, her movements natural, her laughter, gentle and easy.

It was almost too difficult to take this away from her.

Almost.

30

The crowd grew bored and restless. Time ticked by and people broke away. One by one. Little by little. They left the edge of the water as they saw others enjoying the warmth of a bar. The music weaved out of the doors as they opened and closed.

Lacey Lane and her friend had gone below deck. Presumably to take more photographs inside. Having seen her Instagram profile from different locations, it looked as though she only posted one, maybe two images from any one location, and yet, here she was taking tens, maybe hundreds of photographs. It had probably also come as a surprise to these fans who expected a flying visit, a quick snap.

Lacey had known better and had dressed for the occasion. Her imagery wasn't about showing her body, it was all about where she was.

Drew wondered what he would do about the friend. Maybe he would have to call this off tonight, have to find another location, another night. Luck came his way, for once, and the friend waved goodbye, shouted that she'd see Lacey for breakfast and jumped off the canal boat onto the concrete side.

Leaving Lacey Lane alone inside.

The boat was moored on the opposite side to where Drew stood. It was outside the Magistrates' Court. It was outside the twenty-four-hour custody block of Nottinghamshire police. The bland brick building wasn't a police station, but it was filled with cops who took prisoners, arrestees, whatever they called them, there, at any hour they made an arrest.

He had taken a huge risk.

His mood dictated he did this tonight. He'd had enough. He wanted this to end. This thing that had taken over his whole life, that had taken hold and not let go. This was the only way to do something for himself, rather than have others actions ruin his life.

Drew sauntered towards the bridge like he had all the time in the world and not a care to think about. He also had to be careful to not draw attention to himself.

Yes, he had managed to get away with dumping a dead body publicly but this was on another level. If he wasn't careful, his world could end.

He nearly choked as he considered the words that had just slipped through his mind.

His world would end?

Wasn't that why he was doing this? Because his world had already ended?

It certainly felt that way.

If he didn't right it somehow then, yes, an arrest would top it off nicely and he wouldn't even notice any difference. He felt closed in and locked off from the rest of the world as it was. What would being physically restrained in a brick and mortar building change? He'd still be confined and judged harshly for his actions. His life would still be taken from him.

His footsteps felt firmer underfoot as he took the steps down towards the now silent canal boat. A glimmer of light shone out through a crack in a pair of dark dirty curtains that hung at the window.

He looked across the Trent, at the people out to have a good time. Pulled the tip of his hood further down over his face. They were paying not the slightest attention to him. They were too busy engaged in their own lives. Soaking up, not only the beer and wine and cocktails, but any attention that came their way. Like magpies hoarding shiny glittery things. Eager to collect and store. Grabbing at them greedily, regardless of where they came from.

It was sad really, not only were their online lives lived in such a strange and warped way, but, watching them out, like this, free from the constraints of daily life and expectations, they were such different beings. Like changelings.

Drew ducked his head and tried to see if Lacey was visible through the tiny gap in the curtain, but it was little more than a slice allowing light to leak through. He couldn't be taken unawares. She was used to this. She had the upper hand as far as that was concerned.

Gently he stepped on board. Felt the vessel shift under foot. The change from solid ground to water. He took a moment to steady himself and to realign his centre of gravity.

The light shift underfoot immediately took him back. Back to the long weekend he'd spent on a canal boat with Mel. She had been eight months pregnant with Dylan. They wanted to go away before the birth, spend some time out of the house before they were tied there with a crying infant. They wanted to feel real freedom and felt that the water would give them that, rather than the staid walls of a hotel room. Water was going back to nature without having to go camping. It had proper beds. A proper roof over their heads.

Mel loved it. She had been in her element. He, on the other hand, had worried and fretted the entire time, scared that she would go into labour and that if they moved too far they would end up in a different hospital than the one they planned to use. Mel had kissed his neck and nibbled his ear – while at the same time she giggled mercilessly at his concern. There was nothing he could do but allow her to do as she wanted.

Though this hadn't been without difficulties. She was huge and movement was slow. Every time she tried to get on or off the boat he hovered over her, grabbing her and holding her, much to her frustration. Regardless of all of that, they managed to have a blissful three days. Dylan hadn't made an appearance and Mel had been relaxed and happy. Thrilled at the prospect of starting their family and enjoying the last hurrah of coupledom.

Back here and now, with Lacey, on this boat, he had the element of surprise. And he would use it to his advantage. He slipped his backpack off and with a slow movement placed it down onto the deck. He didn't want its bulk to hinder him. He needed to have the freedom to move. Next Drew removed his gloves and pushed them in his bag, pulling out the latex gloves he had brought from the chemist. No need to leave fibre evidence if he didn't need to.

There was music playing inside the cabin. It was loud, which was a positive. This was all going in his direction. Some funky sound with a deep bass and lyrical female voice he didn't know. It made him feel so much older than he was.

With a last look across the river he took a steadying breath.

It would be more difficult than last time. With Seb he had used a knife. It had been quick and relatively painless. Painless for him anyway. Though blood had obviously been an issue. With Lacey he needed to get more in her face and personal.

Could he do this?

As the water lapped quietly at the hull he thought back to that weekend and how happy they had been. He registered what had been lost. Why it had been lost. And how the girl in this canal boat had played her part. He couldn't be sure if she added her voice to the many who called for his dismissal, or arrest – though luckily that hadn't happened because the homeless man hadn't come forward with any complaint and no one recognised him from the very short clip as he was being pushed, but, she may well have joined in for all he knew. That wasn't the point. The issue here was that Lacey Lane was a part of the social media problem, where there was a kind of mania. People seemed to forget their real lives beyond the screen and he needed to remind them.

And Lacey would help him.

He inhaled. Deep into his lungs. Felt the cold air prickle deep within him. Damp from the river. Dirty.

He was ready.

31.

He realised with rising panic that Lacey Lane was getting organised to leave the canal boat. That at any moment she would open the door and come face to face with him and then probably start screaming the area down.

Right in front of the building filled with cops.

The bile rose in his throat as the repercussions flashed forward through his head.

He had to move and he had to move now.

Without stopping to take off his gloves he picked up his rucksack. The light clicked off behind the door, the glow underneath snatched away.

With one long stride Drew was off the canal boat. The handle of the door pushed down. He started to move. He had to be further away, but not look as though he was running away. He couldn't look suspicious. His heart hammered in his chest, like it was about to explode right through his rib cage.

He made it to the metal seat outside the Magistrates' Court and dropped down, pushing his gloved hands down between his legs as he looked up at the canal boat.

Lacey Lane was climbing down from the vessel.

Bile filled his mouth. His stomach constricted and he swallowed the nasty fluid back down.

Dragging the gloves from his hands, he wiped the sweat on his brow with the back of his hand.

That was closer than he would have liked.

He would not give up though.

Lacey was on foot and alone. He could follow her. He'd see where she went and if it opened up any possibilities for him. If it turned out that she went to a club from here then his night was over. He wouldn't give up yet. There was no let up when they were chasing him through the virtual world. Why should he quit in the real world?

He grabbed the suitcase he had secreted by the river wall and lifted. Pulling it by its wheels would cause too much noise and make her aware of his presence. It depended on her level of awareness when she moved around the city. Not everyone was security conscious.

With only a ten-minute walk she was what he presumed was home. A block of nice apartments at the Lace Market.

She hadn't looked behind her once.

It helped that it was a busy weekend night with lots of people milling and walking about. One more behind her and she didn't notice.

Though it was strange that someone of her alleged fame wasn't more attentive. He would definitely drum safety into Libbie as she got older. He wouldn't have her walking so blithely through the city. In fact he wanted to lock her in her room until she was at least thirty-two.

Now here he was, faced with Lacey Lane inside an apartment he needed to get into.

Drew knocked on the door. He was shaking head to foot. It had gone to shit so far. He was taking a huge risk, but she had to be his next play. There was no one else who would fit the plan quite so well. Not here, in Nottingham. Not who he could get to. It wasn't as though he lived in the capital, where everyone who was anyone lived.

He was met by silence.

Had she gone straight to bed? It wasn't even late.

He knocked again. This time hard on the wood. Pulled his hood up further over his head. Pulled his cap down a little more and bowed his head.

'Who is it?' Her voice was soft and gentle.

'Pizza,' he replied, trying to keep his voice low so as to not disturb any of the other residents.

'I didn't order one,' she said.

Now was not the time for her to get security conscious.

'Well I have one here for this address,' he pressed. 'And it's paid for and getting cold.' He leaned towards the door, face downwards so she couldn't see his face. 'You may as well have it. If some idiot made a mistake it's theirs not yours.' He really needed her to open this door.

There was silence.

The door stayed closed.

He clenched his fists. This was not working.

And then a chain was slid in its moorings and a key was turned.

She was opening the door.

He inhaled and filled himself with oxygen. The life-blood of the brain. He had to be ready.

With shoulders back, hands gloved, he was as prepared as he could be.

Nothing happened.

His nerves jangled.

He shook out his arms.

He waited.

The corridor was silent; no one was about. He didn't want to alert any of the neighbours in this block that there were problems here. He had to keep everything quiet.

Then she opened the door.

He was ready for her and with a sudden and rapid movement he pushed with all his might, pushed and kept pushing and he walked forward, kicked back with a foot, nearly tripping himself off balance as he stepped over the threshold and closed the door behind him. He kept the momentum up, driving forward, taking her off her feet. She was lost in the shock and speed of it. Limbs tangled and cut off from her control.

His arm was around her waist and he half carried her into the room in his violent burst of energy.

They exploded into a small coffee table and a vase of flowers crashed over and into the television. The noise in the room loud as the table shifted and the glass smashed.

Lacey yelped as the back of her legs hit the table: the first sound that had escaped her.

Drew pushed her sideways on to the sofa and saw as she realised what was happening.

Her arms came up but Drew was prepared. He didn't want scratching so he weighed her down with his body weight. She struggled and she fought.

He stuffed a rag in her mouth that he'd had ready in his pocket, ready to silence the sounds, and she gagged as her throat constricted and her face darkened. Her legs flailed beneath her and her head thrashed from side to side as she tried to force the rag out of her mouth.

The moment stretched out.

She was beautiful as she fought for her life. There was no question about that. No wonder she had proved to be so popular on a site that revolved around imagery. Placing herself in settings that were not usually known for their beauty was a smart move on her part. Her red hair was like fire around her head. Her blue eyes popped from her now pale face.

She was something else. And the eyes, they held an intelligence. She had worked for what she had achieved. She had known what she was doing, she had an obvious artistic flair and she had worked it well. He felt a stab of guilt for what he was about to do. A young life, striving to live and to live well, to do the best that she could.

Her eyes were wide in terror.

He needed to be quick. Lacey was fighting and struggling for her life. The longer it continued the more chance evidence would be left. Time for stealth was gone.

She was only petite.

This would be easy.

It didn't seem fair.

He had a task to do.

There was music playing. As there had been in the canal boat. And it thumped in his head as he leaned over her.

Her legs kicked out, booted feet wheeling in the air, her body arching and fighting against his grip.

He needed to get control of her and quickly. Had he thought about this part properly, how to keep her quiet? Yes, he had brought the material to gag her but he hadn't considered the noise made as they struggled. He leaned over her more. A heavily booted foot slammed into his stomach. Drew swore. Her eyes glinted and she fought harder. Her breath was coming hard and fast through her chest as it heaved. The music a weird backdrop against the struggle.

Lacey's hands broke free and he realised she was about to go for his face. He punched her. He hadn't wanted to punch her. To hurt her that way. Like a common drunk. But his fist clenched and it happened. She fell back like a puppet whose strings had been cut, her eyes rolling in her head.

This would be easier for him. She wasn't out for the count but she was definitely subdued. He relaxed his grip a little.

The music died.

He paused, standing as still as he could and listened for movement outside.

Then the next track came on.

His nerves were shot. He could feel the adrenaline as it coursed through him, like an electric current. He needed to get this done and then get out. Because that would be the next step. Getting out of here.

He placed his hands around her throat, felt her soft young skin beneath his fingers and his stomach twisted in on itself. He tightened his grip a little. Her head shifted as her subconscious realised what was happening. Her eyes tried to focus on him. Those blue eyes, they flickered as she attempted to get a fix. A groan escaped her throat. The blow to the head had done more damage than he had anticipated.

He applied more pressure. He could feel the muscle in her neck. Could feel as she squeezed back and fought to keep her airway open.

He let go.

He couldn't do it like this. He couldn't do it while he felt everything she could feel.

He looked around the room.

Lacey used a hand to push herself up. He turned. Pushed her back down and she stayed, her lids closing.

The woollen scarf she had been wearing when he first saw her was thrown carelessly over the table with her gloves and coat, all tangled together. He pulled at it, the coat and gloves falling to the floor.

With one hand he lifted her head slightly, wrapped the scarf around her neck, placed a knee on the sofa behind her to get purchase and finished the job he had come here to do.

With a quiet click he closed the door behind him. He looked at his watch. He had spent more time in there than he had hoped to spend.

32

The call came in just as we were about to log off for the day. It had been a slow day. It felt as though we were wading through sludge. We had to work methodically and hope that eventually something would break.

Days like that were long and hard. We craved for that break. For something to show us which way to go. All today had been was legwork. Paperwork and legwork.

Then the call.

As soon as the operator explained what had been found, we knew from the strangeness of it that it was connected. Sebastian Wade had been left in a crime scene. The scene in Hucknall, this scene might be in a different league in how grim it was, and might even be a different MO, but the weirdness of how the body had been left was enough to tell us it was our man.

He had killed again.

And he was making a statement.

I just needed to figure out what he was trying to say.

I looked across, grateful to see Aaron back in the driver's seat, manoeuvring the car seamlessly through the early evening traffic.

'You could have gone home, you know?' I said to the side of his head.

'And left you with this?' His focus didn't leave the road.

'I'd have been okay. Martin, Pasha and Ross are following. The CSU are also travelling. Baxter and Walker are aware.'

'Would you rather I wasn't here?'

'I'm not saying that.'

His focus remained on the road.

'What I'm saying is that it's your first day and you've only just recovered from a heart attack. Lisa would–'

'Recovered.'

'What?' He'd stopped me mid-flow.

'The word in that jumble, the pertinent word, the one you need to pay attention to is, recovered.'

Ah.

'If you're sure.' It wasn't a question. He'd told me he was. He wouldn't have done so if he didn't mean it. Over time I had come to learn this about him. 'I don't want to have several strips torn off me by Lisa though. Did you get in touch with her to say you'd be late home?' Seriously, the way she had fussed over him after his attack, well, I was in awe of the love I had seen. It shone from her every pore.

'I did. She told me to take it easy and to come home as soon as I started to feel tired.'

'And are you?'

'What?'

He knew what I was asking. 'Are you feeling tired?'

'It's just up here.'

The road turned into a dirt track and narrowed. The car bumped along and in the wing mirror I could see a trail of vehicles follow us down like ducklings following their mother.

Up ahead was a row of garages. They were old. Uncared for. To the right of them were a couple of kids. Our headlights picked them out as we wound our way down the cul-de-sac towards them. They can't have been any older then fifteen. Two boys. Skinny, their jeans hanging around their arses. Arms wrapped around themselves as they leaned into each other.

A uniformed vehicle was parked behind them, its light rotating, informing the houses overlooking the scene that we were here. The officer from the car was stood with the boys, a notebook in his hand. His lips were moving and the boys were nodding.

Aaron slowed our car and the cars behind followed suit.

One of the garages had its door wide open like a yawning mouth, stretched wide and dark. A sliver of the police car's headlamp sliced into the edge, giving the chasm a stretched cleaved look and a weird ghostly half-light where you might imagine what was beyond.

Aaron parked and we got out the car.

The boys looked up with panic in their eyes. We walked over to them. PC Hamid Dewan said the boys were Lewis Cotton and Naveed Khan, thirteen and fourteen years of age.

Younger than I thought.

What were they doing here? Where did their parents think they were? I imagined their parents would just be grateful it wasn't them tonight.

'Parents on the way?' asked Aaron. As a father he was always the first to make sure the kids were looked after. I can't say I had noticed this before. Not until his heart attack and I saw how his family rallied around him. How important he was to them and how devastated they would have been if they lost him.

Why was this concept so foreign to me?

'They are,' Dewan said. In the rotating blue light he looked pasty.

'Have you started an incident scene log?' I asked him.

He shook his head.

'You'll have one in your car. If you get it started, then we can get dressed to go in.'

He gulped.

'Not very pleasant?'

He shook his head.

'Get the log. Have a seat while you write in the main details. Get yourself together then we'll get going.'

He nodded his head this time.

'Okay, boys, I need you to tell me what happened this evening,' Aaron said.

They looked to each other. Looked to the open doorway and then back to Aaron.

It took a few minutes, but eventually they told us that they had been hanging around. This was an area they were used to. They would come around here for a smoke, where their parents wouldn't find them. They didn't live here so no one else would see them who would be able to tell their parents. It was just hanging. They saw the open door. It was unusual. All the doors were always closed and locked.

'You know they are always locked?' I asked.

They nodded in unison. They'd tried the doors in the past. When it had rained. Looking for a place to shelter. That's what they were saying anyway and tonight, that's what I chose to believe. They had been through enough.

They saw the open door and as it was getting colder and threatening to rain again they decided to seek refuge. It was dark but they used the torches on their phones.

At first they didn't see it. There was all the stuff around it. It was like a junk garage. Something you would see on *Storage Hunters*. Suddenly it reared out of the dark and it was there, in all its nastiness. They skidded out of the garage as fast as the rain-soaked road would allow, tripping over each other in their rush to escape. Each swearing they would never try to deceive their parents again.

I looked closer at the lads. Saw the soaked patches down their jeans and on their elbows. A wet trail that confirmed their story.

Our own next step was to suit up and make our way into the garage and see for ourselves what lay beyond.

33

Aaron hated not being completely honest with Hannah. He hated not being honest with anyone. But, with Hannah, it felt worse. She had been nothing but kind to him. She was prepared to fight for him against Baxter. An issue he still didn't know what he wanted to do with.

He shouldn't have to *fight* for anything. Not in today's age. Weren't they supposed to be living in a more enlightened era? Though, working in his job he knew damn well that they weren't. There was no enlightenment around him.

He straightened his tie as they moved away from the two teenagers. Hannah hadn't pushed him when he didn't answer her question about his level of fatigue. He knew better than to think she hadn't noticed his lack of response. He fretted on why she hadn't questioned him about it.

He fiddled with his tie again. It helped him feel even, if his tie was straight. It was such a ridiculous garment, so easily moved when it was supposed to be lined up. It was supposed to lie flat and central down his chest with his buttons and from the middle of his chin. If it was all aligned he would feel aligned.

'They're scared,' said Hannah as they reached the line of parked cars. Martin, Ross and Pasha were there waiting for an update.

Why couldn't she just have pushed him? He would have told her what she wanted to know. Aaron flipped open the boot where the forensic suits, gloves boots and masks were stored.

'What do we have?' asked Ross, eager to know the details.

He would have told her he was exhausted and he was ready to go home to Lisa. To a cooked meal, his feet up on the sofa, the comfort of his drawings, and some time to close his eyes.

He would have told her all of that.

Instead, Hannah quietly explained to the three waiting officers what the boys had said.

'Grim,' said Pasha.

He so desperately wanted to close his eyes. His body felt like he was wading through thick mud. He was pushing too hard on his first day. He should have gone home. Lisa told him if he was tired to go home. She would not be happy if she knew how he was feeling. She had known better than to ask. When he called her to say he was going out on a call, she knew he had already made the decision, regardless of what she may or may not say. Any added stress caused by arguing with him would not help. She told him to take care of himself and to come home if he felt he needed to.

Hannah placed a plastic sheet on the ground so they could get changed without getting the suits wet.

Aaron tugged out a Tyvek suit from the box.

He hadn't lied to Hannah about that. In fact, he hadn't lied to Hannah at all. All he had done was avoid the question.

'Aaron and I will go into the scene with the CSIs. See if you can get more details from the boys. Talk to their parents when they get here and organise to do the visually recorded interviews, this evening if you can. Tell them how important it is.' She pulled at her suit, yanking it over her foot. 'If they're against it and want to get their children home, then obviously their welfare comes first. Make arrangements for first thing in the morning.'

Was that as bad? A lie by omission. If it was one of his children he would say that it was.

The CSIs were already suited up and making a beeline for the garage. Small metal plates were being laid down on the ground to step their way into the mouth of the scene. Several huge halogenic lamps were being erected to provide lighting. It was organised and professional.

Should he own up to her? Or keep quiet now?

Aaron still wanted to get into his own bed and sleep. To stay there for a week, that would be preferable. He never imagined his return to work would be this difficult.

He pulled the zipper up on the suit. Collected the paper boots and bent over. A huge fog of fatigue bore down on him and he took a deep breath in an attempt to steady himself.

At home he had been good. But at home all he had done was potter about and sit down when he needed to. Hannah was right, he should have gone home.

It's just there was Baxter to consider. If Aaron gave in and went home, then he was providing Baxter with ammunition to move him out of the department. Regardless of what he had previously said about Occ Health giving him the clean bill of health and Baxter not being able to do anything, if he was unable to do his role, then the situation could easily change and he didn't want that. He liked it where he was.

Hannah shoved the box of gloves under his nose and he pulled a pair out.

Headlights pitched in the dark as two cars roared down the street towards them.

The parents.

Aaron looked at the boys who were both shaking. Martin and Pasha were with them. Ross was talking to the cop and taking notes.

He could feel the urgency as the headlights grew closer.

'You ready?' Hannah wanted to get into the garage before the parents arrived. These weren't victims she needed to spend time with, though they were important and they did need to be cared for, she knew her team was perfectly capable of taking up that task.

Aaron snapped on the blue forensic gloves. 'I'm ready.'

They walked towards the garage. Six sets of eyes followed them as they moved. Two pairs wide and alarmed.

He liked it in this department, no matter what was beyond this door. And he wanted to stay. He pushed through the heavy feeling that filled his bones and carefully traversed the little silver plates.

Into the garage.

34

She didn't look very old.

The scene was warped like a hall of mirrors at a fairground. I suppose the imagery wasn't helped by the fact that she was surrounded by actual mirrors of different shapes and sizes and in all different conditions.

I wondered if we would be able to trace any of them, back to an owner, a previous owner, or a shop. I doubted our killer had made it that easy for us. I also didn't imagine he had left us any fingerprints on them or fibres of any description, but they would of course be seized and forensically examined.

Some were full-length, others half-length and propped up on something that was stacked up in the garage so that she could still be seen, or if she could see, then she'd be able to see her reflection. And there were seven of them around her.

Four were pristine, clear mirrors, three were cracked and broken, dirty and shabby, with pieces missing.

The imagery stood, regardless of the breaks.

Maybe the breaks had been made by the killer to make a point, or perhaps these were the only mirrors he could get a hold of.

Aaron rubbed at his chest.

I turned to him, worry suddenly eating away at my own chest. 'Are you okay? Do I need to call an ambulance?'

He didn't answer. Didn't acknowledge me. 'Aaron!'

His head snapped around. His face was as pale as I had ever seen it. Other than that day on the office floor.

'Aaron?' I asked again.

'No. You don't need to call an ambulance. I don't have chest pain.'

I looked to the girl in the mirrors. 'There is something.' It wasn't a question. I knew him. He was keeping his own counsel.

'There is.'

A screeching broke through the garage as a metal lamp was erected in the corner. Aaron turned to where the sound had come from. His eyes were dark and heavy. The light was switched on.

The girl in the centre of the mirrors now glowed in her macabre stance.

'You okay to carry on or do you need to go and sit in the car?' I asked.

'Carry on.'

I nodded.

We moved closer. She looked to be about twenty-five. Her red hair had been teased out and sprayed in position. It resembled a haystack. Her face had been made-up but not by her. There was bright red lipstick and dark shadow across her open lids. Blush circles filled her cheeks.

Something like a broom handle had been strapped to her arm and was holding out it at an angle. Taped in her hand was a phone.

She was posed taking a selfie.

I looked at the scene closer. Stuck to each mirror was a Polaroid photograph of her in this position at eye level with her. She was surrounded by herself.

There was bruising around her throat.

'It's a different MO. The cause of death, by the look of it,' said Aaron.

'To Sebastian?'

'Yes. An equally bizarre scene to be left in. I'm thinking we're looking for the same killer.'

I let out a breath. 'I'm with you there. Not that I understand it though. What's he trying to say?'

'Beats me.'

'Ah, young Hannah.' The voice boomed from behind me. 'And Detective Sergeant Stone, I see.' I could hear the smile in the voice and when I turned to see the Home Office registered forensic pathologist, Jack Kidner, I saw from the twinkle in his eyes above the mask he was wearing, that he was smiling at Aaron.

'It's so good to see you back with us.' He walked up to us and slapped Aaron on the arm. 'Gosh, old boy, you gave everyone a good old scare, you know. Especially this one here. She didn't half bend my ear, after you were rushed to the hospital.'

Oh no, he was going to tell him.

'Seems I was one of the handful of doctors she knew, even if I did deal in the dead and we were all dreadfully hoping that wasn't going to be you.' He scratched at the top of his head.

Aaron stared at him. He hadn't said a word so far.

Jack continued. 'So, I was the first person she got in touch with. She followed you to the hospital and as soon as she could bear to leave the waiting room she came to find me. Pushed me hard she did. Wanted to know all about heart attacks, survival rates, what caused them, if–'

'Okay, I think he's heard enough now, don't you?' I had to stop him, Aaron knew I had worried about him, but he didn't need this much detail. 'I'm sure you want to have a look at the young lady we have for you here, Jack?'

'Ah, yes, of course.' He peered over to the circle of mirrors. 'Ah,' he said again as he saw what we had been called out to.

'Yes, my thoughts were along those lines,' I said.

Aaron looked at me. I shrugged. Not a lot else I could do. Nothing Jack had said had been untrue. It had been a horrifying time when Aaron had collapsed in the office and the paramedics had strapped the equipment to him and announced he had had a heart attack. A heart attack. He had only just saved me from major injury as I'd battled for physical control of a gangster on the staircase and had fallen with my head aiming for the wall. Aaron had pulled me out of the way just in time and only a few hours later he was on the floor and needing emergency medical help.

He was one of my closest friends. I wasn't sure what that said about my life, my social life, because I didn't see him out of work, other than the occasional work-organised night out. But I did class him as a friend. He always had my back; he could always be relied upon. It was more than just because he was paid to. We had a level of understanding that meant the world to me.

And now Jack made me look not like an adult who knew how to deal with a serious problem, but like a teenager caught off guard with her skirt up.

He was pulling equipment out of his medical bag. Looking down his nose at what he needed. Then he stared at the mirrors.

'What is all this about?' He waved his hand around at the circle.

'I really don't know.'

'Any idea who this is yet?'

'She hasn't been touched until you got here, Jack. We've no idea.'

'Funny business at Market Square the other day.' He looked at the girl again. 'Were you back then, Aaron?'

'No, first day back today.'

Jack stood from his crouched position and turned to Aaron. 'By Jove, Aaron.' His tone turned serious. 'What on earth are you doing here? This late.' He looked at me. A glimmer of accusation crossed his face.

'I don't understand,' I said.

'All those questions you asked at the QMC and you don't understand?'

This time it was Aaron's turn to interrupt. 'Shall we leave you to it, Jack. I'm sure you need to find time of death and take samples.'

'No, she's not going anywhere, we can have this conversation.' I stood my ground with the two of them. Blue strobes from the marked car blinked through the scene as we faced off.

Jack held up his thermometer. He was ready to work.

He was also prepared to let me have it. 'Aaron is recovering but he no longer has complete function of his heart, there has been permanent damage.' He looked at me. 'You did good getting him to the hospital quickly. The quicker a patient is treated the less damage is done, but his heart is still damaged and he will tire more easily because of this. He needs to–'

'Can we not do this here?' Aaron nodded at the CSI photographing the scene. 'I'd rather not have my personal information shared openly. I am a private person in case you two, who appear to like to talk about me, failed to notice.' His own tone was sharp. The sharpest I had heard him. He hadn't even taken this tone with me when I had shouted at him forcing him into the disclosure that he had Asperger's.

'I'm sorry, dear chap,' Jack was conciliatory, his voice quieter. 'Hannah needs to hear this.'

'She does not need to hear anything other than what the time of death was for our Jane Doe,' Aaron snapped, before letting out a long breath.

'Aaron, if Jack thinks I need to know this, and it's about you, then he's going to say it. You can stay or you can leave, but if it's to do with you being at this crime scene, then I am finding out.' My own stance was now combative. The three of us were coming from three different places but were butting heads over something, I wasn't sure what.

'Jack, please, what is it?' I asked.

'You really don't know, Hannah?'

'Jack.'

'At home, he was in recovery mode. Aaron was taking it easy. Having a heart attack takes it out of you, massively.'

Aaron turned his back to us.

'His first day back, anyone's first day back in a job after a heart attack, after recuperating, will be tiring. Coming back to this role, to the police, it will be hard. Doing overtime, coming to a crime scene that is hours after the end of a usual working day, well, Aaron is going to be finding this incredibly difficult, he is going to be utterly exhausted and I for one am worried about him.' He gave me a grave look. 'And so should you be.'

With that Aaron walked out of the garage.

<sup>
</sup>

35.

'She's been dead between one and four hours,' I said to Aaron as I climbed into the car beside him. He was brooding in the driver's seat.

'The kids might have just missed the killer then,' he replied. 'They were very lucky not to run into him. Who knows what he's capable of.'

'Looks that way. We need to get a detailed statement from them.' I looked to where the kids had been standing. 'Do we know if their parents agreed to let us get the interviews done this evening?'

Aaron nodded. 'Pasha and Martin took one of the kids back to the station to do the interview. The other one is booked for the morning. His parents insisted on taking him home. I don't know if it was because he was in trouble or if they were worried out of their minds. Either way there was no way anyone could talk them out of taking him home tonight.'

'Okay. At least we have the one.'

I could see Ross talking to Dewan. He could make friends with anyone. Talk to anyone. He was so easy going. Well, he was now, there had been a time when he had spiralled downwards and Detective

Superintendent Catherine Walker had wanted to kick him off the unit. I'd fought for him and he'd proved to me that it had been the right decision. He brought himself back from the brink.

I glanced at Aaron. And here I was again. Though these circumstances were completely different. This was not Aaron's doing and I would fight tooth and nail for him to stay. Just not at the expense of his health.

'What Jack said...' I started.

'He's right.'

'I know he is. Jack is always right.' I had to have a straight conversation with him. I needed for him to be well. To not put himself at risk this way, plus I needed all the information so I knew what I was dealing with because of the position Baxter had put me in.

'Why are you here tonight, Aaron?'

'Baxter.'

I clenched my fists. My nails dug into the palms of my hands. Sharp pinpricks, pinching at my skin. I'd thought as much. 'What about him?'

'Why would I give him a reason to push me out?'

'Going home at the end of a shift is not a reason to be kicked out of the unit, Aaron. We had this conversation earlier. You were confident that you were good to be here. What happened?'

'The day happened. I didn't realise how exhausting it would be. I thought I could return to work and be the same person I was before I left.' He rubbed at his chest.

'Aaron?' I was scared. My own chest tightened with fear, my breath trapped as I waited for him to respond.

'No, it's fine. I'm just acutely aware of it being there.' He let out a long sigh. 'I feel as though I am carrying around a body filled with heavy metal. As though my bones, the stuff running through my veins is iron. Dragging my own body about is not the meaningless thoughtless activity it used to be. Now it takes effort. It's draining. I can't believe how much it hurts to just walk about, Hannah. How tired I am by doing paperwork in the office today. I feel like a child that needs to go home to their bed.'

He turned to me. 'How do you think Baxter would react to that? Do you think he would support me and encourage me to take it easy until I am back at full strength, because I don't. I think he will use it as an excuse to get me out. We both know he's waiting for one.'

He was right. 'You could always tell him.' If he told him about life with Asperger's, then Baxter would have to be careful in his decisions around Aaron, he would have to make sure every decision was for the right reason and was not a personality clash, which this looked to be.

Aaron shook his head.

'Think about it?'

He didn't answer.

'There's still a lot of work for us to do tonight, and we're only making a guess, but it's an educated one, that this is the same guy.' I made sure he was listening to me. 'We're going back to the station. Jack and the CSIs have this now and Jack is going to supervise removal of the body. And what you're going to do when we get back is go home. Leave the rest of the inquiries and actions to us for today and we'll see you again tomorrow.' I cared more about Aaron and his well-being than anything else right now.

Aaron scrubbed his face. Talked through his hands. 'You haven't read all your emails today, have you? Or the last couple of days for that matter?'

'I might have a few still unread in my inbox. Why, have you requested leave already?'

'Occ Health approved my return to work, but it's a phased return. I'm only to work three days a week for the first two weeks. I couldn't get them to shift their stance on this.'

'For fuck's sake, Aaron.' I was furious with him now.

He turned away and looked out of the side window. At the dark sky and houses beyond. At the people being held back way down the street by uniformed cops who had set up a cordon.

'If you had told me this today then I would have known damn well that you were still in recovery mode and wouldn't have let you come out to this. I would have sent you home. You banked on me not reading it, didn't you?'

'It's my job.'

It was my turn to look out my side window. Ross was zipping his coat further up under his chin. Stamping his feet on the ground. It was cold out there now. I should tell him he could leave and get on with the tasks needed at the station.

The CSIs ferried back and forth between their van and the garage. Boxes and bags, lights and equipment moved with them. They were steady and methodical. In no rush because speed caused mistakes.

'I know it is.' I turned back to him. 'Let's get you back and we'll worry about it when you return.'

Without a word he started the car.

'Let me just have a word with Dewan and Ross.' I climbed out, thanked Dewan, told Ross we were done here and to make sure that the clothing was seized from both boys before they were released, even the one who would not stay for an interview this evening. The clothing was evidence.

'It's going to be a late night,' said Ross.

'It is,' I answered. 'It is indeed.' Wondering how I would deal with tonight's events with Aaron in relation to Baxter's demand for a continual report on his activity within the job. Surely Occ Health would expect this from him and this fell within the extremely normal category and not in a category that could hurt Aaron in any capacity.

36.

Drew kept refreshing his Twitter feed on his phone as he walked. He supposed he should not have left her in such a discreet location. Then again, how would he have been able to stage her and get away without getting caught if he had left her somewhere she could have been found easily and quickly? As it was, breaking into a garage gave him time to get away. It was well away from both the murder scene and away from where he lived which would throw the police. They would have no idea why she was there. They might even presume the killer was local.

It had been genius to do the crime guy in the middle of the night. No one would expect the body to be real. They would never think a killer would walk in right under their noses.

Now he had set their noses sniffing. They were aware of him and he had to be more careful.

He refreshed his feed again.

There was nothing.

Not a word.

Wasn't this what he wanted? For people not to comment, not to turn the affairs of others into some gruesome trial by social media. Maybe they had found the body after all and his plan had worked.

People were so shocked and disgusted that she of all people had been killed they would be silent. After all, it was all too grim. They had turned this girl into what she was and now look.

That's what had happened.

His plan had worked.

He smiled to himself as he unlocked the front door.

'Hey, Drew.' His housemate was in the kitchen and shouted through to the front door. 'Get you a beer, mate?'

The world was a better place tonight. 'Yeah, I'll have a beer if you're having one.' He closed the door behind him and locked it. He wouldn't be going back out this evening. His work was done.

37

Pasha and Martin were still in the interview room with the boy, so we didn't have full details from him yet. We were currently waiting to see if her fingerprints were in the system so we could ID her and then locate her next of kin and inform them tonight. Two death messages in only a matter of days. I didn't understand why this was happening.

I left Ross to chase up the fingerprints and I went to my office to update my policy log from the evening and while I was there I went to check on the email Aaron had told me I had missed.

It was there, halfway down my screen. Still unopened. He was right. Not that I had doubted him.

Damn.

We would have to deal with it as best we could. Even though I felt Aaron was tying my hands behind my back by not disclosing his Asperger's.

Ross knocked on my door and walked in. 'Lacey Nettleton, twenty-two years, the girl from the garage...'

'Tell me more,' I said.

'She doesn't have a serious record just a juvenile shoplifting offence.'

There was a strange look on his face. 'Are you okay, Ross?'

'Yeah, it's just I recognise her now.'

'What? You know her?' I didn't want this to be true, for this to touch one of us so personally. Ross had already been through enough on this unit.

'No, not like that. She's also known as Lacey Lane.' He looked shocked. 'I didn't recognise her immediately from the photograph that came back but then it gradually sunk in.'

'Am I supposed to know who Lacey Lane is?' I asked.

Incredulity crossed his face. 'You've never heard of her?' He came further into the office.

'Grab a seat, Ross.'

He pulled a chair out and sank into it. 'Lacey Lane is Nottingham's very own social media star. She has over a million Instagram followers and has brand names lining up to pay her to advertise their products in her photos.'

I leaned back in my chair. 'What does she do?'

'She's an Instagram star. A social media icon.'

'You said that.' It unsettled me that we had another link to the previous killer: both victims appeared to have a link to the internet. How the hell were we supposed to police that? 'What I want to know is, what she does for a living.'

Ross barked out a laugh, looked at my face then reined himself in. 'You're serious.'

I didn't need to answer him.

'She doesn't have a job, Boss.'

I furrowed my eyebrows at him.

'She makes her money by doing what she does online.'

'How does she do that? How can you make money by talking about yourself online and by taking photographs of yourself?'

'As her social profile grew, products took more notice and, as I mentioned, they then pay for their products to be placed in her photos. They pay for her to visit places and be photographed there. She's an attractive girl and she took great photos. She had a real artistic flair and seemed to take off. People can cash in on the opportunities online. Just look at the diet gurus and the fitness gurus who start on Instagram and YouTube. They're loaded and famous.'

I shook my head. 'Just because she took a good photo?'

'That and she also captioned them well. She had a sharp wit, a sharp tongue. She was a clever young woman. From what I read it started as a pastime, as social media is for the rest of us, but hers took off.'

'Wait a minute. You have social media accounts?'

He flicked his hand through his hair. 'Well, yeah, of course. For nights out with my mates. For being, you know... social.'

To become famous just because you were on social media, that was beyond me.

'Okay,' I said. 'Do we have a home address for Lacey?'

'Yeah, she lives alone. She had enough to buy her own pad.'

Of course she did. 'What about next of kin, do we know anything?'

He shook his head. 'Not as yet. It would have helped if she lived with her parents.'

'We'll do a search of her home, see if there is anything there that can help us. We'll also see if there is a vehicle outside registered to her. It may have a previous address listed if she had it before she moved and that address might be her parents'.'

Ross stood. 'Sounds like a plan, Boss.'

'And, Ross.'

'Yeah?'

'Good work on identifying her alter-ego.'

'No worries.'

We now had a victim and so far, no way to tell her parents she was dead.

38

I sent Aaron home. He argued but I could see he didn't have the energy to put up a long fight with me so I stood my ground and in the end he relented. That left just me and Ross to attend Lacey's.

There were no other people listed for her address on the Voters register but that didn't mean that there would be no one here. Sometimes people moved in after the voters had been recorded.

It was a smart apartment block on Hollowstone, Lace Market, and Lacey's apartment was a couple of floors up. I knocked on the door. There was no response. I knocked again. Harder this time.

Still no reply.

'What now?' asked Ross.

I tried the door handle. It turned in my hand and the door shifted as I pushed. The apartment was insecure. Ross and I shared a look.

'Ready?' I asked in a low whisper. We had no idea if there was anyone still inside.

He nodded.

My heart thudded in my chest. As cops we always moved towards the danger, but we wouldn't be quite human if we didn't feel nervous. This girl had been murdered. We had no idea where and we were about to enter her home which was insecure. Her killer could be behind this door, collecting trophies, not expecting the police to turn up yet.

As quietly as possible I pushed the door open and peered inside. Listened. There was no sound. A silence filled the space.

I nodded at Ross and stepped forward and identified myself. 'This is the police, let us know if you are in here.'

The silence expanded around us.

Ross moved around me and headed to the kitchen.

I shouted again.

'Be careful,' I said as Ross moved further away.

I flicked a wall switch and the room flooded with light. I paused. This was where it had happened, in this airy and open living area. This was the original crime scene. A vase of flowers was smashed on the floor. Water seeped out and petals lay crushed and broken in the glass. The coffee table the vase had fallen from was pushed sideways into the TV stand. The TV hanging off the stand and held upright still by the wall it had fallen into.

Cushions from the sofa were flung round the room.

Ross came up behind me. 'All clear through there.' An intake of breath. 'Shit.'

'Yeah. We need to get the CSU here. And we need to make sure he's not still here while avoiding the main area.' I turned to him. 'Let's check the bedroom and any wardrobes, cupboards, etc.'

'You think he's going to have hung around, Boss?'

'I doubt it, but I'm not asking the CSU to come into a crime scene I haven't cleared.' He nodded again.

In silence we checked the rest of the apartment then left without disturbing anything. Though we had avoided the main living area where the damage was, the CSU team would still not be happy we had traipsed through their scene. I on the other hand was completely happy with my grounds for doing so. Safety over evidence every time.

Outside Ross made a phone call then scribbled a few notes in his pocket book.

'Is a team heading out?' I asked.

His pen stopped in mid-air. 'They're all tied up. It might take a while. They've asked that it be secured until they get here so I've spoken to the control room inspector and requested a uniform presence to guard the door.'

'Good job. Thanks.'

He smiled. A boyish smile. He always looked younger than he was. It sometimes surprised me that anyone took him seriously with his boyband looks. But, they did and he got the job done. In fact, he was good at his job and very enthusiastic about it. It was probably because he was so easy and relaxed about what he was engaged in that others relaxed around him.

'We need to do house-to-house inquiries as soon as we're freed up from guarding this door,' I said.

Ross finished up his notes, flipped the notebook shut and shoved it in his back pocket. He looked at his watch.

'I know it's late.' I was tired too, it had been a long few days. 'But she was killed here. We need to know if anyone saw or heard anything. We can't leave it until tomorrow.'

Heavy footsteps climbed the stairs. I knew these were our uniformed support without needing to see. Round the corner came Tony Hitchen, a young PC who had secured the scene of one of our previous cases. Back then he had been brand new to the job and particularly anxious. I had given him some guidance and attempted to reassure him. And here he now was. Attending another of our crime scenes.

'Hello, Tony.' I smiled at him.

'Ma'am.' He smiled back, still with a slightly nervous look to him. But he had obviously grown in the job, settled in, made it his own. It was natural for supervisors to make young-in-job officers a little anxious.

'It's good to see you again. Even if it's at another crime scene,' I said.

'I won't make such a mess of this one,' he replied.

Ross looked from me to Tony and back again, confused.

'You didn't mess up last time. We all have to learn somewhere and I hope our conversation helped you.'

'Yes, Ma'am, it most certainly did.' He looked at the door. 'This the one I'm here for?'

I told him it was and that Ross and I were going to do the house-to-house. He shoved his gloves in his pocket and opened the scene log. He'd register the location, date and time, everyone who was present and then anyone else who entered and left and at what precise times. He was also responsible for preventing people from entering the premises. That included police officers if they didn't need to be in there. The fewer people inside the crime scene the better. The CSU were always grateful for a strong cordon.

Ross and I began the door-to-door. We split up to make it quicker.

With a loud rap I knocked on the door next to Lacey's. It took two other attempts before someone opened up.

'What the hell?' A male in his early forties opened the door wearing pyjama bottoms and with bare feet.

I explained who I was and that I needed to ask him some questions about his neighbour and he let me in.

The apartment was a mirror image of Lacey's. Identical but turned the opposite way around. I could look at this one and see it for what it was, in a way I couldn't next door. It was a beautiful space. Bright, open and modern. Gorgeous sash windows letting in the inky night. A large dining area was to the side of the living area. Which in itself wasn't shabby.

'You said this was about my neighbour?' he prompted.

'Oh, yes. Can I ask what time you got in this evening please?' I took out my pocket book and pen.

'Can I ask why?' he answered.

It was going to be like that.

'There's been an incident and we'd like to know if you can help us. To know if that's possible, it would be a start if we knew what time you were home.' I gave him a smile. 'And who else is in the apartment and what time they were home.' I looked around again. There were no obvious signs of a female touch. Yes, the place was nice enough, and I couldn't put my finger on it, but it screamed male residence only.

He let out a long sigh as though I was causing him some real trouble.

'I'm sorry it's so late, Mr...?'

He sighed again. I hated these visits. They would be over a lot quicker if people answered the questions without telling us how much of an imposition it was. We knew it was difficult having the police in your house. Though it was a lot worse for the young woman next door.

'Thomas, Dan Thomas,' he said eventually, when he had finished releasing all the air out of his lungs.

'Thank you, Mr Thomas. Anyone else?' I prodded.

'No, no one else. It's just me you're disturbing.'

I did my best not to roll my eyes. 'I'll try to be quick,' I promised. 'So,' I continued, 'what time would you say you have been home since?'

He looked at the clock on the wall. Eleven-thirty p.m. We really weren't going to be popular. 'I've been in since about three today.' He stalked over to the dining table and grabbed a cardigan that was hooked on the back of one of the chairs, threaded his arms through the sleeves then wrapped the front across himself.

I nodded my thanks to him. 'You don't work?'

He looked as though he was going to sigh again, then stopped and just stared at me. 'Day off.'

I continued. 'And did you hear anything from next door between then and now?'

'To be honest I don't even know who lives next door. I pretty much keep myself to myself. I'm a private person.'

I was getting that impression.

'You've never bumped into her when you've been coming or going?' I asked.

'Nope.'

He didn't want to talk to me.

'You didn't hear anything?' This guy was right next door to her when it happened. He was our best bet for a lead and here he was, showing the most disinterest I'd seen from a witness

'I've said that.' He looked at the clock again.

I persisted. 'What about seeing anyone suspicious when you came home at three? Or anyone that gave you cause for concern in the days leading up to this evening?'

He pulled at his cardigan and looked at the clock again. It was an obvious move to tell me he'd had enough. This was important and I wasn't going to let discomfort dictate my job.

'No one.'

'Have any of your neighbours informed you that they've been worried about anything or anyone?'

'Look, what is this?' he asked at last, fed up of trying to avoid giving me proper answers.

'As I said when I knocked, Mr Thomas, there has been an incident next door and we need to know if you have seen or heard anything. Today or in the days leading up to the incident.'

He took in the expression on my face and shook his head. 'I haven't seen anything. I'm not a big fan of people. Like I said, I keep myself to myself.' He moved towards the door. 'Now, if that's all?'

I hated when people were unhelpful, but I couldn't make them talk to me. 'I need to take your details.' He glowered at me. 'For our records, you understand.' His eyebrows sank over his eyes.

With a little cajoling I managed to obtain his contact details and date of birth. I wasn't sure how much I believed his story about not knowing Lacey. I mean, I lived in an apartment and liked to keep to myself, but I still saw my neighbours as we came and went about our business. Not often, but I had seen them. No one lives in a vacuum. How feasible was it that you could never see the person you lived next door to?

I crossed with Ross and we both went to visit a couple of different neighbours and when we were done we met up on the landing again. We had done this floor and the floor below as well as the one above. Several had refused to answer. I didn't believe they weren't in. It was more likely they weren't getting up at this hour and answering the door to strangers.

'We're heading back to the incident room now, Tony. Thanks for doing this,' I said as we walked towards the stairs.

'My pleasure, Ma'am.'

I'm sure it wasn't, no one enjoyed standing on their own guarding a home, but I admired his enthusiasm.

'What did we get?' I asked Ross as we buckled into the car.

'A couple of people said they didn't hear anything, then when they realised we were here and asking because an incident had occurred they were more helpful. Said they did hear something but hadn't thought much of it because it wasn't that loud. There was a crash and a bit of... scraping was the way they described it. Poor people looked horrified to think they heard an event that they could have halted if they had been more concerned but they said it just wasn't that loud. It could easily have passed for a row between a couple or even Lacey moving some furniture on her own.'

I pulled out into the road, which was quiet. The usually busy roads muted for the night.

'Did they see anyone?'

He shook his head. 'Not that they can remember. Though one old woman seems to recall a man she didn't recognise walking out with a suitcase but she figured him for a taxi driver for one of the other tenants.'

I took my eyes off the road and turned to him. 'How big was the suitcase?'

'I asked her that. She said it was huge. Plenty of room to fit everything you need for a holiday, for two people, and more.'

My focus was back on the road but my mind was now elsewhere. 'Did she describe this taxi driver? Would she recognise him again?' A frisson of excitement ran up my spine.

There was silence from the other seat.

'Ross?'

'I'm sorry.'

I turned again.

'She wasn't wearing her glasses. She'd just popped next door to see her friend and was heading back home. She said she's practically blind without them so she couldn't describe him and wouldn't recognise him again. But...' He trailed off.

My mood sunk.

'She said he was wearing dark clothing and one of those tops with a hood and it was pulled up so she couldn't see his face anyway.'

This was our man.

'And the suitcase,' I slowed for a car that pulled in front of me at speed from the road on the left. The problem with quiet roads at night, drivers tended to think no one else was about and drove a bit more erratically. 'Big enough for a petite person.'

39

Aaron sat at the table, head bent over a piece of paper, a steaming mug of coffee in front of him.

Lisa walked into the kitchen. 'Hey,' she said as she dropped into the chair at the side of him and looked down at the drawing he had created so far. The mug with steam rolling out of it, the kitchen units lifting up behind it. The detail was so defined.

She put her hand on his arm. 'Bad shift?'

The pencil scratched gently across the paper. Aaron's fingers relaxed around the narrow stick as he shaded in the corner of the window frame with the shadows that lurked from the night outside.

'Aaron?' Lisa prompted.

He let out a breath. Quiet and slow.

'You're tired?' She leaned sideways onto the table. Looked at her husband. 'The kids are in bed. Talk to me.'

The scratching on the paper soothed him. The soft sound of lead on the 100 lb acid-free drawing pad. He should answer her. He knew that. He finished the shading. The night creeping into the room. The light from above fighting for dominance. The light and shade coalescing.

'I didn't think I would be this tired.' He kept on sketching. Adding details.

'You're recovering from a heart attack, what did you expect?'

'I expected to go to work and be able to do my job.'

Lisa sighed.

Aaron kept on drawing.

'And were you not able to do your job? I thought, from speaking to you earlier, that the day had gone well.'

'The day was fine.'

'What happened?'

'My body is what happened.' He didn't stop. 'The job is fine. My body let me down. I couldn't keep up, Lisa. I really couldn't keep up. I wanted to just stop. Stop what I was doing and curl up into a ball and sleep.' He stopped. For a second. Looked at her. 'Right there at the crime scene, I wanted to curl into a ball and sleep right there on the ground of the crime scene. I was that tired. No matter that there was a poor woman there dead. Murdered. I just wanted to sleep. And I couldn't do a thing to stop the feeling.'

He turned back to the image. Added a couple more wisps of steam as they straggled out of the mug.

'Oh, love. That must have been so hard for you.' She leaned in to him. Rested her head on his arm. Smelt the lingering fragrance of sandalwood from his soap, the smell of him after a long day of work. His warmth. She inhaled him. Felt his body gently vibrate as his right hand moved with the sketching and shading. How she loved this man.

'I know how to be a cop. It's difficult to gauge people sometimes. But, in the main, the job suits me. Especially in Major Crime. It's more analytical. More step based. I've found something that fits me, as a person. I've also found *someone* who gets me. You know how rare that is.'

'Hannah.'

'Yes. Hannah. She wasn't happy with me.'

'Why ever not?' Her tone was sharp.

'I didn't tell her I was on a phased return.'

Lisa bit her lip, she wanted to laugh. It was so like her husband. He would do as he wanted to do. And then when the repercussions happened, he would be surprised. Instead of answering she nodded into his arm.

'I can't lose this job, Lisa.'

'I know, love.'

'I don't know what I'll do if I have to leave the department.'

40.

Several vehicles were parked outside Lacey's home, but a vehicle check had identified which one was hers and we then were able to determine a previous registered address. A voters check had a Mr and Mrs Nettleton living there, Stephen and Shelley.

We had Lacey's parents' address.

As SIO it was my role to go, let them know I was running the investigation and that we would do everything we possibly could to bring their daughter's killer to justice.

It was the most difficult task in the department.

The house we were parked in front of was a neatly kept semi-detached property on Broom Road at Calverton. It was dark, lights twinkled behind curtains up and down the road. Here there was a light on downstairs and one in an upstairs window. They were still up.

I knocked on the door and Ross frowned. Like me this was a part of the job he hated. We all did. My stomach twisted as we waited for the door to be answered, as we waited in that split second, those few moments before the world separates into the before and after. Before their world breaks and after it has broken. When it will never be the same again and we were the ones who would do that to them.

Yes, my head knew that wasn't technically true. That the person who had squeezed the life out of Lacey Nettleton was responsible, but, in the here and now, it was me, me and Ross who were the ones who were about the rip apart the seams of this couple's existence.

There was movement behind the door. A deep male voice asked who was here. Cautious.

'Police, Mr Nettleton, can we have a word with you and your wife please?' I answered. My voice calm. Even. Giving nothing away of what was to come.

Ross shifted on his feet, kicked at the floor. I looked at him and he straightened himself up. This wasn't about us. This was their grief, we had to hold it together.

The door opened and an anxious face looked out at me.

'What is it?' he asked immediately.

'Can we come in please? Better in the house than on the doorstep.' I showed him my warrant card. He glanced at it but didn't take it in. Already a suggestion of what was to come was starting to nibble away at his subconscious.

He opened the door wider and I could feel the warmth from the house with the light that flooded the doorstep.

'Who is it, Stephen?' A voice from above, at the top of the stairs.

We stepped into the house and Stephen Nettleton closed the door behind us.

'It's the police, love. Do you want to come down?' He didn't sound as sure of himself as he did when he first opened his door but he hadn't asked us why we were here.

Shelley Nettleton walked down the stairs fastening a dressing gown around her waist as she did so. She was a slim woman. Her dark hair tied away from her face into a ponytail at the back of her head. It gave her a youthful look.

'What is it?' she asked directly. Worry etched on her face.

'Shall we go and sit down,' I said and we moved silently into the living room. Stephen and Shelley close, sitting down next to each other. Silent, waiting.

Ross and I seated ourselves on the remaining seats near them and I spoke. I confirmed they had a daughter, Lacey Nettleton, and her age, and as I did this I saw the photographs scattered around the room, of her growing up through the years. Alone, and with her parents and family and friends. There were some of what I presumed were her Instagram shots framed because they were square and they resembled the style I'd seen when I'd checked her account out before coming to the address. She really had been beautiful and quite artistic.

One photograph stood out from all the rest, it was larger and framed in a simple dark wood, a birthday party, with a cake in the foreground, a single candle in the middle and sitting behind the cake was an elderly woman. She looked to be about eighty years of age, her hair white and curled around her face which was flushed with happiness and lit up with joy. There was a blur of people behind her in the image, but it was Lacey at the side of her that this photo was framed for. Lacey who was leaning in and kissing the elderly woman on the cheek with such a gentleness and tenderness. A hand wrapped lightly on her other cheek as if the pressure from the kiss might just be too much. The love that fizzed between these two was clear to see. It was a beautiful scene.

I turned back to the couple before me. Shelley clutched at Stephen as I mentioned Lacey. She grabbed his hand and held on, her knuckles whitening with the power of her grip. The words were not yet out but the fear was there and was crawling over their bones.

'I'm sorry to have to come into your home and tell you this tonight,' I started to speak. My stomach tightened and I dug the nails of one hand into my palm, I had to stay calm for them. 'We believe we have found the body of your daughter this evening.'

There was silence. A brief moment as the words worked their way around this couple's minds and were processed and then it happened. It registered. The words I had spoken hit them for what they were. That their daughter was dead and would not be walking through their door to see them ever again. There would be no more family photographs, no more memories. Their life together, her life, it was over.

'No.' Stephen Nettleton said a single word but the power behind it said it all.

A lump formed in my throat. I swallowed and pushed it down. I had to be here for them.

'She was found by a couple of boys in Nottingham earlier this evening. We have opened a murder investigation,' I said to them, drip feeding them information.

A small sound escaped from Shelley, a whimper, like a dog who had been left outside in the rain and wanted to come back in. The sound didn't stop, it changed and escalated in volume as what we were saying sank in.

Mr Nettleton stood, leaving his wife alone on the sofa, unable to sit with himself and the news of what had happened to his only child. 'No, no. No, you have this wrong. It's the wrong girl. The wrong girl. You think it's her. She's well known, so you think it's her, she's well...' tears filled his eyes, his face was grey and he sank back into the seat he had just vacated. Shelley was openly wailing now and he turned and grabbed her roughly, pulled her into him and wrapped his big strong arms around her, pushed her head into his chest and stared at us without managing to see us.

She allowed herself to be man-handled. Her fists clawed at his T-shirt and she grabbed hold of him and cried harder. She called for her daughter, for Lacey.

Ross and I waited. My muscles ached as I held myself together. Still and quiet. The lump in my throat a constant struggle I had to fight against. This was not my grief, this was not my time. It would not have helped them in the slightest if they had seen me break down with them, for me to involve myself in their grief. I was there to be the

240

one who would do my everything for them. They needed our strength.

We needed to speak with the couple, but first they needed to do this, to feel the first flush of grief before the long haul set in. This was the raw unadulterated emotion and it hurt me every time we did this. My heart ached in my chest as Shelley clawed at her husband in an attempt to hold onto something solid and he held on to her as tightly as he could. Disbelief and horror etched on his face. Each line telling the story of his pain. He would never go back to the man he was before he answered the door, before we broke the news of his daughter's murder.

I nodded to Ross and he silently rose to look for the kitchen to make some drinks. They would need something to hold on to when the questions started. Even if they didn't drink a single drop, the act of holding on and keeping it level so nothing spilt would be enough to hold their attention for the short period of time I needed them. They would have questions for us and we had questions for them. And afterwards, when we left, life would never be the same for this couple ever again.

41

I sat with Evie in my living room, a large glass of wine cupped in my hands.

I felt drained after the visit to Lacey's parents. My limbs heavy and tired. My arm throbbed. Her parents had broken and crumbled before us. We had promised that we would do what was in our power to find out what happened.

As far as being able to help us with our inquiries into what had happened to Lacey that evening, they had not been able to help. They had last seen their daughter the previous week. They gave us the key to her apartment and I let them know a family liaison officer would get in touch with them and be their link between them and the investigation.

'One more,' I said to Evie as we drank red wine, 'and we'll have a serial killer on our hands.'

'Jesus, that's grim.' She swirled the drink around in her glass.

'I know Knight was technically a serial killer, but it was a product contamination case, it felt different,' I said referring to a recent case.

Evie nodded as I spoke.

'This guy, he's actually hands-on killing people.' I took a deep swig. 'And he's doing it at speed. I mean, what the hell is up with him?'

'A serial killer in Nottingham.' She nearly laughed. 'It sounds so American. You know we're in the UK, right? And nothing ever happens north of London.'

I tried to focus on her. I was tired. 'Let's hope he doesn't make it three and we don't have to use that word.'

'I have a question.'

I raised an eyebrow at her.

'What's with the online victims? What's his point? And,' she pointed a finger at me, 'why do we always presume it's a male killer? What if it's a female?'

'Is that a serious question?' I put my glass down on the coffee table.

She looked puzzled. 'Which one? The online victims or the female serial killer?'

My upper arm throbbed and I rubbed it. 'I'm not sure, to be honest.' I kneaded harder.

Evie watched me. She knew what I was doing. She worried about me.

'I asked myself that same question earlier, about the online thing. As far as identifying him as a him, it's because it's incredibly rare that a woman is this kind of hands-on killerish. If that's even a word.'

I picked up my glass of wine.

'Okay, but the question needed–'

My phone started to vibrate. I picked it up from the floor, looked at the caller ID.

'Baxter?' I said to Evie, confused. 'He can't be calling for an update, I gave him one before I left.'

The phone rang off before I had a chance to answer it.

'Well, you won't know now because you missed it, too busy asking me why he was phoning, you idiot.' She slapped my knee.

I looked at the phone in my hand. It started to vibrate again and Baxter's name flashed up once more. Persistent. This wasn't good.

'You going to answer it this time?'

'I'm not on call.' I looked at the glass of wine. 'Not officially anyway,' I said under my breath. We were in the middle of a double murder investigation. Shit. There can't be another one. Not already. We would sink.

I pressed answer. 'Sir?'

'Hannah. I just called you.' His tone was accusatory. I rolled my eyes at Evie and put Baxter on speakerphone.

'I'm at home, Sir. I updated you before I left.' As though he didn't realise this. 'Is there a problem?'

'Is there a problem?' he bellowed, cracking up in the air above the phone.

Evie frowned at me. I shrugged. I had no idea what could be wrong. I had done everything we could possibly do before we left for the night.

'Sir?' I prompted again.

'Those two boys.'

'The boys who found Lacey?'

'Yes. Those boys. What other boys do we have?' He was really wound up. There was a serious issue. Was one of the boys responsible for the murder? I didn't see how that was possible. In any case, we had seized their clothing before releasing them and had their fingerprints and swabs for elimination as they had walked in on the scene. We had taken every precaution.

'What's happened, Sir?' To say he was irate, it was like dragging a huge rock out of a well with a piece of string. The pressure against me was immense.

'One of the boys took a photograph of the girl–'

'Lacey,' I interjected, not liking where this was going.

I heard him growl. Evie's eyes widened. She sipped on her wine.

'He took a photo of the girl, of Lacey. And not long ago, when he was finally alone, out of his parents' way, he uploaded it to the internet. Our second murder scene has gone viral, DI Robbins.'

Jesus Christ.

Evie put her glass on the table at the side of mine. She pulled her phone out of her bag and started tapping at it. Her eyes nearly popped out of her head and she nodded at me.

For fuck's sake. 'How the hell?'

'That's what I want to know!' he exploded.

He ranted for a good five minutes. Evie sat, legs crossed, opposite me, listening and reading the comments on Twitter. She showed me the feed for the hashtag #LaceyLane and the ensuing outcry.

With images.

'The boys said they found the body and fled the garage. That was the account from the boy Pasha and Martin interviewed.' I tried to appease Baxter, but it wasn't going to happen. Not with this. Not with another image of another murder scene.

'I've spoken to his parents,' he said.

'Which boy?'

'The one who wasn't interviewed.' He let out a long breath as though conveying this to me was wearing him down.

This just got better. I suppressed a groan at the thought of Baxter, in this mood, making contact with the boy's parents, especially with how difficult they had been at the scene. Who knew what damage he had caused the investigation with his brusqueness?

'They said he told them he had entered the garage with his mate and ran out terrified, as they told us. He went back inside with his phone while they waited for police to turn up. His mate waited outside, which is why there was no mention of this in the friend's account. Though, obviously he did omit to tell Pasha and Martin that the other lad went in.' He let out another breath. It was like listening to a balloon go down.

'So, he went back in,' he was less annoyed now, more into telling me what had happened. 'Creeped up to the girl. Took some quick snaps and then shoved his phone back in his pocket and ran back out. It wasn't until later when he was alone that he checked the photos and realised who the girl was. It was then that he uploaded one of the images. He wanted to be popular. To have people at school think he was something.' Another sigh. 'What do kids think, Hannah?'

'I don't know. I really don't. I had to have Ross tell me about this Lacey girl today. It was the first I'd heard of people earning their money by doing nothing other than what the rest of the country's youngsters are doing.'

The balloon must be practically deflated now as a low short sigh escaped. 'We have a real farce on our hands now. The country is in uproar. I have a message from Walker who has been contacted by the Chief. This isn't good, Hannah.'

So he was rolling the shit downhill to me.

Obviously.

What else was management about? But the buck would stop with me. I wouldn't roll it any further down. I wouldn't lay blame for this error at anyone else's door or start shouting unanswerable questions at anyone below me.

'Has he removed his original tweet?' I asked.

Evie picked up her glass again and took a deep slug. She nearly emptied the glass.

'He has, but from what I understand, it doesn't make any difference. The image is out there. People have saved the image and it's being tweeted from other accounts as an original image.'

'And Twitter?'

'I have someone dealing with that now. Hopefully they will act swiftly to get it off their site, but the damage is done. It's out that she's been killed. People know how she was left. In what state.' There was an air of resignation about him now. The deflation was complete.

'Do you need me to come back in? I've had a glass of wine, but I can get a taxi if you need me.' I hated to admit it, but there were no options.

'No, it's fine. Don't have too much, DI Robbins.' The use of my rank was to remind me of work. 'I want you here early in the morning. We have a lot to be getting on with.'

'What about Lacey's parents?' I asked. They had more than enough to be dealing with, without this on top of it all.

'I'm going to contact the FLO next and ask them to make contact and appraise them of events. We don't want them hearing about this by logging online. Hopefully they're too grief-stricken to be browsing the internet.' He stopped, as he realised what he had said. 'I mean–'

'I know.'

Evie pursed her lips.

'I'll see you early in the morning, DI Robbins.'

'Yes, Sir.'

With that he was gone.

'Wow,' said Evie. 'One of the kids went back and took a photo? He was braver than I would have been in those circumstances at that age.'

I picked up my wine glass and downed the rest of the wine. 'I'm not sure brave is a word I'd use for him right now.' The stupidity of the boy had caused untold damage.

'I'm sure he hasn't thought about what it means to have uploaded it,' she tried.

'That's the whole goddamn problem with the internet. And with teenagers loose on the internet. They don't think about what they're doing or the repercussions of their actions on there. He hasn't even considered that this girl has a family and now he's shared her death image all over the world and no matter how hard we try, it's very likely that at some point in the future, even if it's not tonight, or not this week, but at some point, they'll be online looking for their daughter's memories, and they'll see her death in full technicolour.' I was furious. I sounded like Baxter when he had phoned.

I looked at my empty glass. 'Do you want a top-up?' I asked Evie.

She stood. 'I better not. I'm going to make sure I'm in early with you tomorrow. See what I can do to help. Get yourself to bed, yeah?'

I stared at her. Sometimes she tried to parent me.

'I saw you messing about with your arm before Baxter called,' she said. 'You could do with some rest. I know it plays you up when you're tired or stressed. Get some sleep and we'll start back on this with fresh eyes in the morning.'

I hated being handled. Especially by Evie because she was usually right. I collected both glasses from the table and held them by the stems in one hand.

Evie stepped closer, leaned in, wrapped her arms around my shoulders and hugged me. Her perfume had a slightly floral undertone and was warm and gentle and tickled my nose. 'Get some rest, Hannah.' She kissed my cheek and left. The door closing firmly behind her.

I walked to the kitchen and shoved Evie's glass into the dishwasher. Then I topped my glass up with what was left in the bottle, palmed painkillers into my mouth then walked towards my bedroom. She was right, I did need to rest and another glass of red wine would help me relax before we wound ourselves up again tomorrow.

42

Drew woke up late. His housemate had already left for the day. The house was quiet. It was not like him to sleep in but he felt lighter than he had in a long time. It must be the relief that his plan had worked. It turned out that something terrible could happen and the internet could keep its opinions to itself and not ruin someone else's life.

That, and a beer with his housemate, made for a really peaceful and relaxing night.

He shoved his feet into his slippers, pushed his arms into his dressing gown and made his way downstairs. His first coffee of the day was needed.

The house was tidy, as it always was. His housemate was immaculate, if somewhat slightly obsessive about keeping everything in its place. This had had a knock-on effect on Drew. He had become afraid of upsetting the status-quo and put everything back in its place the minute he had finished using it.

He had been a bit of a slob at home because Melissa had run around after him as much as she ran around after the children and he had accepted it. Like he accepted the way things were here.

He was a people-pleaser.

That's what he was.

He poured his coffee and brought it up to his nose, smelled the start of the day in the deep warm scent, and smiled.

Today was so much better. All the previous days just melted away like a bad dream. If he could keep his days like this then it wouldn't be long before the kids would be enjoying his company again. He could show them that the world was not such a bad place. The internet was not the dog fight it often appeared to be.

Drew walked into the living room, coffee mug in hand, the cold frosty day blinking in through the window. He switched on the television and found one of the news channels. He hated the morning television shows. Full of rubbish. Full of people airing their dirty laundry in public and full of people discussing personal topics that should be kept at home and talked through with loved ones. You wouldn't find him taking his woes with Melissa to a sofa on a TV screen.

They'd offered it as well. A couple of the big daytime shows had been in touch after he had been shamed and lost his job. They wanted his side of it, they said. They wanted to show the world what had happened to him.

He didn't trust them. Plus, it was his business. The whole problem had been other people looking at him, so why would he draw more attention to himself?

They must have thought he was stupid if they thought he would consider dragging it all through the minds of the public again.

As he found out yesterday, his children still hadn't recovered. They would never forgive him.

How did people move on with their lives if they shared every moment of it with TV cameras and strangers?

He found the channel he usually watched. The weather was on. A bleak grey day, starting off frosty then warming a couple of degrees but staying overcast.

He sipped on his coffee. Leaned back in his chair.

The world was starting to feel right. Better.

The female newsreader came onto the screen. Some small talk between the weather guy and the reader before she turned to the screen to go over the morning's headlines again.

An image flashed onto the screen of Syrian refugees, worn and broken from the terrors that ravaged their country. Children wide-eyed but resigned at their way of life.

Drew tuned out. Sipped his coffee and thought about his day ahead.

Should he contact Melissa and Libbie again? Maybe it was too soon. He couldn't expect Libbie to have calmed down this soon. He would have to be patient and give her time. He'd seen that he could change public opinion, so he could certainly sway his own daughter's mind.

The next shot on the screen froze Drew to the chair, his mug halfway to his mouth. The newsreader was saying something about not being able to show the viewers the image that had been online last night, but this was the scene of the crime. The wide-angled shot was of the garage where he had left the girl.

This wasn't what had frozen him. He expected her to be found, of course, and for it to be reported. Though maybe only on the local news, not the national station, but it was that comment about an image online last night.

He hadn't seen anything.

What image?

What had he missed?

Shaking he threw his mug in the sink and fired up his laptop on the kitchen worktop.

She had to be wrong. There had been no chatter online last night. He had checked.

He waited while the laptop woke up. It felt like an eternity as it dragged itself to life.

He opened the browser and went straight to Twitter. Facebook might be where the majority of people spent their time but Twitter was where the news and the gossip and all the harm happened.

There it was, in the trending list again. #LaceyLane – and images. He hadn't expected images this time. Yes, he'd considered it, which is why he had left her in such a posed position, to test the public. It was no good doing what he was doing if he wasn't testing them, but she was also more out of the way so photographs were less likely. Not like last time.

But there were. Just two of them. Both very similar and with a nasty glare as the flash lit up her deathly white skin. Whoever had taken them had done a rushed job. The angle was off. You could only see one of the photographs of her on the mirror and only if you looked closely.

If you knew what you were looking for.

This was Twitter. This was a world filled with people who had nothing better to do than to examine the gory details and also with technically knowledgeable people. People who had blown the image up and had found the photograph of her pinned the mirror. Found the mirror.

It was being called hideous and macabre.

They were calling him hideous and macabre.

He slammed the laptop screen down, felt it shudder beneath his fingers. His own shaking worse, he stumbled backwards to the other counter and fell into it, hitting his back. He leaned onto it. Pushed his elbows on to keep himself upright.

They were calling him hideous.

They were calling him macabre.

They were calling him.

All over again they were targeting him. Calling him. Regardless of whether they knew who they were saying these things about, he knew, he knew these names were aimed at him and his legs could barely hold him up.

Was it shock or fear or anger that made him shake this way?

He had no way to know what the feeling was that was creating the reaction in his body. He just knew he needed to try to pull himself together. He could feel his heart as it raced against his breast bone. His legs weakened and he sank to the floor. Coldness filled his entire core and spread out.

This wasn't supposed to happen.

They were supposed to reflect. See that she had died the way she lived, via social media, that how they lived and behaved online should be considered and not be thrown away like a careless remark that can't be taken back. Here they were, en masse, circling for blood, for his blood.

Again.

What was he going to do now?

43.

I could really have done with Aaron this morning but it was not to be. He was on one of his days off and would be back tomorrow. I had managed without him for the past six weeks so I was sure I could get through a day.

Probably.

Baxter was pacing up and down the corridor in front of my office when I walked in. This was definitely serious if he was not waiting for me to come to him.

'There you are. I thought I said you needed to be here early this morning.' He was exasperated. It wasn't a good start.

I looked at my watch. It was six-thirty. I raised my eyebrows at him. He took my point.

'We'll go in your office, now you're here, shall we?' Still that tone persisted that said he was displeased with my time of arrival.

I pushed the door open and let him walk in ahead of me. The automatic eco-lighting came on as soon as he entered, bathing the office in a dim glow. I stalked around my desk and flicked my laptop on as Baxter paced around the room. Today there was no distasteful look at my desk; he was too wound up about the state of the investigation to worry about how I managed my workload.

'Did we manage to remove the images last night?' I asked as I watched my screen silently load.

'We'll never get them all, but we do have Twitter onside now. They don't want a murder victim on their site, especially a second one, a trend of them, so they're working with us.'

'Good to hear.' I slid my coat off, moved around to the coat stand and threw it over a hook. 'And Lacey's parents? How are they doing?'

Baxter nearly growled at me. 'As you'd expect after their daughter has been killed and then some imbecile decides it's a good idea to splash the image all over the internet for everyone to look at.'

'They didn't go and view it, did they?' I asked, horrified at the thought.

'Amelia Riley, the FLO we're using, drummed it into them what a bad idea it would be. Who knows what goes on once we leave the house. Are they too scared or too sensible to look? Or is the need to see your daughter's last minutes on this earth too much of a pull to withstand?'

He had a point. Those poor parents. No one deserves to see their child like that.

'We need to double down on this, Hannah. It's getting far more attention than I would like. The Chief is watching because of the national press and social media angle. He wants it wrapping up as soon as possible.'

'Well, I'll get right on that then.' I couldn't help myself.

'Look,' he sank heavily into the chair opposite me, 'I know it's not that easy on a large and complex investigation such as this. The Chief is aware of the complexities, but...' he tapped his fingers on my desk. 'From what I've gleaned, he's getting pressure from the PCC.'

Great. Police and Crime Commissioners were publicly elected officials who were in charge of not only the policing budget, but also in how the area is policed, its priorities and targets. Which, in my view was utterly ridiculous considering they knew nothing about policing, or what it took to combat crime. If the PCC wanted something sorting, then we sorted it. If he was looking at this case, because it reflected badly on him, then we were most definitely under pressure. He would want to be re-elected. And the Chief would want to be kept in role too. A decision that was in the hands of the PCC.

It really was a farce. A long way away from how things were when I joined the job. It was true that there were areas of the police that needed to be improved. To put a civilian in charge, well, that was simply going too far the other way.

'And Tierney is not happy with such public scrutiny on his force, I imagine?' I said.

'He is not indeed. Far from happy. So far from happy he's threatening to come and visit the incident room, Hannah.'

I stared at Baxter. 'You're kidding me?'

'I'm afraid not.'

'We're only a matter of days into this. He can't expect it to be wrapped up with a bow in that timeframe.'

'He can and he does. And if it isn't,' he let out a sigh, 'then he will come down and see what we're doing.' He gave me a forced smile. 'For moral support, you understand.'

Damn.

'So, we need to throw everything we can at this. You'll have all the resources we can manage–'

'Is that all the resources I need,' I interrupted, 'or all the resources we can stretch to but with a bow on because it's this job?'

'Hannah, I'm getting a bit fed up of sighing over this case, can we please try and play nice on this? We're both on the same side.'

I relented. Inclined my head.

'Of course we don't have an unlimited budget,' he said in response. 'That's not to say we have to scrimp.'

'Good to know.'

'And now we have that sorted.' He leaned back in the chair. 'How was Aaron's first day back in the job?'

The hairs on the back of my neck rose and I did my best not to stretch my face into a grimace at him.

'I was sorry not to catch up with him yesterday,' he said. 'I wanted to speak to him. Welcome him back properly.'

I could only imagine. He barely paused for breath, so caught up in the spiel he seemed to have rehearsed just for me.

'I wanted to see how he felt about coming back after such an ordeal.'

Now he looked me in the eye. What exactly did he expect from me? Did he think I would be on the same page as him in wanting to replace Aaron? To get another DS on the team? Did he not see how the team worked? I know he had only been here a few months, but come on. He had to see how closely we worked. How loyal we were to each other. And more importantly, how badly everyone had taken it when Aaron had his heart attack.

'He did a great job,' I replied. It wasn't a lie. Aaron had in fact done a brilliant job. As he always did. I had been so grateful to have him back on the team. He put his all into every task he was assigned. You would never worry about a job you gave him. You were safe in the knowledge it would be completed and not left because he was too busy or stressed, as was sometimes the case in the force, in various departments. What with the government cuts many cops just couldn't cope. Aaron though, he was so methodical; he kept his head until he worked his way through any task.

'He didn't have any problems at all?' Baxter probed, with a little too much, what? What was that in his voice? Excitement? At the prospect that Aaron may have struggled.

I had been honest when I said Aaron had done a great job. I had answered that question correctly, but this question, about how he had coped. That was a different question altogether. I flicked my hand through my hair. Looked up at the strip lights in the ceiling. At the one bulb in the corner that needed replacing. Luckily it was over the door and not over my desk. Which was why I hadn't done anything about it yet.

I was not in the habit of outright lying to my supervisors. 'You'll have to ask him how he felt,' was how I chose to go with it. 'All I can do is vouch for his ability to do the job.' I stared him down. 'Which, I might say, was no different to before he was forced off sick.'

He laughed.

Baxter actually laughed.

A short sharp bark of a laugh, but a laugh none the same.

What the hell?

I picked up a pen from the top of a pile of files on my desk. I desperately wanted to throw it at him. Instead I flicked it on the desktop. In a rigid hard rhythm. And stared at him. 'Something you care to share, Sir?'

He cleared his throat. 'I'm sorry. That wasn't very professional.'

Understatement.

'It's just the comment about him performing to the same ability as he was previously.'

I flicked the pen again. It cracked in the silence between us.

'Before he had his heart attack, Aaron was not performing well at all. Not in my estimation, Hannah. He was at risk of being moved sideways. You know that, we had the discussion. Then he went and had a heart attack before we could action it.'

We? I flicked again.

'And now, here you are informing me that DS Stone is performing at the very same level that he was before his heart attack. Knowing his performance was under review. So, for that I thank you. I'll need to speak to him obviously, but you might just have supported a move out of the unit for DS Aaron Stone.'

I flicked the pen again and the lid flew off.

44

I wasn't certain how to describe my mood when I opened up the briefing. There was one sure-fire way I could defend Aaron, but he had argued against it. The only reason Baxter had taken against him was not because of Aaron's work but because of a personality clash. And it was a personality he didn't understand. If he knew about the Asperger's then he could accept Aaron's quirks, like his need to wear earphones when the office became a little too loud and boisterous for him. His sometime blunt responses. Though these, they were no different to what I encountered from anyone above the rank of DCI. Shit, even some sergeants got an attitude as soon as they received their stripes. Rank and perceived power did that to people.

'Okay, quiet down, people,' I shouted above the din.

The smell of grease permeated the incident room. Everyone was in early. It was seven a.m. and the team were here and raring to go. It was Sunday but not one single person complained. This was what they did. A job came in, they came up to the line and worked. If it was a weekend, they did it with breakfast sandwiches. For the second day running.

It was surprising that our waistlines weren't twice the size they were. Martin had texted everyone before he came in, got orders and stopped at an early doors greasy spoon and collected the food. Everyone was chowing down on fried food.

He'd brought me a bacon sandwich, but I was so furious I couldn't touch it.

That was one word for it, furious. But, it didn't do it justice.

Martin gave me a look when I left the cob on the desk at the side of me. It wasn't like me to leave food uneaten. He didn't say anything though. His forte was tact.

'Are we going to have some quiet today?' I bellowed again as the noise continued.

Eventually the racket died down. Mouths were wiped with the backs of hands and napkins. The remains were shoved in and chewed down and pens were picked up.

'Thanks, guys. We have a lot of work to do and I'm not sure if you're aware, but one of our witnesses made our job a whole lot more difficult late last night.'

'Yeah, I saw that,' piped up Ross. I'd forgotten he was a social media user.

'Me too,' Pasha said.

'Anyone else?' I asked, feeling, not for the first time in this investigation, older than I was.

A couple of others in the team nodded, but I was grateful to see I wasn't the only one to not use social media, though I supposed some of them might have just not been on since last night. After all, it was on late and we were up early. Maybe they hadn't had a chance to see it.

'It feels as though we don't have a particularly strong grip on this case and that needs to change,' I said. 'DCI Baxter has Twitter on board and they are keeping on top of the image situation now. But the fact is, it's out there. And even if it wasn't, people know more than we want them to know. The usual case of keeping facts back for interviews of possible offenders becomes difficult when everyone has seen the murder scene.'

I paused as a thought crossed my mind.

It crossed everyone else's at the same time.

'You think that's why he's doing it, Ma'am, leaving the bodies in places they'll get found and photographed? So the murder scene is public property. So the nuts can admit to it?' asked Pasha.

'Not that I'm a fan of the word nuts, Pasha.' A blush crept up her face. 'But, yes, I think it's something we have to consider. That the reason they are left in such public places...' I paused, thought about it some more, 'Though Lacey's scene wasn't particularly public we do have to bear that hypothesis in mind due to the location of the first, of Sebastian Wade.'

There was a few head shakes as people wrapped their minds around how prepared a killer would have to be to think about a scene this way. If it was true, if they did want their dump site or murder site to be public property so any subsequent investigation or trial was skewed, then they were not only intelligent, but this was also premeditated and extremely well thought out, making him a very cold-blooded killer.

'There's an awful lot of work to do. The second boy from last night is coming in first thing this morning and needs interviewing. Many of you still have actions from the Sebastian Wade inquiry. DCI Baxter has authorised more staff. So expect them to be arriving throughout the day. No doubt we'll be using seconded uniform officers as usual. Make use of them. Apparently a young woman called in last night and said she was probably the last person to see Lacey alive as they did some photography shots on the river. She's coming in later so one of you needs to see her and take her statement. Be thorough.'

'And Aaron, Ma'am, he'll be back tomorrow I take it?' It was Martin. Where everyone else was scribbling notes in their Major Incident notepads, Martin was relaxed in his chair listening to the briefing rather than writing anything down. He was not known for being up-to-date on his paperwork. He was particularly good with people, however.

I looked to Baxter who was standing at the rear of the room. Silent. Watching.

He shrugged. Unhelpful.

'DS Stone is due back to work tomorrow, yes,' I replied. And I needed to try to make time to speak to him some time before Baxter got to him.

My phone vibrated in my pocket. As I was still in the middle of briefing and Baxter was here I ignored it. If it was urgent and was job-related they would call the office next.

'Theresa will hand out the actions for today, but we're going to be needing the usual, house-to-house, CCTV collecting, a search for witnesses.' I looked at Evie who was tucked away in a corner. 'We obviously have another online link. I'm going to speak to Evie and the forensic team to see how they can help with.' She nodded.

Baxter gave a short cough and stepped forward. 'We're also going to do a press conference today.'

We were? Shit. I hated press conferences. At least Ethan wouldn't be in the press, sitting in front of me. Ethan, a reporter who had been with the *Nottingham Today* paper but was now working for one of the Nationals in London, and with whom I had been in, I'm not sure what kind of relationship I would call it, but yes, it was a relationship of sorts.

'Will you be taking that, Sir?' I asked. Hopeful.

He preened in front of me. 'I could do.' He flicked away a piece of non-existent lint from his jacket lapel. 'It's been a while since I put on my TV face, but I'm sure I still have it.' He smiled.

Some people lapped up that kind of attention. Me? I hated it. Hated the camera and hated the questions that came with it. I think he was forgetting about that part.

'And what will we be focusing on, with the press conference?' I asked. 'Because, obviously, we need a plan. I'll get Claire to come and see you in your office, shall I?' Claire was our media liaison. Nothing went out unless it went through her.

'Yes, please do. We need to appeal for witnesses to come forward. It's all well and good for them to chat away online with each other and total strangers but we want them to come to us and tell us what they saw, and as far as I can see we're not getting that?' It was posed as a question.

'No, no we're not,' I admitted.

'Good. This might spur them on then. Remind them of their civic duty.' He turned to leave.

'And that extra staff?' I prompted.

He didn't even bother turning back to face me. 'Yes, yes.' He lifted a hand into the air. 'I'll get right on it.' And he pushed his way through the incident room doors.

'I'll contact the morgue and see what time the PM is. You all have something to be getting on with.' A gradual hum rose again as the briefing came to a close.

As I strode out of the office I remembered that I had missed a call on my phone. It must be personal as the office phone hadn't rung. I pulled it out of my pocket. It was a missed call from my dad. At this time in the morning. There was a voicemail. I dialled the service as I walked to my office. As I pushed the door open I saw that the clock on the wall read eight five a.m. and my desk phone was ringing.

My dad's voice clicked into my thoughts. Panic lifted the tone. 'Hannah, it's Dad. Oh, oh, I really wish you had picked up. Oh, you must be, oh erm busy. It's just. Oh, Hannah. She's left the house. I couldn't stop her. I thought I would tell you. I thought you would want to know.'

There was the briefest of pauses as he inhaled. 'Oh, Hannah. It's such a difficult situation. I didn't know if you would want to know or what I should do. I'm sorry, love.'

The call ended.

I was puzzled. Why would he call me to tell me Zoe had left the house? Was he worried she had gone out to score? Was she in trouble? Shit, I would kill her. He really didn't need this in his life. He had waited patiently for her release. It had kept him going after Mum had died. And now she was doing this to him. Wait until I got my hands on her.

I snatched up the phone on my desk before it rang off.

'DI Robbins.'

'Ma'am, it's PC Mitchell.'

'What can I do for you this early on a Sunday, PC Mitchell?'

'I was just walking into the station when a young woman outside said she wanted to talk to you, says she's your sister.'

45

I yanked her by her arm and pulled her towards the door. She let out a small yelp as my fingers dug into her arm. My eyes shot towards PC Mitchell who was still hovering. She dropped her head and looked down as soon as I turned.

'Come with me,' I hissed then paused. Where should I take her? Into the corridor where any of my colleagues, from anywhere in the station, not just my office, could overhear us? Or outside where a member of the public could hear us?

It was a Sunday. The station was quiet. There was only uniformed staff about as the majority of civilian staff only worked Monday to Friday. Better to risk a colleague or two than a member of the public.

Again I tugged on her arm and made for the internal door. This time she moved with me.

With my free hand I unlocked the door, pushed my way through it, pulled Zoe through then let go of her as the door slammed closed behind us.

'What the hell?' I turned on her.

She stood in front of me with a puzzled look on her face.

'I wanted to talk to you. You wouldn't talk to me the other night so I thought this would be the only way to make you hear me. Why are you so mad?' she asked.

Seriously. 'You need to ask?' I whispered at her, my voice a hoarse snarl.

'I told you. I've changed.'

I looked around me. At the narrow corridor we were in. No one was about. The walls were freshly painted from the repair job that downstairs had needed after it had been damaged in a fire. It all smelt fresh and new and here was Zoe trying to tell me she was fresh and new.

I looked at her. She had put on a little weight. No longer the rakish drug-addled women I had housed before her arrest. Her jeans fitted her and a scarlet polo neck jumper clung to her frame giving her a healthy glow. Her hair was washed and hung gently around her shoulders.

'You know Dad phoned me to warn me you were coming.'

She looked shocked. 'Why would he do that?'

'Because he understands, Zoe. He understands my job and what it means to me. What is it about you that makes you unable to grasp the situation?'

She ran a hand through her hair. A move I also made when I was getting stressed.

'I came because I need you to see that I've changed, Hannah. I need you to believe me and I need my sister back. I can't take back what I did but I am sorry. It wasn't me.'

I glared at her.

'It... it was me. What I mean is that the drugs, they had control. I needed to get that control back.' She took a step closer. 'And I have.'

Voices came from behind me. I shook my head at her. I wouldn't do this with an audience.

'You won't forgive me?' The colour drained out of her face.

'I'm saying wait a minute, you idiot. Someone is coming.' I shook my head and she looked past me, lifted her chin in acknowledgement and kept her mouth shut.

'And when he's in custody we'll do a Section 18 straight away. See what we have before we go into interview.' Two officers moved past us with barely a pause as they discussed an offender they had locked up.

Once they'd rounded the corner and were out of earshot again I turned to Zoe. 'Why should I believe you this time, Zoe? I believed you last time and look what happened.' I gritted my teeth at the memory of the search team going through my apartment. Fellow officers searching my home. A senior officer attempting to soothe the situation for me, but nothing could have calmed my rage that day. My space was being violated and it was all Zoe's fault.

Her eyes teared up. She swallowed hard. 'Do you really think I would come here,' she waved her arm around at the surroundings, the corridor we were standing in, 'to a police station, if I was still in that life? Do you think I would risk it?'

I paused.

'Do you think I would be that brazen?'

Ah, there was a question. She'd had me doubting the sincerity of her words until she said that. I looked her up and down. She stayed still and took it.

'I'm clean, Hannah.'

'What do you want?' I didn't get it. Why was she so desperate to talk to me, to resolve this? So much so that she would come here while I was working. And on this particular case. Was that it, was she interested in the case? No, she had made moves before Sebastian had been found.

'I just want a chance.'

I pursed my lips at her.

'Okay, I want a second chance. Because I want my sister back.' She paused. Thought about her next words.

I looked behind me, checked for anyone else who might come down this way. It was clear.

'Dad would be over the moon, you know.'

'That's a low blow, Zoe,' I said. 'Using Dad that way. You know I'd do anything for him.'

She smiled.

'Fuck, Zoe.'

She smiled again. It wasn't smug. It was small. Cautious. Hopeful.

'I have work to do. You have to go,' I said to her.

The smile slipped.

'I suppose we can talk again.'

Her face lit up.

'I'm not promising anything, Zoe. You need to be aware just what happened after you were arrested. What happened for me. How your actions impacted on me. You can't just sail through life, having Dad pick up the pieces for you.'

'You think prison is sailing through...' She stopped. I glared at her. 'Okay. Thank you.'

I let her out of the door.

'Don't let me down again, Zoe.'

She put her hand on my arm. 'Hannah, you mean the world to me. It broke my heart when Dad told me something was going on for you at work after I was arrested. That was when I hit rock bottom. When I knew it wasn't just my life I had screwed up. I want to make this better.' Her hand slipped away and I closed the door behind her.

46.

This was the second press conference I had been a part of this year. Luckily, Baxter had agreed to take the lead. I felt so exposed when I led a press conference.

This time the national press was here as well as the local press. This case had garnered interest because of how Sebastian had been found. We hadn't yet made a definitive link between the two cases but we believed it was the same killer and so did the media.

As did the people on social media who played by their own unique rules.

We held the briefing at Headquarters, because we needed the space, and the room was rammed. We had been upstairs to see the Chief Constable before heading down to this melee and he hadn't been happy. This I had already been aware of, but coming face to face with him was a different matter. Luckily, I was shielded by Baxter who, as senior officer, took most of the flak. He was even less happy than the Chief by the time we were excused from his office.

'I want this man caught,' he said to me as we walked down the stairs.

'We're doing everything in our power,' I replied, two steps behind him.

'Do more,' was his curt response.

I ignored it. There was nothing I could say.

I looked out at the room from my spot at the side, behind a couple of stands. It was heaving with people carrying cameras and microphones, notepads and pens. Items with which they would be able to scold us with later today.

Baxter looked down at himself. Picked at something I couldn't see on his suit jacket and brushed downwards. 'Are we ready?' he asked.

I really didn't want to be. This was torture. 'Yes. Into the devil's den,' I answered.

He stepped forward, leading me into the fray. The cameras flashed immediately. It stops you being able to see the people behind them. Dehumanises them. Not that they need help in this regard. Their social skills at one of these things seem to take a hike as they push each other in an attempt to get their question answered before time runs out.

Baxter introduced us. Told the expectant crowd he would give a prepared statement and then take a few questions.

Then he waited for the room to quiet.

Gradually the noise eased. The flashing of cameras lessened and everyone stilled for what came next.

Baxter read from his sheet.

He told them that there had been a murder and identified Sebastian Wade. He expressed his deepest sympathy to the family of Sebastian Wade and I wondered if Nick would be watching or if he would avoid this. I imagined he would be glued to it. Attempting to prise any single piece of information out of it that we may have withheld from him.

The shutter swish of cameras could be heard through Baxter's monologue and the flashes were bright in the tightly packed room.

Baxter went on to say that Wade had been left in Market Square and that the police tape had not been left by Nottinghamshire police but was tape you could buy from a shop or online. He then went on to say that, yes, there had been another murder and at this time we were treating them as separate incidents but it was an evolving situation and we would provide more information as and when we had it. He identified Lacey as her family had been informed and her image was all over the internet. Again, he offered his condolences and asked that both families be given peace at this time as they grieved for the loss of their loved ones.

He stated that the public could expect to see a high police presence at the site of both scenes and in general to reassure members of the public that their safety was of the utmost importance.

The inquiry was at a very early stage, he informed the recording crowd, and at this time we were not in a position to discuss any leads that we were following or any possible motive for the attacks.

Baxter finished by asking the public that no more images be shared online as it perpetuated the crime, it gave the killer what he wanted and hurt those left behind. He also asked that if anyone had any information they should come forward or contact the help line that had been set up.

He closed.

The room exploded. More lights, and voices all at the same time. Hands in the air. Microphones pushed ever more forward. You could feel the pressure of the people as they tried to get closer without jumping on the table in front of us.

'Okay, okay, one at a time,' Baxter bellowed.

I was lucky. I was here for support. This was his show. I stayed still and watched.

The room subsided into an awkward hum as the journalists continued to vie for attention.

Baxter pointed to a woman on the front row. Her dark hair tied away from her face.

'Gillian Reaves, BBC,' she said.

I wondered if she was from the local station or if they had sent someone up to cover this.

Baxter gave a brief nod of his head.

'Sebastian Wade was left out in a crime scene. He was a true-crime blogger. What do you take from that, Detective Inspector Baxter?' Her notebook was poised on her lap, pen hovering over it. She peered at him, ready to take in every word he said.

I was so glad this was his event.

He cleared his throat. I wondered how much he had prepared for this or if he was just winging it. It was a rough one to wing. It was complicated and difficult.

'Obviously I can't talk about specifics to do with the investigation, Gillian.' He smiled. His whitened teeth glinted in the darkened room. 'Of course it's something we're aware of and have as a line of inquiry.'

He pointed to a male further back, dark black hair slicked across a bald pate.

'Glen Davids,' he mumble, the rest and I didn't hear it. That or the hum of his colleagues around him drowned him out. 'There is talk that the killer wants these victims to be found and photographed. What do you make of that?'

Baxter paused. Steepled his fingers, then spoke. 'As I said previously, we haven't linked the two murders, so we can't say that *the* killer intends anything. What I can say is that it looks as though he was trying to make a point with Sebastian Wade, definitely. But Lacey wasn't left out in a public place, so I'm not sure that hypothesis stands up.'

He was feeling more relaxed and in his stride, I could tell, as he leaned back in his chair.

'Okay, one more question.' He leaned forward again. 'At the back I think this time. The gentleman standing in the corner.'

I peered through the gloom and the lights to see who he was pointing at, it was an older guy I didn't recognise. He gave his name and paper then the question came. He lifted his chin to be heard better over the heads of his colleagues. 'There's a lot of furore online about these murders,' he started, on the most difficult part of the investigation. 'Is the public sentiment having any bearing on the investigation at all? And do you think the public sentiment, the outrage, will have any impact on the killer, either singular killer or both?'

He'd managed to ask two questions, which was more than anyone else. They were good questions. The whole of the room turned and looked at Baxter, including me.

'As this is DI Robbins' investigation, I will allow her to field this question.' He in turn looked at me.

For a minute I was stumped, his words not quite penetrating my mind. Baxter was fobbing his questions off onto me.

I stared out into the field of faces, saw them all staring back at me, all focused, ready for what was about to come.

Shit, again.

I shifted in my seat. Tried to kick-start my brain into gear.

The online activity. The investigation. The killer's reaction.

My thoughts?

'DI Robbins?' Baxter prompted.

'Yes,' I said. I had this. I would answer. I had nowhere else to go. I looked out to the room. 'It's true that there has been a huge interest in these murders, and not just from yourselves, but in today's world, we do have to be aware of social media and how news is picked up and reported, but as far as social media having an impact on our investigation, we can't allow that. We will follow the evidence where it takes us. Nothing more, nothing less. As for the killer or killers, I can't speak for their state of mind or how they will perceive the reaction to their crimes. It's very possible they knew they would get a reaction when they left Sebastian Wade on the steps of the council building, but what reaction he expected, I can't comment. I do reiterate what DCI Baxter stated earlier though, and that is to request that anyone using social media should not share any of the images as it is detrimental to the investigation and to the memory of both victims and their families.'

I had nothing further to say and relaxed my shoulders, realising they had gradually crept up so they were around my ears. I heard Baxter whisper, 'Good work.' Easy for him to say when he had shirked the question.

I looked to the reporter who had asked the questions and he gave a single nod and a slight smile.

Baxter and I stood to a chorus of, 'Sir, Sir, Sir,' as the crowd vied for more time and for more questions. He'd done what he wanted and we were out of the room.

47

I pushed some files to the side and made a space for the fresh mug of green tea I had made. I had a heap of paper work to catch up on. It had barely been five minutes and one email cleared from my inbox when Evie knocked on my door and strolled in.

'I'm always glad of a distraction,' I said, 'but I'm never going to get to this elusive inbox zero if you come in and sit down, you know.'

Evie dropped into the chair opposite me, notebook in her hand, so I knew this visit was work related.

'You don't have chocolate biscuits I see,' I said.

'I knew there was something I'd forgotten. Want me to go back and get them?' She was deadpan.

'Whatever you're holding in your hands must be pretty compelling if you forgot the biscuits, Evie.' I picked up my tea and sipped.

'Ah, this, you noticed.' She lifted the notebook and waggled it about in the air.

'It's not biscuits, of course I noticed.' She had a habit of fetching biscuits with her if she came to see me – as well as keeping them in a drawer in her own office.

'I might have something of interest for you,' she said.

'The biscuits gave that away,' I reminded her. Still aggrieved I didn't have any with my tea.

She gave me another smile, opened her notepad and pulled a pen from out of her hair. 'You know you asked me to look at Sebastian Wade's true-crime blog?'

'I do.'

'Well, it didn't take long for the service provider to come back to me when they heard it was a murder investigation. There was a contact form on his website. And the hosting company provided his website email address when we requested it. I got access to his messages.'

'Okay, following so far. But,' I warned her, 'if this gets too technical, remember to speak in English.'

She tapped her pen on the pad. 'Most of the messages were from people wanting him to look into specific crimes that interested them but that they were too lazy to do it themselves.' She looked up at me. 'One even asked him to investigate a live crime because they didn't trust the police to do a proper job.'

'Seriously?' I was shocked. Yes, I understood that people didn't trust us, but to go to a blogger and ask him for help? What kind of person would do that? 'Was that one of ours?' I asked.

'No. It was a Met job.'

'They get a bad rap.' I put my mug back down on the desk.

'Indeed.'

'So, nothing in his messages?'

'As I was saying, there was nothing of interest–'

'I'd say it was pretty interesting that people try to circumvent the police by going to a true-crime blogger,' I said.

'You know what I mean.' She screwed up her face at me in a show of absurdity.

'Okay, you were saying,' I waved my hand for her to continue.

She inclined her head. 'There was nothing of interest until recently.' She had my attention now. She knew she would have and she continued. 'Someone contacted Sebastian and told him that he was wrong to publish his blogs, that he shouldn't bring the crime stuff up so publicly.' She looked up from her notebook. 'It was a lot more rambly,' she said.

'It's okay, I get the gist, carry on.'

'They said that it wasn't right or fair on the people involved. On the victims and their families for this stuff to be dragged out in the open. He even said it could be unfair on the families of those who had committed the crimes. They have to live with the terrible consequences as much as the victims. In fact, you could class them as victims too, he said in his messages.'

'I don't entirely disagree,' I said. 'It has to be hard to find out your husband or son is a deranged killer. Just look at Mrs Knight from earlier this year. She was a lovely woman who had already been dealt a difficult hand in life and then she had to find that out.' I picked up my mug again. 'Do they say anything else?'

Evie looked down at her pad again. 'That Sebastian was in the wrong and something bad would happen to him if he continued to cause untold damage to others in this way.'

I raised my eyebrows. This was a promising lead. 'Do we have an email address of this person? A name? Any other details?'

'We have an email address and a name.'

'Perfect. I think we have someone of interest. Email me the details please. And email them to Martin and he can get the paperwork completed for SPoC so we can ID them. Thanks, Evie.' SPoC was

293

the single point of contact team who dealt with the phone and electronic identification work.

We would be onto this guy very soon.

I pushed the incident room doors and was met by a wall of sound. The sound of everyone hard at work. A full and busy incident room. I sought out Martin's desk and made a beeline for him.

'Did you get the email from Evie?' I asked.

He looked up. 'Yep. All sorted. SPoC just came back to me. I'm doing some intel work on the address now.'

It didn't take SPoC long to obtain details if the job was urgent. After all, the information was held on a database and all it took was a few keystrokes to access it.

'What do we have so far?' I asked.

Martin rummaged around on his desk and found some bits of paper he needed. 'As you know, he signed off with the name David Cooper, and that's correct according to who the internet is registered to.'

'Good start. Stupid mistake on his part, to sign off to Sebastian with his real name. Especially as Sebastian was capable of doing his own investigative work.'

'Yeah. You don't antagonise someone like Sebastian who puts everything out there on the internet and is fascinated by crimes. Harassing him would have been potential fodder for his blog. In fact, I wonder if he was considering writing this up.'

'So we have a potential motive for the first murder.'

Martin leaned back in his chair and looked at me. 'It looks that way.'

'If Sebastian had indicated that he was indeed going to write this guy up for harassing him. Do we know if he did mention it to him, or not?'

Martin turned to his screen, switched to his emails and flicked to the one from Evie. 'Evie doesn't say anything about that, but it's not to say it didn't happen. We have two good reasons to talk to him now. He's already angry with Sebastian for posting in the first place and if he was worried about being the subject of his blog, that could have tipped him over the edge.'

'I'll check with Evie. Okay, what do we have on Mr David Cooper?'

'He lives in Arnold and has no criminal record.'

'It's a big jump from no record to murder.'

Martin agreed.

'Though, as we saw previously with Knight, it's not impossible if there's a big enough trigger.'

'It's the scene thing about this that's pertinent though, isn't it?' Martin said.

'It is and this guy fits the bill. Do some more work on him, Martin, and then we'll make a decision on what we are going to do from there.'

Two hours later Martin and I were standing on David Cooper's doorstep. The sky was leaden and the pressure heavy.

Martin had not been able to find anything else about Cooper other than he had a traffic offence and not a lot else. That and he was a regular complainer. We had records of him on our command and control system because he called in to report his neighbours for too much noise, for their dogs, for their children, for the vehicles and for any behaviour he considered suspicious.

Martin knocked on his door and we waited for a response.

'Maybe he's at work?' Martin said as we stood staring at the closed door.

I looked at my watch. 'It's five-thirty. I would have thought he might have been home by now if he did have employment.

'Hello, can I help you?' a female voice called from next door.

'We're looking for Mr Cooper. Have you seen him?' I asked.

The woman stepped out of her home, eager to see what this was about, no doubt. Tired looking rabbit slippers flapped on her feet. 'He should be in. Not sure what he does, but you can usually catch him. Seems to work funny hours, that one. You need to knock harder. He doesn't like answering the door.'

She peered at us, squinting through the dark. The street lights casting a dim glow by which she could see us. 'Can I help you with anything?' She wanted to know who we were.

'We're good, thanks,' Martin answered with one of his lazy charming smiles.

'Okay. Well, if you need anything, you know where I am.' She waved an arm back to where she had come from.

'That's really helpful. Thank you.' Martin waited for her to leave.

She stood her ground. 'You need to knock harder for him to hear,' she prompted again.

'Yes, we get that, thank you for your help. We appreciate it.' I used my more cold harsh tone now. I knew some people found me cold, but it was more a fact that I was engrossed in the job than not having feelings. It came in useful at certain times though, and this was one of them.

'Ah, okay then, I'll leave you to it, shall I?'

Martin couldn't help but chuckle. 'That would be great, Mrs?'

She warmed up again and took a step closer to him. I glared at him and he shrugged.

'Mrs Kowalski, but you can call me Alek. And you are?'

'Busy,' I said.

'Yes, yes, of course.' She turned away, back to where she had come from. 'Just keeping an eye out for my neighbours, you understand,' she threw over her shoulder as she stepped through her door. Then with a click she was gone.

Martin laughed again.

'Really, did you have to encourage her?' I asked as I rapped hard on the door in front of us.

'She's probably lonely,' he said with a trace of humour still in his voice.

'Or she has a house full of people in there and is just bloody nosey.'

Martin gave a full-throated laugh just as the door in front of us was yanked open and a tall slim male was standing before us, looking disgusted.

'I don't want whatever you're selling,' he said, a poisonous look on his face.

I pulled my warrant card out of my pocket, held it in my palm. 'Mr Cooper?'

'I told you. I'm not interested.' The door started to close.

I pushed very gently against the door. We had no grounds for entry, but we did at least need him to know who we were before he sent us away.

'What the hell?' He spat the words out.

'DI Robbins and DC Thacker.' I raised my ID so he could see it. 'We'd like a word with you if that would be okay? Preferably not on your doorstep.' I looked to next door where the woman had appeared from not a couple of minutes previously.

'What's it about?' The door was still almost closed. He was talking through a small opening.

'I'm not sure you want us to discuss it out here?'

He huffed out a lungful of air. 'Wait there.' The door was slammed shut in our faces.

'Well he's a charmer,' said Martin.

'If it went on personality alone I'd say we had our man.'

'It would make our job so much easier,' he agreed. 'What do you think he's doing in there?'

'Whatever it is he's hiding, or covering up, we can't stop him. We don't have a warrant. We're just here to talk to him about the emails, which in themselves aren't an offence. So, we'll see what he says, assess it and go from there.'

It wasn't particularly warm stood on this doorstep. We had been made to wait when he'd refused to answer the door and now we were being made to wait while he did something inside the house. Which was obviously suspicious.

I rapped my knuckles against the glass pane again, my temper fraying as the cold air tucked itself inside my coat.

Again Cooper yanked the door open with the finesse of a walrus ballet dancing. He stood back and I took the invitation and stepped inside.

'Well?' he asked without moving further into the house. If we were just going to stand in the hallway why had he made us wait outside while he covered up or hidden whatever it was he had been hiding? It would have been nice to get a look around.

'Shall we go and sit down to have this conversation?' I asked.

'How long is it going to take?' He really wasn't happy about us being here.

'Not too long,' Martin tried to placate him. 'But neither is it a one-minute issue.

Cooper looked around him, as though the answer to all this lay on the walls or up the stairs, then walked through the nearest door into the living room. We both followed him in. He'd obviously done a good job with his cover-up because I couldn't spot anything that we should be concerned about.

The room was fairly sparse. There was a three-piece suite and a television as well as a laptop on the arm of one of the chairs. Lid down. Now that was probably what we would be interested in.

Cooper sat in the chair with the laptop. 'Are you going to tell me what this is about now?' His patience was wearing thin. Though I wasn't sure if it was impatience or worry.

'Did you hear about the death of Sebastian Wade the other day?' I asked, getting straight to the point.

His face gave nothing away. Whether he had killed Sebastian or not, he had still interacted with him, harassed him and yet here he was cool and calm.

'I heard that someone had been killed. I couldn't have told you the guy's name. I don't follow the news that much.' He was perched on the edge of the chair. Not relaxed at all. He looked ready for flight. Not that he could go anywhere from here.

'You don't recognise the name now we bring it up?' I tried again.

'No, should I?'

I felt Martin turn and look at me then back to Cooper. 'The reason we're here today is your contact with Sebastian.'

There was a silence. Cooper stiffened. He paled and his fingers laced into one another in his lap turning white where they gripped too tightly.

'Would you like to tell us about that?' I asked him.

'Am I...' His throat caught, his mouth dry. He licked his lips and tried again. 'Am I under...' This time I could see his mouth sticking together as the saliva had drained away. 'Arrest?' There was a slapping sound as he forced the words through his now dusty unworkable mouth.

'Should you be?' I asked. Interested in this reaction. Wondering where this would go.

Cooper gave a ferocious shake of his head. His tongue slid out again as it tried to add moisture to enable his power of speech.

'Can I get you a glass of water?' Martin stood. It wasn't so much a question about the water, more a question about the direction of the kitchen.

Cooper pointed the way, a grateful look on his face.

Not a minute later Martin was back, a glass of water in hand. Cooper grabbed it greedily. Slurped at it, licked his lips. This time they glistened as his tongue moved around his mouth. The only sound in the room, that of huge gulps of water as he swallowed before he was ready to try to talk again.

'Okay?' I asked once he had drained half the glass of water.

He nodded. Silent still.

'Ready to talk?'

'I'll ask again,' he said. 'Am I under arrest?' He was a different man to the one at the door who had been brash and confident. This man was afraid and quiet.

'You're not under arrest, Mr Cooper, what would make you think that you are?' The minute that he said anything that indicated he was involved in a crime, we would have to stop the questions and make the arrest he was so very obviously afraid of. We could not continue to question him without him being cautioned and without the right to a solicitor, but at the moment, we had no idea if he had done anything. All he had done was speak to our victim. He was a... I could hardly call him a witness, this may be thin ground, but it was ground I was happy to stand on. For the moment.

'You come here, the two of you, try to trick me with a question before telling me you already know the answer.'

'Why would you lie about knowing Sebastian?' I asked.

'Why do you think?' He took another deep mouthful of water and swallowed again.

'I don't know, that's why we've come to talk to you. To find out about your relationship with him.'

He snorted at this. Water flew out of his nose. His hand shot up to his nose and his cheeks bloomed. 'I'm so sorry,' he mumbled from behind his hand.

'Don't worry about it. Take your time and tell us, first of all, why you lied about knowing Sebastian and then about your relationship with him.'

He wiped at his face with the back of his hand, playing for time. 'Do I have to answer your questions?'

'You don't, no. As I said, you're not under arrest, but, it would be really helpful if you could. This is, as you know, a murder investigation. We just want to follow all the lines of inquiry, follow up on all contact Sebastian had before his death and rule people out or find further lines of inquiry we can follow. You would make us more suspicious if you decided you didn't want to help us. If you have nothing to hide, then I don't see that there's an issue.'

The thin ground I was now on was starting to crack. Pressuring people this way was not supposed to be the way we did things. I had to back off now if I wasn't going to go the route of arrest.

Cooper thought some more. 'I'm sorry, I don't think I can talk to you,' he said eventually.

I paused a minute. Wondered if I had enough grounds for arrest. He had sent the victim some emails to his website, and the victim had ended up dead. The problem was, the emails hadn't been particularly threatening. They could have been classed as harassment should Sebastian have wanted to pursue that if he'd have been alive, but they didn't make any specific threats towards him. Not liking what he did didn't give me enough grounds. I had to walk away.

'You're sure about that?' I tried again.

'I'm positive.' He stood.

Our cue to leave.

Martin and I rose.

I handed him my contact card. 'We could really do with your help,' I said. 'If you change your mind, please do get in touch with me. Leave a message if I'm not available. My email is on there as well.' The irony was not lost on me.

He took the card from my hand and shoved it in his jeans pocket.

'Thank you for your time.'

He shut the door in my face. Yet again.

'That wasn't strange at all,' said Martin as we walked back to the car.

'I want to know what he's hiding,' I replied as I climbed into the car and clipped myself in. 'He's now made his way to the top of my suspect list.'

48.

Drew thought his housemate believed himself a young man because right now he was sitting downstairs watching some shit on the television. Some reality TV shit that the youths watch. When the reality was he was a similar age to him. They had never had the conversation about their ages. You just don't, do you, as blokes. It's more of a woman thing, to consider and compare ages. Blokes, they don't really care about that kind of thing. If they're adults and working together or living together or drinking together, then all was good.

There was a line to be drawn at teenage television programmes when you are obviously not a teenager. Grow the hell up.

Because of this crap on downstairs, Drew had taken himself to his room to watch the news. He wanted to bring himself up to date with what was going on with the police investigation. Social media and the news channels were the only places he could find his information and it was either a trickle or outrageous rumour. He knew what was rumour and what wasn't as far as the offence was concerned, but he needed to know more about what the police were doing. He needed to be able to protect himself so he could protect his children in all of this. They were his priority after all. To finally show the craven keyboard warriors what they were and in doing that, show his children that these people were nothing, what they said and did was not worth dictating their lives over.

The newsreader was talking about a new policy that the PM was attempting to push through but which was getting a lot of heat from the opposition. Drew was not interested in the slightest.

He picked up his phone and opened the photo app. Scrolled back a couple of years. To when they were a family. Photos of the kids. Just snaps of them in the house doing mundane things, homework in the kitchen, Dylan tormenting Libbie, Melissa hugging Dylan when he was ill. Which he would hate if any of his friends got hold of that image, at his age.

They were his whole life.

The TV screen in front of him changed and Nottinghamshire police headquarters was in view with the banner Police run media appeal.

Drew snatched up the remote control and pressed feverishly at the buttons to turn the sound up. He turned it up so loud the set vibrated and echoed. He pressed at the remote again, turning it back down a little.

The picture changed to a panel inside the police station, a table of officers with serious expressions. He shuffled forward, compelled to be near the screen, near the officers and near the media appeal. Even after the fact.

The main officer, a DCI Kevin Baxter according to the ticker tape running along the bottom of the screen, was calm and relaxed. This was the opposite of how Drew felt right at this moment. He was about to find out what the police knew and what they thought about what was happening. Straight from their mouths, not from the gossip and fake machine that was the social media sites.

On the screen Baxter pulled himself up taller, dropped his shoulders and took a visible breath in. Then he read, in a steady and strong voice, from a prepared statement. He named the victims. Sebastian Wade and Lacey Nettleton, otherwise known as Lacey Lane.

Drew nodded along with the speech, his own breathing short and shallow.

DCI Baxter asked that the victims' families be given peace at this time as they deal with their grief. Drew barked out a laugh. He had to be joking.

Whether the press listened to him was one thing, but the public and their appetite for the emotional pain of others was insatiable. There would be no stopping them. What they did not know they would simply guess, conjecture and make up. They would not let the small issue of facts or loss or grief stop their blood sport. Their daily fix of someone else's emotional pain.

Baxter went on to ask that no more images be shared online.

Drew stood from where he had been perched on the edge of the bed. He didn't know what to do with himself. The irony of this man sitting here outright asking these people to do exactly what it was he had been attempting.

They were deaf though.

Baxter moved on to ask anyone with information on the murders to come forward and gave out a hotline number.

Drew paced the room. He scratched at his arms.

How could this DCI be so calm and ask such stupid things? Did he not realise what he was asking?

The room was then opened for questions. Drew attempted to rein his emotions in so he could listen. Maybe he would learn more about the investigation now because nothing of note had been offered so far.

The first question was about Wade being a true-crime blogger and did the police think it had any bearing on the offence, particularly as he'd been found the way he had, in a crime scene.

Drew dropped back down to the bed and waited for the DCI's response. His breath held in his chest. Baxter skirted the issue. Said it was a line of inquiry. That was it. Drew wanted to vomit.

The next question was about him, about Drew. And about whether he wanted the victims to be found.

Clever, clever journalist.

Again the DCI skirted the question, failing to give a straight answer. They didn't have a clue.

Then another question and the DCI said this was the last one. Drew wondered if he would actually answer this one, if he would learn anything this time, or if this would have been a giant waste of his time.

The question was again about him. It was strange to hear. To listen to the journalists asking questions about him, on national television. To be sitting here and to know that it was him they were talking about but that no one else knew it was him. It was his little secret. It gave him a warm glow.

To be the centre of attention this way. To know it is you. For no one else to know this fact. He wanted to go and tell his housemate that they were talking about him. That this guy on the TV everyone was discussing was him. He clapped his hands together and held tightly. He couldn't do that. He didn't want to get caught and leave his family, be any further away from them than he was now.

He missed the start of the next question. His mind had wandered, but as he caught up he realised it was to do with social media, something about whether it had any impact on the investigation and finally if the DCI thought public sentiment would impact him.

It was a good question and he was eager to hear the answers.

The DCI passed it over to the female officer, DI Hannah Robbins. Drew recognised her. She didn't look comfortable to have the question foisted on her this way. After a bit of a pause she spoke. Drew leaned forward.

The social media outcry would not and was not having an impact on the investigation and though she couldn't speak for the killer's state of mind, it was likely he knew what would happen when he left Sebastian Wade out on the council building steps that way.

She was spot on.

He did know.

She was pretty intuitive. He liked her and would be interested in her thoughts on him if it didn't mean his freedom was at risk.

49.

Aaron walked into the incident room. There was no one else in. The light was on in Hannah's office but he didn't bother to stick his head in. He was desperate to get back to work. The enforced days off created by the phased return grated on him because of his need to be back at work, but how it was all planned out and organised, he could work with that. It balanced him out. Allowed for him to follow the plan.

Now it was his day to be back in the office, he was eager to show he was here and able and willing.

That was not to say he hadn't made the most of having yesterday off. The need to gather his energy had been strong. He had been overwhelmed by the level of fatigue. Shocked by how weak his body was. How much it had let him down recently and continued to do so by not allowing him to go back to the person he used to be.

Sitting at his desk, he switched on his computer and waited for the screen to load. Yesterday had been a busy day for the incident room. He had watched the press conference on the news. He had followed the conversations about it afterwards. And Lisa had told him what social media was saying that evening as he did some more drawings at the kitchen table.

With the screen loaded he checked into HOLMES and read through the entries.

They had their hands full. They had no substantive evidence on either case as yet. No witnesses other than an elderly woman who couldn't see very well and wouldn't be able to do a sketch or ID the man she'd seen. And, they had no link between the cases. Other than the brief description from the old woman which could have been the male from the CCTV from the night Sebastian Wade was dumped.

A suitcase? That hadn't been mentioned in the press. Not surprising really. Very movie like, wasn't it? It seemed a bit crass to Aaron, but then again, this guy, if they were one and the same, had wheeled a dead Sebastian Wade across Market Square and dumped him in front of viewing eyes. Brazen if ever the word were needed.

'Hey, I thought I heard someone moving about,' Hannah said from the doorway. 'It's great to have you back again.' She smiled. 'It feels like I only just said that to you.'

He returned her smile. 'It's good to be back. It really is. I just want to do my job. Not sit at home all day.'

She moved further into the room, a mug in her hand.

'Want me to make you one?' she asked, lifting her mug up.

He shook his head. 'I want to catch up on yesterday's workload so I'm good to go when everyone is in.'

'Is that a hint for me to leave you in peace?'

'It wasn't, but yes, I could do with the space.'

She pulled a chair from the desk next to him and rolled it over, sitting down making sure not to spill the contents of her mug.

'I need to work,' he reiterated.

'We need to talk,' she countered, then looked around the room and towards the outer door.

'Am I in trouble?' He hadn't been here to be able to be in any trouble, but he never understood conversations that started with the phrase *we need to talk*. They made him nervous. It never seemed like a good four words to him.

She didn't smile, but told him that he wasn't.

Aaron looked at HOLMES. He really needed to read this, he needed to know what was happening so he wasn't lagging behind everyone else. 'Will it take long, Hannah?'

'It's important.'

He let go of the mouse he had still been gripping. 'What is it?'

'It's Baxter.'

Those words. He hated them. More than *we need to talk.*

'He's back to the conversation he was having before you were off sick. Yesterday, when he realised you were on a phased return, he...' She struggled to find the words.

'He wants me gone,' Aaron provided.

'Yes,' said Hannah.

He nodded. He knew this was coming.

'We could talk to him. Explain.' She pleaded with him now. 'He wouldn't be able to do anything then. He would have to accommodate you. And that's what this is. It's a lack of accommodation. It's nothing to do with your work.'

She slammed her mug down on the desk. 'Because if it was, then I would have had an issue, and I can't do without you, Aaron.'

He was touched by her words and by her passion.

'Can we see how it goes?' he asked.

'We can't leave it long.'

He could hear voices coming down the corridor. He needed to bring this conversation to a close.

'Let's get through today. One day at a time. See what happens. It's not something he can do on a whim.' He looked to the door again.

Hannah followed his gaze. She stood. Collected her mug. 'Okay, but if you have any problems, or if you want to chat about it, let me know.' She stared at him. 'Okay?'

The door opened and Pasha and Ross strolled in.

'Okay, Aaron?' she pushed him.

He brought his computer screen back to life and turned his back to her. 'Okay,' he muttered.

50

Drew knocked on the door. Dylan answered. The minute he saw his dad Dylan grunted, opened the door wider so he could step inside, but he didn't say anything, didn't welcome him, just turned around and walked up the stairs, phone in his hand. Peering down at the small screen, the glow lighting up his face.

It was Monday morning. The kids were getting ready for school. Dylan's shirt was half buttoned, he had no tie and was barefoot.

With a sharp click Drew closed the door behind him and went in search of Melissa. He could hear the television on in the living room so went in there first. She was sitting with a mug of tea in front of the news, which was turned down low, a friend, one of their old neighbours in the chair. He said old friend because she was obviously an old friend of his but still a current friend of Mel's. They were engrossed in conversation. Mel's face lit up with laughter.

At the sound of him entering the room she stopped, turned and saw him. The smile slid off her face to be replaced by a much more serious expression. She no longer looked relaxed. Drew turned to the friend, Gina, who had also stiffened. Why had they changed just because he had walked into the room? There was a time when it wouldn't have mattered and they would have told him what the joke was, included him, and he would have laughed along with them. Now they stopped as though a stranger had entered their den.

'Hey,' Mel said. 'I wasn't expecting you. Did I miss something? Do we have a school meeting for one of the kids?' Her voice was pleasant enough. He hated how she was doing okay. That she could sit here and be okay and sit and laugh while he was alone and pining for his family, for the old times. How did she do it? Had he, had they, their family unit, meant nothing to her?

'I was in the area,' he started. It was hardly a realistic lie at this hour.

The look she gave him said she knew it for what it was, a chance to see them without having pre-organised visit.

'And I thought I'd stop by.' He hated the expression in her eyes now.

Pity.

He wouldn't make this about her. 'I wanted to see if the kids wanted to go out for something to eat later when they get home from school. I thought I would catch them now.'

'How are you?' Gina asked, finally speaking up. Acknowledging he was here, in his house. The house she was sitting in, drinking tea in and laughing in. Without him.

'I'm good, you know, keeping busy.'

She looked surprised, as though she expected him to be sleeping on the pavement like the homeless guy he had supposedly pushed over. 'Right.' Her eyebrows lifted up into her hair. 'That's great to hear. What are you doing now?' A slight tone of incredulity slipped in.

He ignored it. 'Still teaching.' That's all he would give her. It's all she deserved.

Her eyebrows nearly flew off her head now. 'Oh,' she squeaked. 'You managed to get another job?' She flushed beetroot red. 'It's not that... I don't mean...'

'It's okay, Gina,' Melissa leapt in to save her. 'He didn't start working in another school.'

He glared at her. What was she even doing here at this hour anyway? He wouldn't have her know that the baying crowd had destroyed his life.

He jumped in before Mel could go any further. 'I'm a tutor now for an online university.' It wasn't that he was banned from working with kids. It was a decision he had made and the irony was not lost on him that he was working online when it was the online world that had destroyed him. 'I'm teaching adults in an adult world.' He stared at Gina, defying her to say something derogatory. 'It's very rewarding,' he lied. He would not admit to anyone, especially this woman or Mel, how much he hated it. That he so very desperately wanted to teach children. To show them how much there was to learn about the world. To set them up as they grew, ready to go out on their own, but he was afraid to apply to other schools for fear of rejection. It had been hard to leave his last school and he wanted to steady his ship for a while.

'How did you get in?' Mel changed the subject and he felt himself shrink an inch or two by having to answer this question.

'Dylan.'

She nodded. 'I'm having a late start so Gina came round for a breakfast catch-up. It's been too long.'

Libbie sauntered in, face down, looking at her phone. She nearly walked into him as he hovered in the doorway behind the sofa.

'Hey, love,' he said as she manoeuvred around him.

Libbie grunted a hello back at him and sank into the sofa next to her mum who wrapped an arm around her. Libbie leaned into it. A crushing pain enveloped Drew's chest as he watched. This used to be them. The three or four of them in the room just chilling out. He stared hard at the interloper, still supping on her mug of tea. Not in the least uncomfortable in her place in his home.

A report popped up on the TV about the recent murders. His eyes caught it and he looked away.

'Have you seen this?' asked Gina to Mel. 'It's awful what he's been doing.'

Who the hell was she to make comment? Not only was she sitting in his home, but now she had an opinion on this. She was no better than the rest of them.

Libbie looked up from her phone to see what Gina was talking about. Took in the screen then looked back down.

'Yes,' said Mel, 'I've been following it. It feels so much more real and less like the news when it's local, don't you think?' She looked to him as well when she spoke, trying to include him, he could tell. She was always kind, even though they'd had problems, she was never malicious.

'Do you want to go for something to eat after school?' he asked Libbie.

She didn't even look up. 'Naaa.'

'Another time?'

A non-committal sound escaped. It could have been an affirmative noise. He took it as such.

'Yes, I've been scared to go out, to be honest,' Gina answered Mel about the locality of the crimes. Scared to go out indeed. Such a drama queen. As if anyone would want to drag her off the streets. He'd like to drag her out of his house.

'It's the kids I was afraid for,' Mel said. 'After that young Instagram star was killed. You know they're all on it. It's their thing. I worried that if they started commenting on it, they would be targets. I told them not to but you know what they're like.'

Gina nodded vigorously. She had a couple of teenagers at home. It's why they got on so well. He did used to get on with her. He just begrudged the fact she was here now and he wasn't. 'What do you think?' She turned to him.

'Me?' He was surprised to be included in the conversation. Surprised he hadn't been kicked out of the house yet.

'Yes, Mel was worried about the kids. It's local. You must have an opinion.' That was the thing.

Everyone had a goddamn opinion and thought they had the right to it.

'Not really,' he shrugged. 'The kids know about strangers and to keep themselves safe.'

Melissa turned on him. 'This guy is crazy, you know that, don't you?' Her tone was cold now. Freezing him out. He'd said the wrong thing.

'What?' was all he could manage.

'This guy. Did you see what he did to the first victim? On Market Square. I mean, how crazy do you have to be to do something like that? You must have seen the CCTV footage the police released?'

'Well, yeah, but it didn't tell us anything about him. We don't know what's going through his head, do we?'

'Come on. To be that bold. He's lost the plot. And if you've lost the plot, that makes you dangerous. And to have a dangerous killer in our area, well, that makes me nervous. How can you not be anxious about that?'

'You think he's lost the plot?' he asked, focusing on only a few of her words and not the ones she wanted him to hear. His hearing tunnelled. His focus narrowed. This was the woman he loved and this was him she was talking about. This was what she thought about him.

'You don't? Of course he's lost the plot.'

'Yeah, Dad.' Libbie didn't look up from her phone, but managed to slide in two words that sliced through him like a butcher's knife through a fresh piece of meat.

'He's killing people and leaving them in disgusting set-ups. His mind is lost. That's scary as hell. He scares me.' She shivered.

'I have to go.' He turned.

'Don't you want to ask Dylan?' Mel asked.

He was halfway to the door. 'No, I'll try again another day,' he said and was gone. He couldn't handle this. The mirror held up to him by the people he held most dear. And what he saw in that mirror he didn't like, he didn't like at all. It was ugly, grotesque and needed cutting out.

51

The office was quiet and Aaron was catching up with some work. Hannah was in her office. Some of the staff were in the CCTV viewing room, others were out, attempting to mop up the house-to-house inquiries that hadn't yet been fully completed as not everyone had answered their doors, and a few were taking statements.

Aaron liked it when the office lulled like this. The peace was perfect for him. He could work and focus without the distraction of gossip and laughter and loud voices breaking through his thought processes.

'Aaron?'

The voice came from behind him. Baxter stood in the doorway.

'Do you have a minute?' He'd walked down the stairs to ask him rather than phone down for him. This was unusual.

'Sir.' Aaron stood and Baxter turned on his heel and headed back to his office.

Aaron waited in the neat room for what was coming. Hannah had pre-warned him. It wasn't as though he wasn't aware. He took a deep breath.

'How was your first day?' Baxter asked. A voice of calm and reason.

'It was like any other day,' Aaron replied.

'You felt good?'

It was a direct question and Aaron squirmed. He knew what answering this would do to his career. It was also natural to feel as he had. How could an intelligent man like Baxter not know this? 'I was exhausted,' he said.

Baxter leaned back. Steepled his fingers. It reminded Aaron of a spider about to pounce on a fly.

'It was a tough day?' Baxter clarified.

'I did my work but it exhausted me as is to be expected after a heart attack, Sir.'

Baxter tickled under his chin with his steepled fingers. A noise thrummed in his throat. 'I have a proposition for you, Aaron.'

Aaron didn't like the sound of that. He waited.

Baxter looked at him.

Aaron waited some more.

Eventually Baxter spoke again. 'Training.'

'Sir?'

'The training department.'

'What about it?'

'It is a Monday to Friday job with no overtime, no staying late and no having to come in at the weekend because a case demands it. You've been through a lot and a vacancy has just come up in the training department and I think you would be perfect for it.'

Aaron didn't react.

'Hannah tells me regularly how methodical you are, how much she values you. Your talents would be perfect in the training department. Think of all the experience you could impart to the new probationers and to the trainee detectives. You would be perfect.'

Baxter leaned forward now. 'Aaron, the fact that this vacancy has come free now is a sign that it's made for you.'

'Yes, Sir.' He couldn't think of anything else to say. He didn't know how he felt about it.

'Will you at least give it some thought?'

'Yes, Sir.' And he would. He would give it some serious thought. Could he really do the same job any more after this heart attack? Should he move to a different department? Should he be taking things easier? Lisa would probably be happier without the worry he would keel over again because of the long hours.

'Just think of how little stress you'd be putting on your body in the training department,' Baxter said, as though he had been reading Aaron's mind.

Aaron nodded.

'I'm offering this in your best interest,' Baxter went on. 'You're a valued member of the team and I would hate to lose you, but if it means you're kept safe and well and are not prone to another heart attack, then I will be more than happy to put you forward and recommend you for this position. And I have no doubt you would get it.' He smiled. 'I have a bit of pull, you know. And if it's a matter of your health, then that will take precedence over fairness in any interview procedure.'

His health. Was he really that bad? It had certainly felt that way on his first day back. He would never have believed being at work would make him feel so dreadful had he not experienced it himself.

'Will that be all?' he asked.

Baxter looked perplexed. 'Well, yes. Of course. But, you will think about it? This offer needs to be acted on before they start advertising the post. I've heard about it before any action has been taken.' He let out a small cough.

Aaron didn't understand.

He stood. 'I will think about it, Sir. Thank you.' And he walked out of the office.

52

Drew's mind was all over the place. It was freezing outside, but he was burning up. He put the car temperature down, tried to cool himself, but the sweat beaded on his forehead and slipped down his back. He wriggled forward, uncomfortable with the sensation. The car jumped forward as he fidgeted and he tried to steady himself. Gripped the steering wheel in the ten two position. Held on and told himself it would be okay.

But his wife and his daughter, they had called him a monster. He pulled up to the roundabout and looked right for traffic, the road was quiet, he pulled out and took the second exit onto Mapperley Plains. His stomach rolled.

How had it gone so wrong? This hadn't been what he wanted. This hadn't been the point of it all. If Melissa and Libbie couldn't see it then no one would. He had failed and those people had died for nothing.

Melissa and Libbie could usually be trusted to see the bigger picture but this time, it was completely invisible to them. How had he managed to screw it up so badly?

The winter sun was low in the sky and dazzled him through the windscreen. He squinted and pulled down the visor. He really hated this time of year. He hated everything at the moment.

When he originally came up with his plan, he had been afraid that they might figure out it was him. Mel in particular, because of her big picture viewpoint and because she knew him so well. He hadn't envisaged they would miss the point altogether and call him a monster. And Mel, Mel had said she was afraid of him.

His Mel. His beautiful beautiful Mel. Afraid of him. How the hell had that happened? He had to right this.

He would right this.

He would right this for his family.

He had put them through enough. He hadn't done it intentionally, but, because of him, they had been through a lot. He would stop their fear. He would cut out this ugliness.

He had another plan and it would show once and for all if the world had any decency and this plan couldn't fail because for this one to work he had to tell the world he was the killer.

53.

'You're doing what?' I bellowed at him.

Everyone in the room turned to look. Aaron looked down at the floor.

'I'm sorry,' I said. I was. Not for the sentiment, but for shouting at him.

Again.

This wasn't the first time I had done this. Shouted at him. But this time it was because I cared and I couldn't believe what he had told me.

'I'm considering Baxter's offer.' His voice was low, his face still downturned.

'Come with me,' I whispered through clenched teeth, reining in my very real need to grab hold of him and strangle him. I turned to the door, stalked a few steps then checked he was following.

He had more sense than to push against me right now but the look on his face told me I had a fight on my hands. He was serious and I wasn't sure he was in the mood to back down. There was no arguing with him when he thought he was talking sense. He usually talked sense, but he wasn't now and I needed him to see that. Baxter was playing him.

I stomped down the corridor, slammed into my office. Waited for Aaron with my arms crossed and chin jutting out in fury.

He walked in, calm and steady.

'Close the door,' I demanded.

With the gentlest of touches he pushed it to and looked at me. Looked at the anger that flashed across my face, clear for him to see.

'What do you mean, you're considering his offer?' I could barely get the words out of my mouth, my face was clenched up so tightly.

'Just that, Hannah.' He waved at the chairs. 'Can we sit? Talk about it?'

'No.' I sulked. 'Tell me.'

'What don't you understand?'

'How you can even consider going to the training department, Aaron? That's what I don't understand. You're a born cop. You're meant to be here, talking to witnesses, to criminals, looking at crime scenes. Not locked up in some classroom talking to snotty-nosed probationers and shiny new detectives who think getting out of the uniform is a step up in the world.'

I let out a breath and my body relaxed as I expressed my fears. 'This is your life, here, with us.'

He didn't say anything.

'You do know Baxter saying there was a space open at training school wasn't an offer, don't you?' I said.

'What do you mean? There isn't a position?'

'I'm sure there is,' I snapped. 'What I mean is that it's not an offer, Aaron. He's sending you there whether you like it or not, he's just dressing it up as an offer, in the hope you'll jump.' I glared at him. 'Which you damn well look like you're doing.'

His silence continued. 'And if you turn his kind *offer* down, he's going to send you anyway.' I raised my voice. 'And you're making his job a whole lot easier. Why the hell would you do that?'

He sank down in one of the chairs opposite my desk. 'I'm tired, Hannah.'

It was that simple. Three little words. They were like daggers in my chest. He was tired. Aaron was tired.

I dropped into the chair at the side of him. 'Oh, Aaron. I'm so sorry. I should have done more to help you out.'

He shook his head. 'There's nothing for you to do. It's my body that's letting me down. There's nothing anyone can do.'

'I can take the load off you a bit more. Give you time to recover. Jeez, you've not two months ago had a heart attack and here you are back at work. Lisa would kill me if you had another one, you know.'

He smiled. A sad, resigned smile.

'You don't have to do this alone. We can do this together. We'll get Occ Health to assess you again, see what support they can put in place. See if there's any practical help they can offer, not just the phased return stuff, but physio etc. to strengthen your body, get it used to being fit.' I didn't know enough about heart attacks. Just some stuff I had read online after Aaron had had his as well as talking to Jack. I didn't know what he needed but I would find out and I'd give it to him.

'We can do this, Aaron. And you have to really consider telling them about your diagnosis. We could even talk to Walker if you don't want to tell Baxter. I know she's a bit brusque herself sometimes, but Baxter, well, he's just on another level with how much he wants this department to perform.'

'What if I told you it's not what I wanted?'

'What do you mean?' He didn't want to go to Walker? He'd rather talk to a man, Baxter?

'To stay on this department.'

'You're kidding, right?' I stood. Not sure what to do with myself.

'I think maybe it's time.'

'Time to what exactly?' I railed at him. 'Time to give in. Time to let people walk all over you.' Shit, I really needed to stop turning on my friend like this. But, fuck, I wanted him to stay and he was throwing away his career because some dickweed decided he wanted him out. It was all fine before Baxter had turned up.

Aaron stood now. 'You can't control everything, Hannah.'

'You don't mean this,' I tried again. 'I'm sorry I shouted. I'm emotional. You know that about me. It's because you mean a lot to me. Sleep on this decision, Aaron. Don't make it yet.' A thought sprang into my mind. A last chance. 'Have you spoken to Lisa about it?' Surely she wouldn't let him throw his career away.

'Hannah–'

'When you've talked to Lisa and when you've slept on it, we'll talk and go from there, okay?'

'This is not something you can figure out and resolve like a work problem. This is me. This is my problem and one I have to evaluate, and I'm tired.

There is structure and regular hours in training. It's perfect for me.' He walked out the door.

54.

I felt bereft. A tiredness overwhelmed me. A feeling that Aaron himself explained to me. I made it to the other side of my desk, sank into my chair, stuck my elbows on my desk and put my head in my hands. What the hell would I do without my friend? It wasn't just about me. How would he survive without the puzzles of work to keep his brain active? He would shrivel up and die. I knew him. He loved this department. We worked well together.

I wanted to shake some sense into him. I hoped that Lisa would be able to, but maybe she was behind him all the way, supporting him in whatever decision he made, as a good wife did. But I wasn't a good wife. I was his boss and his friend and he was throwing a good career away. I couldn't let him do it. I didn't know how to stop him. I needed some time to think about it.

It was an interesting move on Baxter's part, to offer Aaron the slide sideways rather than waiting for any report from me. He was probably a little worried that there wouldn't be anything he could write Aaron up on so this was another way of getting the same result. An Aaron free office. I would speak to Occupational Health myself before I handed over any report if it came to it anyway. There was no way I would throw Aaron under the bus. They wouldn't give me specifics on Aaron but they would help me understand what was normal for his settling back into the department. I would not go down without a fight in this situation.

Though it looked possible that might just happen.

I looked at my desk, at the notes scattered all over the piles of paper and Post-its tacked around my laptop screen. In the meantime I had work to do.

So much work, I wasn't sure where to start.

I looked at the whiteboard where I had listed the pertinent facts of the case. A habit I had started after the Talbot case a couple of months ago when a night in with my whiteboard had resulted in a lightbulb moment.

The list was a mess. There was no making sense of it this time. No break-through Aha! moment here. Just a list of actions we had already taken and some that still needed to be done.

I ran through them and saw that we still hadn't received the list we needed from Andy Denning, the guy who ran the true-crime book club for Sebastian, of the members of the group who had now left. Who were members in Sebastian's time, but no longer attended. Denning had been helpful, but he appeared to have forgotten this one crucial piece of information. And that could be our Aha! snippet. Our guy could be hiding in amongst the people Sebastian knew. After all, it started with him and it had to have done so for a reason. Yes, there was the significance of the crime scene. And we were still working that. I had to do something. I had to get out of the office. I needed some air. Maybe I could get some clarification on two things at once if I popped out and did this small task.

Grabbing my coat and scarf, I yelled down the corridor into the incident room. Told them where I was headed. An arm was waved in acknowledgement.

It was good enough, I supposed. They were aware I existed at least.

The temperature had dropped outside. I pulled my scarf tighter and climbed into the car, ramped up the heating and willed for it to warm up faster than the journey would take. I wasn't hopeful.

I wasn't sure what Denning did, I'm sure we had his occupation logged somewhere on our system. I'd hate to have driven out here and for him to not be in this time. I was in luck. His car was on the drive. There was a light on in the house.

The car was warm now and I didn't want to leave. A couple walked past with a baby wrapped up in a pram, their breath spiralling around them as they spoke. It really was bloody freezing out there.

I tightened my scarf again and clambered out. Knocked on the door. Jumped up and down on the spot to keep warm.

'DI Robbins.' He sounded surprised to see me.

'I'm sorry to disturb you,' I said. Please just let me in. 'It's just that we never got that list of old book club members from you.' I looked more closely at him. He looked terrible. It seemed I had appeared at a bad time. 'I won't take up much of your time,' I added.

He looked thoughtful. I jigged up and down again to show him how cold it was out here.

'It's no trouble,' he said finally. 'Please, do come in. Your timing is perfect actually.'

He stepped aside and I walked in. Out of the cold.

55

Aaron was sitting at his desk with his earphones in. Regardless of what Baxter would have to say about it. It didn't matter now.

He allowed the gentle sound of raindrops to soak into his mind and quieten the frenzy that had seared through it during the conversation with Hannah. The natural sound lowered the blinding whiteout so he could think and function again.

He flicked through HOLMES and checked to see where they were currently at.

Hannah yelled down the corridor that she was heading out to see Andy Denning to obtain the list he hadn't provided yet. He didn't have it so loud that he couldn't hear the work world around him. He added the task to HOLMES.

'Get you a coffee?' Pasha appeared in his line of sight making a drinking motion with her hand.

He pulled an earphone out of one of his ears.

'Coffee?' she said again.

'That would be great, thanks,' he said.

She nodded and moved off, around the room getting orders from everyone.

Evie strolled into the room with her laptop under her arm. She headed straight for Aaron and stood above him until he pulled his earphones out again.

'Hannah not in?' she asked.

'No, she's gone out to see a witness, the book club guy, Denning.'

'Okay, do you have a minute?' She searched around for a chair. Saw one further in the room, wandered off to fetch it without waiting for Aaron's response, then pulled it over and sat beside him, placing the laptop on his desk. He hated when Hannah came and sat on his desk and put her mug on it, now Evie was here, dumping a large laptop on it. Was there no peace to be had here? He kept his thoughts to himself. She obviously had something she wanted to show him.

'What is it?' he asked, rolling his earphones up and shoving them in his drawer.

'Remember when Hannah asked me to have a look at the blog Sebastian Wade ran?'

'Yeah.'

'Well, I found something of interest. Do you remember that bloke who shoved the homeless lad over and the internet went wild about it?'

He remembered something about a homeless male being pushed and some guy losing his job, but he'd heard about it on the news, not on social media. 'I think I know what you're talking about,' he gave her.

'Guess who blogged about it?'

'Sebastian Wade?'

'Bingo.'

'And what does that have to do with our case?' he asked. Not following at all.

'It's probably nothing, but it's a local case and it's the most recent local one he's blogged about, so I thought it was worth mentioning and there's a photograph. It's not very clear but you can just make out his face. I know it's a long shot, but it is someone Sebastian blogged about and not in a very polite manner. It was a lead Hannah suggested we look at and he seemed to say that the guy deserved to lose his job because he was a school teacher and we need our teachers to set an example, but then went on to say that he didn't deserve to be vilified in the way he was being on social media. It was a real mixed post, to be honest.'

Martin had turned round and was listening. 'Even though he was currently using him for fodder on his blog?' he said with a laugh.

'I know, right?'

Ross was paying attention now too. 'I watched this incident unfold, with my mouth on the floor, it was awful what they did to him, whether he did push the other guy or not,' he said.

Pasha came back with a tray and put a mug down on Aaron's desk. 'What are we talking about?' she asked.

'The guy who pushed the homeless kid,' answered Ross, leaning over and picking up a mug.

'Wow, that was nasty. How's he involved?'

'We don't know he is,' said Aaron. 'Evie has found a post about it on Sebastian's blog.' He turned to Evie. She was pulling up the post and the photo. 'Do we know who the so-called offender in that case is?'

'Yeah, his name is Drew Gardner.'

It didn't ring any bells. 'Okay.' He made a note of it. 'We'll have a look into him. Do we have any more details?'

'There's this photograph from the day of the incident.' She pushed the laptop closer to him, turning it so he could see the screen better.

She enlarged the photograph to fill the screen and the two men were clear as day. The homeless male who the whole country had been up in arms about had his face turned away from the camera as he stumbled to the ground. The other male, the one that had hold of him, his face was clear. No wonder he had been identified. His face filled the screen and seeped into Aaron's brain. 'Nope, nothing from me.'

There was a gasp from where Pasha was standing with a mug of coffee in her hand. Everyone looked at her. She had paled and her hand was shaking.

'Where did the boss say she was going when she went out?' she asked.

'To see Andy Denning,' replied Aaron.

Pasha pointed at the screen. 'That's Andy Denning. That is the guy from the book club who supported Sebastian in running it. The boss has just gone to visit him on her own.'

56.

The plan was simple. He would put this all right. See if the social media crazies were in fact crazy or if they were human.

He had opened a browser window on his laptop. He logged into Twitter using his own account and had his profile photo attached. The account that had not had a single tweet sent from it for well over a year. This time would be different. He was about to have his say and this time they would listen.

He drafted the tweet and attached the hashtag they were still using for the murders. Then he created a poll.

I am the killer. I killed Sebastian Wade and Lacey Lane because of what you did to me last year. Now it's up to you what happens. #crimescenemurder

Poll:

Kill myself

Hand myself in.

He kept the message in the draft folder and collected his car keys. He would hole up somewhere where they couldn't find him. This was his final act. Let's see what their final act would be. And he was fully prepared to carry out whatever they decided.

He selected the sharpest knife from the kitchen block, held it up to the light and watched the blade glint. It would do the job if necessary. But, he hoped they would finally turn into human beings.

Then there was the knock at the door. He put the knife and the car keys down on the kitchen worktop and went to get rid of whoever it was. He could be as rude as needed, he just had to get out of here.

He didn't expect to see the detective inspector standing on his doorstep, a pleasant smile on her face, asking for his help. He had forgotten to give her something she said.

He was confused. What was it she needed? All that was in his head was the message in his drafts folder. The knife on his kitchen counter. The plans for the rest of the day how it would end. Maybe she would have something to do with it. Well, she would in one way or another, either with an arrest or collecting his body.

Then it crossed his mind. She could be a part of this in another way. A more direct way. She could help him. The social media frenzy had not been kind to the police. It never was. This would be more interesting if he could pull this off.

'Come on in,' he said. And she did.

As she stepped over the threshold and he closed the door, her phone rang. They carried on walking. He moved them towards the kitchen.

'I'm sorry,' she said. 'I just need to get this. It's the office.'

He didn't want her to answer the call, but, if she didn't, they might get concerned too early for his plan to be put in motion. He moved to the kitchen counter and she answered the phone.

'DI Robbins. Yes, yes, I'm here now.' Silence. Her eyes darted to him. He felt uneasy. Her body stiffened but she kept a smile on her face as she looked at him.

Something was wrong. He could feel it.

'Uh huh,' she said. 'Okay, yeah, that's great.' She smiled again.

He gripped the knife tightly. She knew. They knew. He didn't know how. Her eyes slid to his hand on the knife and she kept quiet to whomever she was talking to. It didn't matter now. All that mattered was getting out of here and quickly before they could get to them. Once they were out of here then he could put his plan into motion and it would end the way he wanted. Not the way they wanted it to end.

With one long stride he was in front of her the knife pointing directly into her stomach. 'We need to go,' he said to her.

'Andy, what is this? Let's talk about it.'

He was done talking. He had tried to talk last year. He was all talked out. He grabbed her arm and pulled her over to his laptop. 'Carry that.'

She picked it up, a confused look on her face.

'Andy, you don't want to do this. You'll get yourself into more trouble than you're already in. We can sort this out. Whatever's happened. Let us help you.'

He kept the knife pointed at her. Close enough to lunge and penetrate her stomach at a moment's notice. She did as he directed.

'We need to go to the car.' He pushed her towards the front door. 'Phone,' he demanded.

'Andy,' she tried again.

This time he pushed the knife into her coat slightly, the coat offering some cushioning, but she would know he meant business if she didn't follow through. She handed him her phone. He threw it to the floor. He didn't care if they came here. He was about to admit it all anyway.

He pushed her again. 'Make a sound and I'll kill you.'

She walked in front of him, carrying his laptop. They loaded themselves into his car. He made her drive so he could hold the knife and he held it into her groin where there was a main artery. All he had to do was slide it across, he told her.

And that was it, within a couple of minutes of the phone call they were out of there and his new plan of action was about to be set up. Only now they weren't about to vote on whether he died or was arrested. No, now they were going to vote on whether he died or she died.

57

Andy forced me into the driver's seat, making me climb in through the passenger side door and over the handbrake so he could follow me and stay close with the knife. It was somewhat like an assault course while carrying the laptop but once I had folded myself in and we were both settled he took the laptop from me and put it down in his footwell.

At all times I was conscious of the large bladed kitchen knife he was threatening me with and how much damage it could cause. I wasn't blasé that it was a blade and not a firearm. I had seen first-hand just how much devastation a knife could cause as one of my own DCs had lost her life to a one and I had been injured in the process.

To say I was fearful was an understatement but I had to keep it together. It would be the only way out of this, if I kept my head about me.

'Where are we going?' I asked as I drove away from his house.

Andy was quiet. His shoulders hunched.

What was it Aaron had said on the phone? Pasha had identified Andy as someone else altogether. Andy wasn't his real name. By that point in the conversation with Aaron I had seen the knife in Andy's hand and had missed the alternate name Aaron had given me.

'Keep driving and I'll direct you in,' Andy said, giving me no idea of what was to come.

Were we to go to a derelict location where he would attempt to dispose of me or was he aiming for a more high profile event as was his first kill?

My stomach twisted and I gripped the steering wheel tighter in an attempt to keep my nerves in check.

Aaron and the team knew where I had been and who I had been with. They would be on the ball. I was not alone no matter how it felt. This, as always was a team effort. I simply had my part to play.

And that part was to stay alive.

Andy twisted the knife in his hands and turned his head to look at me several times reminding me he was paying attention to what I was doing.

I turned right onto Calverton Road, a fairly quiet road surrounded by fields and bare trees and hedges. This didn't give me a sense of where we were going yet as we were still heading out of Mapperley.

I looked down at the laptop and wondered the part this would play in unfolding events.

'If you talk to me, I can help you,' I said.

'Just keep driving. You're helping me anyway.' He wasn't engaging, it seemed he had one thing on his mind and that was to get to the destination.

Ten minutes later and I pulled up outside of a three-bedroom semi on Surgeys Lane in Arnold.

Whatever was going to happen, it was happening here.

My afternoon had taken a dark turn. I had come for a list of names and now I was in a strange house being threatened with a knife. Wasn't getting stabbed once in this job enough? I had no intention of going through this again. I had to keep him calm.

I'd noticed while in the kitchen in his house, not the one we were now standing in, that there were two empty spaces in the knife block. He had one of the knives in his hand, but the other, could that be the knife that killed Sebastian? I would have to check when I got out of this.

If I got out of this.

I was unnerved by how calm he was. He looked organised, like he knew what he was doing.

He stuck an internet dongle in the laptop to provide internet service and tapped away at the keys. The knife only mere inches away from his hand. The door completely secure. He had the key in his pocket. The key for the front door and the back door. I had no idea whose house this was but he'd had a key to get in.

'Aren't you expecting anyone to come home?' I asked. I really didn't want someone to walk into this and get tangled in this mess and become injured, potentially killed.

'No, they're all out. They won't be home until later.'

I looked around. There were photographs on the walls. Young children who grew up in the images and were teenagers in the most recent ones.

'Are these your children?'

'Just keep quiet will you,' he snapped.

Then he stopped from what he was doing. 'All done.' He smiled. This made me nervous. 'Would you like to see how this is going to end?'

I'm not sure I did, but it was better to be informed about your situation. 'I'd like to know what I can do to help you,' I answered.

'You can't help me,' he said. 'It's in their hands now. They'll decide if you're going to be helped or not.'

I didn't understand.

'Come on. Have a look.'

I walked to where he was and looked at the screen. He had Twitter open and a tweet in the middle of the screen.

I am the killer. I killed Sebastian Wade and Lacey Lane because of what you did to me last year. Now it's up to you what happens. #crimescenemurder

Poll Option 1: Kill myself. Option 2: Kill the police officer leading the investigation because I have her.

Shit. He had publicly outed himself and had decided one of us was going to die. It didn't look as though tweet had been sent yet though. That was good. I had time to talk him out of this.

'Andy, that seems a bit drastic. Let's–'

Before I could finish he grabbed hold of my hair and yanked my head towards him. Pain shot through into my eyes. I gritted my teeth and tried to keep my balance. With a swift movement he let go of the knife, picked up his phone and took a selfie of us together.

This was my one chance, I stamped down hard on his foot with my heel. With a sudden reflex to the pain he jerked forward. His hand still in my hair. Stars flew behind my eyelids.

I had to keep my eyes open. I had to keep my eyes on the knife. I slammed my elbow up into his face. Felt it connect with skin and bone. A grunt escaped as blood flew from his nose across my cheek. His fingers dug in harder and it felt as though my scalp was going to be dragged straight off my head.

With a deep breath in I did a half twist to face him, pulled back my arm and with as much bodily momentum as I could manage I forced my fist upwards.

He saw it coming. I was too slow. The twist and the backward swing, gave him time to shift slightly to his left, the punch grazed his jaw, I heard the click as it swung past just catching. Then I was going down. He was going with me. He was doing the only thing he could do to gain control of the situation and that was to take me down. With his hand still wrapped tightly up in my hair he had full control. I screamed at the top of my lungs and swung with both arms. I had to stop this descent to the floor. If he got me down then it was lost and he would have the upper hand.

With my face bearing down I couldn't see a thing and bile was rising in my throat. The hair he didn't have hold of fell over my face now, blocking all view of him of the room, of where the knife was.

So much for not wanting another knife wound.

My fists connected but nothing that was causing him any injury. Our breath was coming thick and fast as we struggled to come out of this on top. I wasn't causing him any pain now and I was doubled in half and he was still pushing and pulling my head to get me down. You can't pull against your own hair. Your own scalp. It's attached to your head and it's excruciating.

Then he was on his knees and I was on the floor, on my hands and knees. Panting hard. Air pushing through my lungs in ragged breaths. My face pushed down to the floor. I tried to lock my elbows, refusing to give in completely and lay flat for him. The carpet brushed into my nose. I could taste dust.

His grip tightened even more, the pressure hardened and my face flattened against the ground. He was grunting as hard as I was. I felt the stretch of him as he reached forward and then it was there. The knife. The large kitchen knife. He pressed the blade against my cheek, slid it down to my throat.

'You really want to go out like this?' he asked, his voice ragged in his throat. 'Why'd you have to do that?'

His knee pressed in my back. I was locked down tight. How would I get out of this? 'I'm sorry. I shouldn't have done that,' I panted. 'I saw what you wrote and reacted. I should have just talked to you. Let me up and we can talk about it. There are obviously things you want to talk about.' I struggled to get the words out in my position and after battling with him, but I forced them. I needed to get through to him.

There had to be something he wanted to talk about otherwise he wouldn't be telling the world he had killed those people. I had to get him talking. It was my only way out of this. This was me and him.

My life was down to me.

58

He kept me pinned to the floor for a moment and I caught my breath. He was obviously thinking, there was no rush in his movements. I still had a chance here.

'If I let you up you won't try anything like that again?' he asked, his mouth inches from my ear. The threat implied in his tone.

I tried to shake my head but it was difficult. 'No. I just want to talk to you.'

He wasn't used to physical activity. The exertion had taken his breath away and it was taking effort for him to talk.

His hand let go of my hair and I relaxed. This was forward movement.

'I still have the knife, DI Robbins,' he said before removing his other hand and standing up over me.

I sat up and rubbed my head. 'I know. Thank you for letting me up.'

He gave a curt nod, his face closed and immobile.

We stayed in this standoff for a couple of minutes trying to get the lay of the other and then he moved. Seemingly satisfied that I would keep my word. He stood in front of the open laptop and indicated I should follow him over.

I climbed up from the floor. My arm from the old incident throbbed. I gritted my teeth and tried to ignore it. I had to focus on the here and now and not get dragged into the past.

The screen was still open on Twitter. The tweet he had written was there in the middle of the screen.

He turned to me. 'I wanted you to see this.' And with the press of one key the poll was out in the world for everyone to see.

'Let's talk, Andy, while we wait,' I had to do something. I had no idea what impact that tweet would have on my situation.

He turned on her. 'My name is Drew. Not Andy.'

'Yes, sorry, my colleague did mention that when he phoned. Do you want to tell me about that?'

'I changed it after they made my life unbearable. Everyone knew the name Drew Gardner. I couldn't use that name for anything. So, when I joined Sebastian's book club, I used a different name and hoped no one recognised me. I needed to get out of the house at least once a month, which is what the book club offered, and I like true-crime. Everything seemed to be okay, Twitter is more about the words and the hashtags than images. And no one realised.

Drew is short for Andrew so I chose Andy. Both were still my name.'

Of course, I hadn't realised Drew was short for anything. He was talking though and that was a good sign. I needed to keep him talking, create a bond with him. 'Shall I make us a drink?' I asked.

'I don't see why not,' he said.

Relief flashed through me. I was a jumble of tense muscles and this one response gave me further hope.

He leaned down and refreshed the page. He only had 142 followers. It was possible this would not go far.

When the screen reloaded I could see it had been shared six times, with shock and disgust voiced with the retweet. He checked the accounts of those who'd shared. None of them had large followings either.

I wasn't sure how he would feel about this. I needed to distract him. 'Come on. Let's get that drink.'

The kettle boiled and I organised the cups. Drew sat with the knife in full view. In control.

'So, do you want to tell me about it?' I poured the boiling water into the mugs.

'You read the message,' he said.

'I did,' I agreed. 'It didn't say a lot, did it? Why Sebastian?'

He let out a sigh. 'Top the drinks up with some cold water, I don't want you throwing it over me.'

I inclined my head in acceptance and took the mugs over to the sink.

Drew continued, 'He wrote a blog post about me. It wasn't very polite.'

I turned from the counter. 'About you?'

'Yeah, the homeless man incident.'

I remembered that last year. There was a real uproar online apparently and it had made it into the *Nottingham Today* because it was a local story. Was Drew one of the men? I squinted at him as I handed him one of the mugs. 'You're the homeless man?'

'No. I was the other guy.'

'You pushed him?' I was surprised. Yes he had killed people but for some reason he didn't seem like the type of guy who would randomly go around pushing people in public.

'No. Yes. But, not how it looked. There was a car coming behind him, I was protecting him. The photograph doesn't pick that up though. I was vilified. My life was ruined.' Drew dropped his gaze for a moment then suddenly jerked his head back up and shot me a look.

I hadn't moved. I needed more than a momentary lapse after the way it had gone last time.

'I lost everything,' he said.

'And Sebastian wrote about it.' I paused and thought it through. 'You were in a book club with him. Didn't he recognise you?'

'No. Well, not straight away.' Drew continued, 'I only joined about eight months ago, so after he'd written the post and he was on to other things then. That post was history. Then eventually it came to him where he had seen me before. He took me to the side and asked me about it. I told him what really happened and he promised to keep it to himself.'

'He was your friend then?'

Drew nodded.

'I don't understand. Help me understand.' I cradled my mug in my hands and stared at him.

'My life was still over. I was pretending to be someone else. My kids wouldn't see me. My wife was living without me and it was all because of the online drama.'

'So, you want to take everything away from? Who? I don't get it.'

'They turned on me like my life was a computer game they were playing. They demanded I lose my job. I did. I lost my wife and my children stopped talking to me.'

'I'm sorry. That must have been hard.'

'I wanted to show them that...' He scrubbed his hands across his face.

He was struggling to put this into words. I waited for him.

'They behave as though everything they put online is meaningless, as though it doesn't have consequences. I wanted to show them that it does. Look, I wanted to say.' He waved one arm out, the knife circling in his hand. 'Look at this crime scene, this is real, but it's not real, this is your world now turned into something deadly. How does it feel when you get your kicks online and they turn out to be so very real? It's not so good, is it? But,' he pleaded. 'It didn't work. They lapped it up. They loved it. It was like the best thing they'd had to talk about for a long time.'

'So why did you do it again with Lacey?' I asked.

'I wanted to shock them. Show them it wasn't good. Maybe one example wasn't enough. Just, look. Look at this. She spends all day showing herself to you. Now look at her, showing herself in such a grotesque way. Is this what you really want? Think about what you want on here, in your internet world.'

I let a soft sigh. 'It didn't work, did it? You'll never stop them or make them think about their actions, Drew. And killing people is not going to make the difference you want. If you go through with this, you're just going to give them more fodder. You're going to make their day more exciting. It will give them something to talk about. To share. You can stop this now and we can talk this through. Without them.'

He put his mug down. Not a sip had been taken. 'They won't listen to me, will they?' he said.

'They won't. This isn't the ending you want. Let's talk about this. Me and you. I promise you'll be safe.'

He nodded. 'I'll delete that message first. No point leaving that out there.' His shoulders slumped. His arm hung heavy by his side, the knife nearly falling from his hand. He was tired.

We walked into the living room and the laptop and he clicked on the message, it reloaded. He stared at the screen. Stretched back out. He stood taller. His shoulders broadened. The grip on the knife tightened.

I couldn't believe what I was seeing.

He turned to me. 'It's been shared over twenty-two and half thousand times. We're not going anywhere.'

59

Aaron, Martin and Pasha walked back into the office after going to Drew's address, the guy they had known as Andy, to back Hannah up.

'There was no one there.' Aaron was grey as he spoke to the rest of the team. 'Her car was there, we forced entry, but they've gone. Uniform now have the scene and the shift inspector has promised to start a search to see if there is anything there that can point us in the right direction of where to go now. But we had to come back here to continue inquiries from our end. He's assured me he'll get in touch with anything they find and won't close the scene until we've been back and had the once over.' The room was quiet; staff were getting on with what they needed to do but were subdued, the DI was missing, this was not easy to process.

'Aaron, you need to see this.' Evie's face was white, the colour drained away.

'Martin, get onto SPoC and see if we can triangulate Hannah's phone will you?' Aaron said, still trying to crack the problem they had in front of them, worry obviously working away at him.

Evie tried again. 'Drew has posted a photograph, Aaron. He has Hannah and he's threatening to kill her.'

The silence in the incident room was heavy now. Anyone on a phone held the mouthpiece in mid-air, mouths agape. Tapping at keyboards stopped. Aaron turned on the spot. Then turned again. Unsure what the hell had just happened.

'I don't understand,' he said. 'How can this have gone so wrong so quickly?' He stood shocked for a fraction of a minute, then he pulled himself together.

'Let me see it, Evie. Let's see what we're dealing with.'

She brought up the tweet.

I am the killer. I killed Sebastian Wade and Lacey Lane because of what you did to me last year. Now it's up to you what happens. #crimescenemurder

Poll

Option 1: Kill myself.

Option 2: Kill the police officer leading the investigation because I have her.

The image showed Drew with his hand wrapped in Hannah's hair, her head pulled in close to him.

There was a look on her face that said this was not a stable situation.

'Fuck,' he muttered under his breath. 'Have you spoke to SPoC yet, Martin? We need to track down Hannah's phone.'

Martin put the phone down. 'They're on it now. They'll be back to us shortly.'

'Do they know how urgent it is?'

'Yes, I told them.'

'We need to inform Baxter and Walker,' Aaron said. 'And get this image to digital forensics, see if we can get anything from it, see if they can get a location from anything in the background.' He turned to Pasha. 'Research this guy, I want to know everything about him. Particularly locations. I want to know where he might have taken her. This looks like it's a house, a home. We must have it listed for him somewhere.'

'On it.' She sat down at her desk. Started tapping at her keyboard.

'Why the hell do we not have this guy flagged in the investigation?' he asked to no one in particular. And got no response. A couple of shrugs. Guilt filled the room. No one had seen this coming. Everyone had missed it and now the Boss was at risk.

Aaron looked at the message on Twitter again. It was now he noticed there was a time limit on the poll. Drew Gardner had given the people of Twitter just two hours to decide who should die, him or Hannah.

60.

'Where are your family?' I asked Drew. I had figured out this was his home. It was the only way he could have a key and know his way round the house so well. Plus, with the story about him losing everything, it made sense.

He looked at the photographs on the wall. Sadness filled his eyes. This was a man in pain. I had to get through to him.

'Mel is at work and the kids are at school.'

'You still love her,' I said. I had to remind him of everything he had, of all he had to lose if he went through with this.

'Of course I still love her. Why do you think it hurts so much that I lost this? This is my home. Not that other soulless place you visited. That isn't a home. It's a place with walls and a bed. This is home.'

He was passionate. 'What would Mel think about all of this if she knew?' I asked, not sure if I was pushing him in the wrong direction.

There was silence as he continued to look at the family photographs on the wall. I hadn't spotted any with him in, but then, in the corner on a side table,

I saw it, a family of four; he was there. And they looked so very happy. His world had been shattered.

I looked further around the room. What could I use to gain control of the situation if I needed to? There was nothing I could see. With a huge kitchen knife in his clenched fist he obviously had the upper hand. But, I wouldn't die here today.

'Drew?' I prompted.

'She would be furious.' He stared at me. 'What do you want me to say? That she would be okay with this? Of course she wouldn't. She's a good woman. She couldn't cope with the public scrutiny on us when it was all happening, that's why our marriage broke down. She wants a quiet peaceful life. This would break her. I know that. And yet...' He looked back at the photographs, at the memories. 'I did it anyway.'

'You can stop it though. Prove to her that you're sorry. Bring this all to an end. It doesn't have to end this way. How horrified would she be if she knew what you have planned?' I was grasping at straws but he had given me enough information to make an assessment of her thought process on this.

He shook his head. 'It's too late.' He moved to the laptop, refreshed the screen again. His jaw went slack and his eyes widened. I could see him reading through comments on the screen. Shock registering on his face. I was scared to think what was on there. Did people hate the police that much that they were voting for me to die? Or had they seen sense and closed it down? Had the public proved him right or wrong? And which was which? Is this what was shocking him so much now? That they refused to engage in his game?

Surely people would not vote on someone dying. This wasn't a dystopian fantasy drama. This was real life and this was my life and his life. No matter what he had done. No matter what they thought he deserved, they were not the ones to make a decision on who lives and who dies.

I inched forward. Slowly. Afraid to startle him. I wanted to see what he was reading on the screen.

'Have a look.' He waved me over with the knife. 'See what they think.'

I moved next him. He was stressed. I could smell the body odour seeping through his T-shirt. Sour and strong. Dark circles had formed under his arms. I tried not to wrinkle my nose. Instead I focused on the screen.

At first I wasn't sure what I was looking at. I wasn't used to Twitter. It took me a moment to understand the list of tweets.

Let her go. You deserve to die. You deserve more than death.

Do us all a favour and kill yourself now. Don't wait for a stupid poll result.

Just die.

Die.

Kill yourself now.

Kill the killer.

Die now.

Let me come and kill you. I'd do a good job of it.

Give her the knife. Let her stick you.

They were baying for his death. You could practically hear the chanting tone of the messages. He kept scrolling and the messages kept on coming. Hundreds of them. Thousands of them.

Then he clicked on his original tweet. The poll. It had been shared over three-hundred-and-twenty-eight thousand times and had two-hundred-and-fifty-one thousand votes. Ninety-five per cent of those for his death.

I wasn't sure what he expected, but by the look of his face, he had held out a faint hope that they would prove him wrong. Prove that they were decent and would not engage in this game of his. Would he really carry this out or just resign himself that the world was not a good place?

'Dad!' There was a scream from outside. 'Dad!' And again. Followed by banging and the door handle being attacked as someone tried frantically to get in. 'Dad! Stop, let me in!' The voice was distraught and loud. Wanting to be heard. She banged and banged and banged.

And then there she was, at the living room window. Peering in. At her dad holding a knife. With me just standing here. Her face was streaked with tears, a mottled mess of pasty white from shock and bright red from crying. Eye make-up slashed her cheeks with the tears.

This was his daughter.

61

Drew looked at Hannah in blind panic. 'Libbie! How the hell? She should be at school.'

Hannah looked from the window – from the girl with the tear-streaked face, screaming and banging at the glass, to Drew. 'I presume she has a smartphone,' she said.

His hands went up to his head, the knife in his hand waving about in the air.

'Dad, noooo!' she screamed again. 'Let me in. Dad.' Her voice was high and terrified. Here she was, a young child on her own, facing her dad through a window as he threatened to take his own life or that of a police officer, publicly on social media.

Suddenly two more faces joined her. Dylan and Mel. Mel looked in. Saw the state of Drew and stared at Hannah. She was trying to keep Dylan calm. Talking to him quietly. Then she grabbed Libbie and wrapped her arms around her in a bear hug, dragging her away from the window into an embrace that shoved her face into her shoulder.

Dylan stood there. Confused. 'Dad?' A quiet whisper Drew could barely hear.

'Drew, you have to close the curtains,' Hannah said quietly. 'We can sort this out, but don't let your children see this.'

Drew started to pace the room. Becoming more and more erratic. He hadn't wanted it to turn out this way. This wasn't what he had planned.

'They were supposed to be at school,' he moaned.

'They're kids. Something like this was bound to get at least one kid's attention and then it would sweep the school in no time. Don't let them watch this, Drew. Close the curtains. You can see them when we walk out of here.'

With heavy and slow footsteps he walked to the window.

'Drew, what are you doing?' Mel asked through the glass.

'I'm sorry, Mel. I never wanted it to go like this.' His own eyes were now flooded with tears. Would this be the last he saw of his wife?

'Drew, please, just come out. You're scaring the children. Come out and tell them you didn't do this. That you're hurting in your head and you made it up, that you're going to seek help. They'll understand a breakdown, they're good kids, Drew.'

He shook his head. Tears fell down his face and he drew the curtains.

'Dad!' Libbie screamed.

62.

Aaron called for attention in the incident room. 'We've had a call from Melissa Gardner, she says the man behind the tweets is her husband, Drew Gardner. He's currently holed up in her family home she and the kids have arrived there and she's seen Drew and Hannah alive through the window, but that he's now drawn the curtains.'

There were sharp intakes of breath and a couple of groans in the room.

'We're going to the scene. A few of you will stay here and work the intelligence systems. Pasha, Martin and Ross, you come with me. The rest of you, I need you here. Baxter and Walker will be attending as will the ARV. DCI Baxter is a trained hostage negotiator so he'll be taking the lead once we're there.'

Evie stood. 'I'm coming with you.'

'You need to stay here, Evie.' Aaron pulled on his coat.

Evie moved to the door. 'I'm coming with you, Aaron. She's my best friend. I'm not sitting here doing nothing while people vote on whether she lives or dies. I'm going.'

'I need you to get the tweet removed.' He stared at her. 'It's important.'

Evie wasn't backing down easily. 'Could you stay here with her out there in trouble?'

'Please, Evie. I can't worry about you as well as her. You figured this out for us. Now I need you to close it all down. I don't understand why it's not happened yet.'

'Because Twitter are working on US time and they get a lot of complaints. This is one of many. They'll get to it, but whether they see it in time is another issue.'

'Will you stay and chase them?'

Pasha looked between Aaron and Evie. Evie relented. 'Bring her back safe, don't make me hurt you.'

Aaron nodded. 'She's my friend as well.'

They closed the street off at both ends. Between the taped cordons uniform and plain cars parked all over the road, like sets of dice rolled randomly across a table. The armed unit were having another briefing on site. The officers were all kitted up in their vests, weapons strapped around shoulders.

Serious expressions on faces. This was what they trained for. They were ready.

Officers were clearing residents out of the houses adjacent to Drew's house or opposite, moving them out of the cordoned area, much to their very vocal annoyance. They had no idea what access he had to weapons. The officers back at the station were working on that.

Aaron shepherded Mel and the two teenagers to an empty vehicle and they clambered in, Mel in the middle with two traumatised looking children, each side of her. They might be teenagers but they very much looked like small children right now.

Aaron sat in the driver's seat, twisted himself round so he was facing Mel. 'Melissa Gardner, isn't it?'

She nodded.

'What can you tell me about today's events?'

She was as pale as her children. 'I can't tell you anything. The first I knew about it was when Dylan texted me and told me to look on Twitter. I don't have a Twitter account so I had to look on a colleague's account and then I saw it. I knew the kids had made a beeline home, that they'd run out of school, I left work immediately and phoned you when I saw him there.' Her hand went up to her mouth and a sob escaped. The daughter leaned her head into her mother's chest and allowed more tears to flow. The son attempted to be the stoic man of the hour and stayed rigidly still as the two women of his life struggled.

'What about weapons?' Aaron pushed.

'I saw a knife.' Her hand was still up at her face.

A band of pressure went around Aaron's chest. 'What was he doing with the knife?'

'Nothing. He was holding it.'

'He wasn't threatening DI Robbins?'

'No.' She shook her head. 'She looked fine. Well, as fine as she could in those circumstances,' she added.

'He wouldn't hurt her,' Libbie chimed in, lifting her head and looking at Aaron. 'He's my dad, he wouldn't hurt her. He's a good man. He didn't do what they said he did. He told me. I was just angry because of all the stick I got at school about it. I was angry at him because it had gone viral and made my life hell. I believed he didn't do it and was helping that man.'

'I believe you,' Aaron told her. 'But, right now, he does have a knife and he does have one of our officers in there with him and we need to know what we're dealing with.' He turned to Mel again. 'What about firearms, does he have access to those?'

'Oh my God, no.'

'No!' both teenagers burst out at once.

Mel tightened her grip on them. 'Where would he even get one from? He's not that kind of man.'

They all looked towards the house. Where Drew was now, with a kitchen knife and a Nottinghamshire police officer held hostage, having launched a Twitter poll threatening to kill one of them in the next hour. He most definitely was that kind of man.

63

The tension in the room was dark and thick, ever since his family had turned up. He had changed. Where I had thought I was getting through to him, now there was a wall up around him. We heard the commotion outside and Twitter confirmed the arrival of police and the cordoning off of the street, the removal of some of the neighbours and the use of the armed officers.

I was close to the laptop now. My eyes flicked to the clock in the corner of the screen, checking how much time we had, I wondered what he was going to do when the clock ran out.

The house phone rang.

'That will be them,' I told him. 'You need to answer it.'

He shook his head.

'Drew, talk to them. Let them know what's going on. Let them know I'm okay in here. That you're okay in here. That way they won't do anything dramatic that you don't want.'

He looked at me, a silent stare as he contemplated what I had said. The phone continued its shrill call. He didn't move.

Then it stopped.

Damn.

'Drew, you really need to speak to them. We might be able to sort this out. Your children. They're out there. You don't want this to be the worst day of their lives.' It was going to be anyway, no matter how it was resolved, but I wasn't going to tell him that.

The phone started to ring again.

'Drew?'

'Shup up,' he yelled.

I was quiet. This was spiralling out of my control. Not that it had ever been within my control. Drew himself was losing it and that was bad news.

He snatched up the phone. 'Yes.'

He listened. 'Yes, she's fine.' He held out the handset to me. I went to take hold of it but he shook his head. Instead I put my ear to it.

'DI Robbins here,' I said.

'Hannah, are you–' The phone was ripped away. Baxter's voice. Baxter was out there. My team was out there. They were close.

'That's enough. You know she's okay. That's all you need. Now leave me alone.' And with that, he put the phone down.

Shit. This wasn't going well.

The phone rang again.

Silence from Drew.

Then again.

Then again.

He yanked the phone from the wall.

'Drew.' How the hell were we going to resolve this if he wasn't going to engage with them?

'It's too late for all of that,' he said. He looked at the laptop. 'I think the dregs of society have spoken.'

'No, Drew, they haven't. They aren't society. They aren't the whole population. They don't speak for everyone. They're simply keyboard warriors who think it's fun to hassle people from the safety of their homes without considering the impact. Normal people like me and you, we don't use social media like that. We would be, we *are* horrified by this behaviour. You don't have to listen to them or make decisions based on their words.'

He paced around. I could see he was listening, but his pacing was erratic. I had to talk him down. One of us was about to die.

He refreshed the screen. The messages hadn't changed. The percentage of people who wanted him to kill himself was now at ninety-eight per cent. His hand and his knife went up to his head again.

If it came to it, I was going to damn well fight for my life. I was not going to die here today. There were armed officers out there. I would scream my head off. I would protect my major organs with my hands until they got here. I'd been stabbed before, it wasn't pleasant, far from it, but life was life as I knew. I didn't know what he would do, no matter what the Twitter feed said. He could easily decide to dispatch me to prove another unhinged point.

He refreshed the screen again, but the tweet and poll were no longer there. His account had been deactivated. He couldn't see the Twitter feed at all. We both stared at the screen for a minute. Taking it in.

Then I started to back away from him. Very slowly.

One small deliberate step at a time.

He looked up.

I lifted my arms in front of me. I had nothing. I stepped again. Closer to the sofa. To the cushions. They would help. Anything. I had to defend myself.

He stared for a moment. I wasn't even sure if he saw me or not. It was a blank far-off stare.

'Don't worry,' he said. 'They voted for me.'

'You don't have to–'

He lifted the blade and brought it down hard into his stomach.

64

'Shit. No. Drew.'

He yanked out the knife and blood spurted from his abdomen. He was still standing. Still with the blade in his hand. Bent over a little. He raised it again.

'Drew. No.' I looked around in panic. Why did people live so tidily?

The laptop.

He stabbed down again, and again the blade entered his stomach. A grunt, a huff of air was released. He was sinking at the knees.

I ran for the laptop. Grabbed it and with a sideswipe I hit him. The casing smashed into the side of his head with a resounding thwack. He was weak and a third stab wound had now been administered. The knife fell from his hand and dropped to the floor. His T-shirt was soaked with blood. It ran like a sheet down the front of his jeans. The carpet, once a dusty mat for my face was now puddled. Drew's face was grey.

I let go of the laptop. It bounced on the floor. I pushed the knife under the sofa with my foot and grabbed Drew under the arms as he sank into the puddle of blood. He was losing a hell of a lot of the stuff.

'Oh, Drew.'

I screamed for help and pushed my hands over his stomach.

I screamed out again as I pressed down.

Memories of doing this in the past seeped into my head. Of a dark seedy basement. Of a young colleague.

I was here again. The blood seeped through my fingers.

'Leave me,' Drew whispered.

I wasn't sure how much longer he would be conscious.

'This is what they wanted. They probably would have voted for this from the start when they saw the original photograph, the one on the street when I was pushing him away from the car.' He coughed. Blood ran from his mouth. This wasn't good. 'If they'd have had the option,' he finished.

'Drew.' I pushed down harder, spreading my hands in an attempt to cover all his injuries. 'You give them too much credit.' I yanked off my sweater. Pulled it over my head and pushed it down on his stomach. I screamed out again.

The screams of last year echoed through my head when I'd screamed out that there was an officer down.

If I let go of him he would definitely die. If I didn't get him help... he would most probably die.

I looked down at Drew's ashen face. At the blood I was now kneeling in. That surrounded us.

The blood that his family would come home to.

I didn't see how this would end well for him.

I had to make a decision.

I pulled on his hands. 'Drew. You have to push down on here. You have to fight. You have two beautiful children to fight for. The people who voted for this, they are meaningless. Your children, they're not. PUSH.' With the faintest movement I could feel, he pushed down. I let go and ran to the door. Scrabbled for the key which he had thrown on the floor. My hands shook as I struggled to fit it into the keyhole. Eventually it was in and turned. I flung open the door.

'I need emergency medical help in here. NOW.'

I flew back inside.

Drew's arms had slipped down to his sides. His eyes were glazing. My jumper on his stomach, now slick with his blood. It looked like a butcher's shop in here. I skidded down beside him. Applied more pressure. Blood pooled up.

Footsteps pounded through the door as police and paramedics ran in. I was pushed aside as they started to work on him.

Aaron was by my side followed quickly by Pasha and Martin and Ross.

'Are you hurt? Is any of this yours?' asked Aaron.

I shook my head. 'None of it. It's all his.'

I heard the paramedics call Drew's time of death and I turned away.

Epilogue

Aaron knocked and came into my office. I looked up from the professional development reviews I was attempting to complete for the team without much enthusiasm. They were supposed to encourage them to improve themselves, but it was another piece of red-tape that was added to their working day.

'You done with those yet?' Aaron asked.

I scowled at him. 'They've got them in on time and now I have to add my comments to all of them. It's not as though we're busy and have something better to do is it?'

Aaron laughed at me. 'You're not enjoying yourself then?'

'How did you guess?'

'Your face,' he answered as he dropped into one of the chairs in front of my desk.

'I see you managed to add your comments pretty timely,' I added.

'I don't mind the paperwork side of the job.'

He did and as always I appreciated him for the alternate tone he added to our working relationship.

'I thought we'd lost you,' he said, relaying, again, the fears he had about that day with Drew.

'You don't get rid of me that easily,' I said and looked at him, serious and grateful. 'Thank you.'

He looked confused. 'For?'

'Being there. You're always there when I need you.'

'And I'll always be there,' he said.

'You will?' I was surprised.

'I realised when you were missing that this is where I belong. Here with you and the rest of the team. I am needed here. I am good at my job. If it means I have to let a couple of people know then so be it,' said Aaron.

I let out such a deep sigh that I practically melted into my chair. 'You don't know what that means to me.'

I flipped the lid down on my laptop, happy to close the PDRs for now.

'I've just closed the file on the job,' he said.

'Filed as detected, yes?'

'Yeah, we had all the evidence ready to go had he survived. The missing knife from his knife block matched up to the wounds in Sebastian Wade. It would have gone through to court if he had lived.'

'I'm glad about that,' I said. 'It's closure for the families. They don't have to be dragged through a trial. Though no outcome is the best one for his own family.'

I stopped and looked at Aaron. 'And what about you? Are you sure about your decision, about staying?'

Aaron nodded. 'It was difficult coming back after the heart attack, Hannah. I still feel exhausted every night and it may be that I do have to take a gentler role if I find I can't do this and these hours, but I'm going to give it a try before I jump. Stress didn't give me a heart attack and Lisa is behind me all the way.'

'Have you spoken to Baxter yet?'

Aaron nodded. 'He wasn't happy.'

I was worried. 'You know we're going to have to deal with it, don't you?'

He nodded again. A slow steady movement. 'I don't want to leave the team so if he forces the issue then I'll do what needs to be done, Hannah. And with you and Lisa by my side then I can do it.'

I smiled at him. I was lucky to have Aaron and I was grateful he had decided to stay. Now we just had to keep him here and hope that Baxter didn't win this battle.

Books in the series;

Three Weeks Dead (Prequel novella)

Shallow Waters

Made to be Broken

Fighting Monsters

Other books by Rebecca Bradley ;

Dead Blind

About the Author

Rebecca Bradley is a retired police detective who lives in the UK with her family and two Cockapoo's Alfie and Lola, who keep her company while she writes. She needs to drink copious amounts of tea to function throughout the day and if she could, she would survive on a diet of tea and cake.

If you enjoyed *The Twisted Web* and would be happy to leave a review online that would be much appreciated, as word of mouth is often how other readers find new books.

DI Hannah Robbins will return next year, but in the meantime if you're interested in meeting the team again and finding out how they got to where they are on the Major Crimes Unit, then you can read the prequel, *Three Weeks Dead*, a short novella where a young DC, Sally Poynter, has to get through to a desperate husband before he commits a crime that will have far-reaching consequences. You can claim your free copy on the blog rebeccabradleycrime.com

Twitter: http://Twitter.com/RebeccaJBradley

Please look Rebecca up, as she would love to chat.

Acknowledgements

A novel is never written in isolation, it takes a team to put a book together and this one has been no different. Therefore I have several people I need to thank.

Jane and David Isaac for reading an early copy of the manuscript and for help on how Aaron would be feeling after his heart attack.
Denyse Kirkby as always for her support with Aaron's Asperger's. It's important that he is as real as any of the other characters and Denyse supports me with that.
Marie O'Hara in discussing school disciplinary procedures and Anne O'Hara for her keen eye.
Debi Alper for her skill with a pencil and for her clear thoughts on the book, and my early readers for supporting me on my journey.

Last but by no means least my family, without whom none of this would be possible. I love you.

Printed in Great Britain
by Amazon

30329590R00229